Beyond the Skyline

Brody Lane Gregg

Cover Art:
Michelle Crocker

http://mlcdesigns4you.weebly.com/

Publisher's Note:

This is a work of fiction. All names, characters, places, and events are the work of the author's imagination.

Any resemblance to real persons, places, or events is coincidental.

Solstice Publishing - www.solsticepublishing.com

Beyond the Skyline

A Novel

By

Brody Lane Gregg

Part 1

Something Resembling Normal Life

Chapter 1

December 21, 2013

I t's difficult to preface the story of my life, to put it into words in a way that displays genuine honesty and integrity, yet is interesting enough for someone to pick it up and read it. I mean, who really has such an amazing life that others would want to read about it? I guess one could argue that there are people like rock stars, movie stars, reality TV stars, and a million other "stars" that we just can't get enough of. Even some criminals have autobiographies. But how many of those stories are actually one hundred percent true? Everyone knows fiction sells better than the mundane, boring truth.

But I'm not everyone. I'm not trying to sell a million copies or blare out copious amounts of grossly misinterpreted and otherwise fictionalized headlines. I'm all about the truth, whether it is mundane and boring or something more. I know what you're probably thinking: "These are the worst first two paragraphs I've ever read."

Well, I can admit that I've never been much in the way of introductions. So I'll keep it short. No, as a matter of fact, I'll just skip it altogether.

So here it goes.

My name is Alex and this is my story.

Wait. I guess this is an introduction.

Chapter 2

August 9, 2013

I t was July of 2011 when I first put pen to paper. I'd like to say it was sparked by way of some profound thought or prophetic vision, but nothing could have been further from the truth. Honestly, I just needed some way to pass the time and put my mind to use, because hours upon hours of staring at the wall seemed like a rather poor way to stay sharp.

What I didn't know then was that writing would become an integral part of my life. Not only in keeping my sanity, but as a release—a high, if you will. Not like taking a hit or doing a line, but something more sustained, more fulfilling. Writing became important to me. Almost necessary.

And anything that could take my mind off my current situation was welcomed. At the time, I was in Hillbrook Juvenile Detention Center in upstate New York. I had just started my stay and by way of accident came upon a pen—a blue and white ballpoint with Planned Parenthood stamped on the side—and a college-ruled notepad. I was told by a fellow delinquent that some kid named Carl could get me cigarettes in return for favors later on. At the time I didn't know what he meant by favors. Needless to say, I received pen and paper instead of cigarettes, and Carl found the wrong end of my fists.

And so I began to write. Like I said, I can't particularly say why, but I know it was for a purpose…like, it was meant to be.

But that's all I'm going to say about juvie. There's nothing of real value to be learned from that experience except that it was filled with violent and disgusting people—including myself—and others who were merely scared for their lives. All you need to know is that Hillbrook was the place where I finally grew up. Writing was one of the tools that moved my growing-up process along. I'm sure my thoughts will come back to this place someday. Until then, you can just use your imagination.

**

I stepped out of Hillbrook two weeks after my eighteenth birthday—a free man. I swear, the first thing that hit me was the air. I know what you're thinking. It was the same air that I'd been breathing for the last fourteen months and four days. Well, it felt different. This time, no walls were holding me captive. It was an amazing feeling.

Second, I felt an overwhelming sense of anxiety. I'd longed for this moment every day I was in lock-up. But now what? Where did I go from here? Part of my growing-up process included a decision to change. And the change I envisioned for myself was simple: not to be a criminal anymore. But that was easier said than done. I really didn't know how to not be a criminal. And I still don't. But I knew I'd made a choice, and I had chosen not to go back to that life. I didn't want to be that violent and disgusting person anymore.

Certainly, the anxiety also stemmed from my belief that I wouldn't have any help changing, that I was lost and alone in a world that wasn't keen on offering opportunities to people like me. That I would have to make it on my own.

Of course, life has a way of turning our thinking upside down.

That's kind of how my story begins, upside down and confusing.

I know, right now, most of you are thinking, "What did this guy do?" And that's an understandable question. But I'm not taking the time to write about it. I don't even want to think about it.

So moving on.

I never imagined that when I left Hillbrook someone would be waiting for me, so when I saw a black car at the end of the paved drive, I brushed it off as some rich visitor, probably visiting their snobby, spoiled-rotten child. Like Carl, for instance, who seemed to think that it was an injustice to be locked away for stabbing his father's housekeeper after she threatened to disclose to daddy his son's advances on her.

On a side note, it was an absolutely beautiful car. It looked brand new and way out of the price range of your average nine-to-fiver. It was definitely foreign, a make I wasn't familiar with. As I passed it, I ventured to look into the windows, but the tint was too dark to make out much of anything inside. The only thing I could ascertain was that the car was not empty. I caught the figure of a person in the driver's seat.

But I thought nothing of it, save that whoever was in the car was probably freaked out, having a newly released prisoner peering into his or her window.

I started walking away, just me, the clothes on my back, and a trash bag full of notebooks.

But then the car's engine started. I turned around just as the driver's side door was opening, and a well-dressed—no, *immaculately* dressed—man stepped out of the car. He was tan and wore large sunglasses. A very shaggy beard covered most of the rest of his face. He was dressed to kill—literally, when I saw the pin-striped suit, I thought mobster or hit man.

Strangely enough, he just stared at me.

With no actual out-of-lockup interaction in forever, I managed to say, "I'm sorry," before turning around and continuing to walk. It felt stupid to apologize to a grown man for peering into his windows. But really, what else could I have possibly said, besides asking a rude, "what are staring at" question?

"Alex, where are you going?"

I managed a few steps before the question sank in. The voice sounded very familiar. I turned back around. Now the bearded man was smiling.

"You don't recognize me, do you?"

"Not at all," I said. He definitely wasn't someone I used to run with. They were all locked up, too. Or dead. "I can't say I do," I added. "But your voice?" For the second time, I managed to sound stupid.

The man shut the car door and started walking towards me. "It probably sounds a lot like our father's voice," he said. He took his sunglasses off, and I immediately made the connection. He had my eyes.

"Brandon?" was all I could mutter before I dropped my bag.

I met him with a hug. It was quick, one of those embraces where two men are uncomfortable and would rather separate prematurely than hold on for too long.

Brandon reached for my hand and shook it firmly. "I'm probably the last person you expected to see."

That was an understatement.

"Why are you here?" I asked.

"To pick you up."

But that didn't answer my question at all. I tried again. "Why are you here, Brandon?"

His smile turned flat. "Because you're my brother. That's enough, right?"

Before I could say anything, he turned around and started walking back to the car. "Come on, get in," he said over his shoulder. "We can talk in the car."

How could I refuse?

***

I now find myself sitting in a room the size of four or five of the cells—I mean rooms—at Hillbrook. In the corner is a mirror pinned with carved leaflets and pearl-like beads. It's an antique, for sure, and probably worth more than anything I've ever owned. Or stolen.

The bed I'm sitting on feels like a cloud—literally what I would dream a cloud might feel like, as compared to what I'm used to, which I must say isn't much. And like those British films about royal families, I'm sitting under silk bed curtains attached to gold bedposts. Yes, I said gold.

Better yet, everything else in the house—no, mansion—looks exactly the same: antique and expensive. I have to be dreaming, right? How else could I explain how I woke up in a cell this morning and will be sleeping like a king tonight.

But before I start ranting like a twelve-year-old girl, let me take you back a few hours.

The car ride was strange to say the least. I practically fell into the very low car—which I later learned was a Maserati. There were no back seats, so I had to hold my bag of notebooks on my lap. And then I couldn't figure out where the seatbelt was, which forced my brother to reach over me, trash bag and all, to grab it and click it for me. So picture this. I'm in dirty blue jeans and a white T-shirt, with a trash bag full of my belongings, riding in a $100,000 car.

And then came the silence. I hadn't seen nor spoken to my brother in five years, and it didn't look like we'd be hitting it off anytime soon. The roar of the engine became the only noise, as I guess he didn't feel like turning on the overly-complicated looking stereo.

Mile after mile without a word. I stared out the window, surveying the rather drab scenery of Syracuse, New York. And then we left the city. Then through several more towns. And we kept driving. And we drove, and we drove, and we drove some more. Almost four hours later, with only two quick stops for gas, I saw New York City's skyline in the distance. Seeing Manhattan staring back at me was like a breath of fresh air.

As if the sight of the city were the key to communication, Brandon said one sentence. "I'm rich now, you know?"

No, I couldn't say I inherently knew that, but I wasn't ignorant. "I gathered that," I responded. "As soon as I saw the car."

Brandon laughed.

One self-centered statement, and suddenly the flood gate opened. And for much of the remaining trip, Brandon never stopped talking. He told me about his career as one of New York's premier financial investors. His greatest career achievement came when he had a full bio in the *New York Times*. He told me the title was "The Young Gun in Finance."

"And I actually held a gun in one of the pictures," he said. "Can you imagine the *Times* doing that now? I'd be condemned as a terrorist by the liberals and turned into a hero to everyone southwest of the state. And of course, the *Times* would be neck-deep in lawsuits."

It sounded like a rather shady business to me. But what did I know? I never had enough money to invest any of it.

As Brandon spilled out his entire life story, even some things I knew, his smile never faded. He was proud of what he had accomplished. Pride was something I had never felt.

"But my greatest accomplishments, Alex, are a beautiful wife and the most wonderful daughter. They can't wait to meet you."

"What are their names?" I asked. I have to admit, I really didn't need to know half the information I asked for.

I really didn't care about every little detail of his career, and, honestly, at that moment I didn't care about the names of his wife and daughter. The most pressing question in my mind was why I was sitting in his car, riding to his house—the brother I'd barely even known before I left home five years ago. The brother I definitely didn't know now.

But I kept asking questions because I definitely didn't want him to ask me anything. There was no way I wanted to divulge where my life had been, was currently, and where I was headed. First of all, I was ashamed, and, second, I couldn't answer the questions myself, let alone give an answer to someone else.

"My wife's name is Jennifer," he said without skipping a beat. "Most people just call her Jen for short. She's absolutely beautiful. And when I say she's beautiful, I don't mean the supermodel type, but sweet and innocent, you know? And she's passionate, whether that is for our family, a project she's working on, or just the latest fashion trend that she has to be a part of. It's hard for me to even put into words how amazing she is."

She sounded perfect. Otherworldly perfect.

"And our daughter's name is Ally," he went on. "She just turned five, and she's about to start kindergarten. She's everything of her mom in heart, but she has the looks of her father. She has my eyes—actually—*our* eyes, Alex."

The way he talked about his family seemed strange to me, especially since our family growing up had been as dysfunctional as a family could get. Along that line, I had other questions.

"How's Kim doing?" Kim was the middle child. Unlike my brother, she actually had something to do with my early childhood. She was three years my senior and four years younger than Brandon. To me, she had been my only true family. The last time I saw her, she had just dropped out of high school and was leaving for rehab due to a cocaine addiction.

Brandon looked pained. His smile disappeared and he put his hand on my left arm. "Kim's dead. She overdosed two weeks after you left. The drugs, coupled with you leaving, well, it was too much for her. I'm sorry. If I had been able to find you earlier, I would have told you."

I'd learned to take nothing as a shock, but hearing this was difficult. As I'm writing these words now, I feel emptier inside. If I could think of some way to explain it, I'd put it into words so you could understand. But I can't. So for anyone who has lost someone they hold dear, I'm sorry. I mean it.

It was different when my parents died. They were less than worthless. I have the scars to show it, and the nightmares to forever remind me, too. Kim was all I had. And even after I left, she was all I held onto.

Until now. So what could I possibly hold onto with her gone? I guess this is one of those things a person can't understand until they've been through it.

By the time Brandon's lips uttered "she's dead," we'd been in the Bronx for at least twenty minutes. We passed streets I knew, places I'd lived, alleys I'd be afraid to go back into again. It was as if Brandon was driving me through the projects to show me where I didn't want to go back to before bringing me into the neighborhood where he thought I belonged. As we started passing gated communities and fountains of colored water, I definitely didn't feel at home.

Finally, we pulled up in front of a long line of brick buildings that jutted right up against the street, leaving only a narrow sidewalk between the cars and the stairs. They were all attached, each one seemingly squeezed in between its neighbors. But they all had character. Wealthy character.

The neighborhood was north of Manhattan, away from the sprawling downtown, and much quieter.

"This one's mine." Brandon pointed to one of the smaller squares, a brick face with pillar-like trim. It looked like his home had been thrust in between the others.

My first reaction was, "That's it?" But when I stepped through the double front doors—which I swear are ten feet tall—I realized I had entered a mansion. I was in an oversized foyer that narrowed into a long hall, with dual staircases that followed the rounded walls until they met at the balcony above. It was like a movie set, not a home.

"Do you like it?" Brandon asked.

Do I like it? I thought. How did he expect me to answer that? *It's too big for my taste?* "I've just got out of a juvenile detention center," I said. "What do you think?"

He laughed and laid his suit jacket over a white chair by the door. "I guess you're right. Come on. Follow me. I'll show you where your room is. I don't think the girls will be home for a few hours, so you can get settled in."

I grabbed my trash bag and followed him.

***

I've had many strange days in my life, but none stranger than I what I just told you about. I'll probably have to sleep on it just to give it time to sink in. That's if I can sleep at all. Although this cloud-bed will definitely help.

I know most people would be happy to be in my situation. But I'm not. I don't know if it's the fact that three hours ago I found out that my sister killed herself or if it's just this strong feeling that I don't belong here. If it's the former, I assume the feeling will pass. Time heals all wounds, or so I've heard.

If it's the latter, I don't know how to make it go away. As I sit here, I don't even know what I should do next. Do I leave the room and try to figure this place out?

Or do I follow my instincts and pull out the massive ivory inlays on the face of the grandfather clock against the far wall? They've got to be worth something.

I could just go to sleep now and see what tomorrow brings. Judging by the sky outside the enormous window beside me, it's probably late enough. Or is it? If only that fancy grandfather clock actually worked.

I guess—wait, someone's knocking on my door. And, surprise, a lady with a thick accent just called through the door that she's the housekeeper. Yes, my rich brother has a housekeeper. I guess I'm supposed to let her in.

Chapter 3

August 10, 2013

When I think of a place called home, several images come to mind. First, I see my worthless father on top of my sister, Kim, pushing her down hard on her bed with his right hand while unbuckling his belt with the other. I see Kim's tear-filled eyes looking at me—pleading—before my father notices me in the doorway.

"Get out!"

And then I see my mother sprawled out half naked on the couch, the needle, or sometimes needles, still hanging from her arms. She would lie there for hours before someone—usually my brother—would have the decency to cover her.

I see Kim telling my father for the first time that she wanted to go to rehab. He yells from his chair, "You're a crack whore and you always will be. Just like her." He points to my mother, still on the couch, her eyes rolled back, drool pooling out of both sides of her mouth.

And then I see Brandon leaving the house early in the morning and not coming back until long after I'd fallen asleep. He was gone every day. He left us all alone with *them* so Kim could be raped and I could be beaten. Gone, day after day after day. And for what? So he could get a college degree and become a millionaire, while we were the ones being abused? He was out in the world making a new life for himself while we were drowning in the life we could not escape on our own.

Trust me. I could think of a hundred other pictures that would thoroughly disgust you. Think of the worst things in the world. That was probably a normalcy in my childhood.

But that was *home* to me.

So it doesn't matter if Brandon, or Jen, or even little Ally tells me this place is my new home. I don't care. It's not home. When I left that filthy house at thirteen, I decided no place would ever be home to me again. That's because home was a terrible reality—a nightmare that never goes away.

***

I woke up this morning in a daze. Contrary to what I expected last night, I slept soundly. The ultra-soft bed actually came through for me.

After the tiny housekeeper—who I learned was named Ariel—came in, I lay down and faded instantly. No dreams, no worries, just dead sleep. And I slept until the sun hit my face this morning.

The aforementioned daze was a mixture of *How did I get here?* and *What do I do now?* And then there was still the overarching question. *How and why is this happening?*

Dazed or not, my only option was to leave the room. I couldn't hide forever. Fortunately, Ariel was kind enough to fill me in on her "client family's" normal Saturday schedule before she tried to turn down my bed, which I declined, much to her chagrin. She also informed me that I would probably see an older "white" gentlemen named Charles around. (Ariel was Hispanic. We were white people to her.) "My client family calls him Butler Charles," Ariel said, "but he's actually the groundskeeper and maintenance manager for the estate."

Because everybody needs a groundskeeper and maintenance guy for their house, right?

Saturdays for the "client family" were unorganized do-as-you-please days. So, I decided to do just that. The first thing I needed to do was find the kitchen. My stomach ached for food. Anything would suffice. I just had to find it.

Walking down the hall toward the movie-set staircases, I counted eight doors, four on each side, each one set between large, golden candelabras and maroon curtains. That meant if the hall on the other side had the same number of doors, there would be a total of sixteen rooms on the second floor alone.

I walked down the first staircase, which was on the left side of the foyer. At the bottom, I had three choices. There were doors on both the left and right and a hall between the sets of stairs. It was strange, as all the doors were closed. Maybe I wasn't supposed to see what was behind them. Who knows? I'd lived in a facility that had hundreds of locked doors, so it wasn't necessarily out of the ordinary for me.

I chose the hall. It was not as long as the hallways upstairs, but it was decorated much the same. I passed only two doors on my way to a large open doorway at the end. I reached it just as a woman walked by. She had an apron on with blue jeans and a tank top underneath.

She didn't notice me standing in the doorway, as she began to knead a large ball of dough on the island countertop. Yes, I had found the kitchen if you were wondering. She looked up just as I took a step into the room.

"You must be Alex!" she said with a wide smile. "Welcome home."

"Hi," I muttered.

"I'm Jen, Brandon's wife," she said, wiping her hands on a towel. "Are you hungry? I bet you are. Here, have a seat." She pointed to a small table next to the island and in front of a large bay window.

"Actually, I'm starving," I replied. As I sat down at the table, Ariel walked through another door to the right of the small dining area.

"Oh, my!" she said. She looked up at the ceiling. "God help me," she added, before walking through the door I'd just come through.

"Excuse Ariel," Jen said. She untied her apron and laid it on the chair across from me. "Every day is a crisis for her."

I smiled because I thought it was the right reaction.

On a side note, Brandon had stated that Jen was "not the supermodel type." I beg to differ. She was absolutely gorgeous. She had long blond hair and beautiful blue eyes. Her frame was so small, it was impossible to believe she had borne a child.

"What can I get you to eat?" she asked, laying her hand on my arm.

I pulled away immediately.

"I'm sorry," she said.

"No, it's okay," I said. But it wasn't okay. I hated to be touched. "I just figured you would have someone around here to cook."

She laughed. "Well, Alex, you thought wrong. I only work part-time, so I can at least cook." She walked back to the island. "We have cereal," she said. "All kinds. Or I can cook up some eggs, only scrambled though. Toast. Or cold pizza from last night."

"Cold pizza," I said. I hadn't had pizza in *forever*, and the thought of pepperoni, or sausage, or a thick layer of cheese was unbelievably tempting.

Jen laughed again, but this time it was one of those "you're kidding me…that was a joke" laughs.

"No, seriously," I responded. "I haven't had pizza in so long I can barely remember how it tastes."

"Well, in that case, cold pizza coming right up. Just let me put this dough away. I could warm it up if you want?"

After assuring her at least three times I didn't need it warmed up, I took a bite of heaven. I hadn't tasted such flavor in forever. Hillbrook's food just didn't compare. My first meal out of juvie couldn't have been better.

Jen sat down beside me and took out a slice of her own. I didn't know if she actually liked cold pizza or if she was just trying to make me feel more comfortable, but after thinking about it, I decided it was probably the latter. I doubt she kept that slim figure by eating pizza and downing a Coke every day. I had requested Coke to go with my pizza, which she wholeheartedly accepted as an okay choice, pouring herself a glass, too.

After five slices I was full, the kind of full that requires a moment to relax before you try to do anything else. Jen finished her first slice, and then she closed the box.

"So," I asked, more sarcastically than seriously, "what is my agenda?" Part of me really wanted to try and figure out what I was expected to do here.

"Well, Brandon took Ally to her piano lesson, so they'll be gone for a little bit." She picked up the box and stood up. "So I figured we could go shopping."

I almost laughed until I realized she was serious. "Wait. What?"

"Yeah, I figured you'd need some new clothes. Brandon said you only have what you're wearing."

"And what's wrong with what I'm wearing?" I responded, feeling a little judged.

Jen set the pizza box on the counter. "You slept in those clothes last night, didn't you?"

I wanted to say no, but I knew it would be an easily detectable lie. "Yes."

"Well, then, that settles it." She walked back to the table and pushed her chair in, then leaned over, putting herself eye-to-eye with me. "One thing you'll learn if you're living in this house is that I usually get what I want." She said it seriously, but had such a sweet smile, probably that sweet and innocent part Brandon had talked about. But I wanted to tell her that I didn't plan on living in this house. And that I didn't take well to commands. For some reason, though, something inside me told me I probably didn't want to get on this woman's bad side. And, honestly, I don't think I want to.

***

It's amazing how many stares one can get when pulling up to a strip mall in a Porsche. I can tell you, it's a lot.

I would have thought the Young Gun's wife would be a classier shopper, but I didn't ask any questions. At first I suspected that maybe she was trying to give me a lesson in humility. Or frugality. But, believe it or not, while I was sent to find clothes on my own, Jen actually shopped for herself. In a chain store! I'd pictured her in downtown Manhattan, shopping at Saks or somewhere like that.

Although I'd been locked away for over a year, I knew what I liked. I picked up a few pairs of jeans and some T-shirts, mostly black and gray. I couldn't imagine that styles had changed much in the time I'd been locked away. Thankfully, by what I saw, I was right. After getting a few more things, including underwear, which I stealthily hid between my other things, I waited. I walked around for what seemed like hours as I waited for Jen to come and get me. When she finally did, she had two things in her hand, a sweater vest and a pair of shorts. "How do these look?" she asked me.

They didn't look like something she would wear. I was about to say "fine," when I realized they were for me.

"No…that's not me at—"

"And that stuff is? What are those? Skinny jeans?"

"Maybe they are," I answered.

"No, you are not wearing that. Come on, this would look nicer." She held up the vest.

"I'm not wearing it," I said.

"But you need some color," she said. "Look, maybe not this, but there's so much more here in the store than just this."

"No."

"Just a little bit of col—"

"NO."

People were staring at us. It didn't seem to faze Jen in the least, but I felt a little self-conscious.

She lowered the outfit. "So you just want all those blacks and grays? Are you trying to look like a freak?"

There was no reason to continue arguing when I could show her exactly what I wanted to say. So right there, in the middle of the store, I took off my shirt and tossed it on the closest rack. Jen's mouth dropped open. People who were taking in our public display had the same reaction.

"I'm not trying to be a freak," I said, maybe too loudly. "I *am* a freak. So let me show you." I pointed to the swastika tattooed on the left side of my chest. "I got this tattoo right after I left home. It covers two of the cigarette burns my dad gave me."

Then I pointed to the large American flag on fire that covered the right side of my abdomen. "This one hides the scar where my broken rib punctured the skin. That happened when I was pushed down the stairs by my mother."

I turned around and showed her my back, which was covered with German phrases from *Mein Kampf*. "These hide the scars from my father's belt," I said. "And all of these other tattoos—" I had a lot of them "—do the same thing. They cover up the wounds of my past. And you know why I picked these tattoos? Because they're pictures of hate. All I do is hate. I'm one of those people that

22

doesn't belong with normal people like you, so that makes me a freak. So, please, just let me dress like one." I pulled my shirt back on, acting like my show had been part of a normal conversation.

Jen was over the shock factor and had an inquisitive look on her face. "And what was the other scar on your chest?" she asked. "And why isn't it covered up?"

That scar is my prized possession. It's my salvation. I've never told anyone what that scar was. Or what it means to me.

But since I had already made such a public display of myself and her, I thought I owed her an explanation. "That scar came when my mother burned me with her iron. It's the scar that saved my life."

"How so?"

"Well, it got infected right away. My parents, thinking the infection could lead to discovery of what was going on in our home by my teachers or friends, which could possibly lead to law enforcement, decided to go to the store one night to buy some medicine to put on it. Well, my mother was strung out on cocaine at the time, and my father was drunk as usual. They didn't even make it out of our neighborhood when they ran a red light and were struck by another car. They were killed instantly. Therefore, this scar saved me."

"I understand," she said. "Your brother never told me how your parents died."

"Yeah, well…Brandon wasn't much of a role model back then, either. But it doesn't matter. You've seen all of my scars and now you know why I'm such a freak."

Jen had a smirk on her face. "You're right," she said. "You should wear what you want to wear. But no more sob stories." She held her right arm in front of me and turned it over. There were scars all over her forearm and wrist. "The ones on my wrist were self-inflicted. I could never commit fully, even after three tries. And the scars up higher were from my dad's cigarette lighter. I've got them all over my body."

I'd been one-upped. And now it was my mouth that had dropped open. There was no way I could look her in the eyes and tell her my life was worse, or that somehow I'd been through more. But then again, she was rich and drove a Porsche now, so it was hard to feel sorry for her.

But I can say that I quickly found respect for the sister-in-law I barely knew. Which is lot more than I can say about my brother.

Jen bought all of the clothes I'd picked out and took me to several other stores. I did my best to see what she paid at each stop, and by my best calculations, she spent well over a thousand dollars on me. Every part of my being wanted to tell her to stop spending money on me, but she couldn't stop telling me how happy it made her feel to be able to do it.

And as much as I hate to admit it, I enjoyed shopping with her. Yes, I just said I *enjoyed shopping*. And I enjoyed the lunch she bought for me, too. And I also enjoyed all of the stories she told me about her family, especially since they were mostly focused on her "baby girl" and not on Brandon.

But just so you know, this doesn't change how I feel about my current situation. I still don't belong with them. Not in this house, not anywhere near them. I just wish I could have found the way to express that to her today. And the more I think about it, the more foolish I feel.

***

I have a feeling I'll be dreaming Disney tonight. Which I guess isn't the end of the world. It's a lot better than the nightmares that I've had in the past; the nightmares I still have occasionally. If I do dream Disney, I'll have to remember to thank Ally for that tomorrow.

I guess most do-as-you-please-days in the Lane household end with a movie. Ariel didn't tell me that part. Which is understandable the more I get to know her. I've got to say, the housekeeper is crazy. I watched her talk to God several times tonight. Just randomly during the movie, she looked up at the ceiling and started to talk. More like demonic possession, if you ask me. But after my public display of skin earlier, who was I to judge?

The whole movie thing was Ally's idea. Jen said that the family didn't often have much time together, so they always made up for it on Saturday nights. So at seven o'clock, we gathered in the living room. That's the room to the left off the foyer.

The first person I met was Butler Charles. I swear, at first glance I would have guessed he was a hundred years old. When I walked into the room, which, much to my surprise, didn't look like the Victorian Age threw up on it like the rest of the house, Charles gave me a salute. It looked like it hurt him just to raise his hand to his head.

I had no idea how this white-haired, wrinkled, old man could do anything physical. I guessed he was probably more of a family member than an employee at this point.

Butler Charles only spoke one time tonight, and that was to say, "Excuse me," when he thought one of Ariel's rants was directed at him.

Ariel never shut up, so between her random conversations with God and countless questions about the meanings of English words, I got pretty annoyed with her. Everyone else seemed just fine with it though.

The saving grace of the night was meeting Ally. When she walked in with Jen, she immediately crawled up onto my lap and looked me in the eyes. "You must be my new brother," she declared in the tiniest voice I've ever heard. "I'm Ally." She rubbed my shaved head and felt my cheek bones. "You look like Daddy, but your bones are pointier and you don't have any hair."

"Hi, Ally," I responded, unsure of what to do with this little girl sitting on my lap.

"Okay, Ally" Jen said, noticing my discomfort. "Come sit with me." She was sitting on the large couch set perpendicular to the one that Charles and I were sitting on. "And he's your uncle, not your brother."

"But, Mommy, I want to sit with Alex."

"Yeah, it's okay," I said. I'm not sure why I said that. I didn't mean it.

"Are you sure?" Jen asked.

Everything in me said no. *Just say no, just say no.* "Yes, it's fine."

"See, Mommy? I told you we'd be best friends."

I'm not sure if an eighteen-year-old criminal and a five-year-old self-proclaimed princess can be best friends, but I'll tell you one thing. After meeting Ally, I know it won't be her that pushes me away from this house. And, frankly, it won't be Jen, either, or Butler Charles or Ariel. If anyone is going to push me away, it's Brandon.

When my brother decided to grace us with his presence, his first order of business was to make sure I felt even more uncomfortable then I already did. He didn't say, "Hi" or "How was your day?" He grabbed his daughter off of my lap, and looked at me with a stare that didn't for a second hide what he was thinking. I saw disgust in his eyes, as if I were some pedophile holding his precious daughter. It wasn't the smiling Brandon that picked me up from Hillbrook. I'm not sure where that Brandon was.

"But daddy, I—"

"You can sit with your father, young lady." He threw her up in the air and caught her. She quickly went from questioning him to giggling uncontrollably.

Brandon threw her in the air a few more times before gently tossing her on the couch. He kissed Jen and sat down between them. "Hey, everyone," he said, not particularly looking at anybody.

Charles saluted, and Ariel awkwardly said, "*Hola*, hi."

I didn't bother to answer.

He looked at me. "So, I hear you had an interesting day."

Ariel started to answer. "I sure d—"

"No, not you, Ariel. Alex. I'm talking to you."

I didn't look at him. "You did, huh?"

"Yeah. Jen said you made quite the scene. I kindly brought you into my house, so please don't do it again."

I think I could have strangled him right there. What gave him the right to scold me? "I didn't ask you to bring me here," I fired back. "And are you mad because I might have made a fool of you or because your wife liked what she saw?"

Brandon started to stand up, but Jen put her arm across his waist. "Now boys, not now."

He glared at me, his jaw clenched. Finally, he exhaled. "Maybe it was a bad idea."

"Maybe."

Ally stood up. "Okay, no more fighting. I want to watch *Snow White!*"

And to Brandon's dismay, she ran back over to me and leaped onto my lap again. She stared up at me with her father's eyes. My eyes. "Do you like *Snow White?*"

Ally had the same smile on her face that Jen had had before she showed me her scars. I understood what Brandon meant when he said she was "everything her mom in heart."

"I don't know," I told her. "I've never seen *Snow White*."

A true look of shock fell over her face.

"It's a classic," Brandon said, obviously trying to diffuse the situation.

"Isn't it, like, fifty years old?" I asked Ally. "Like your father?"

"No," she laughed. "It's ummm…how old is it, Daddy?"

Brandon smiled. It's probably as old as Butler Charles."

"That's ancient!" Ally said.

Charles just smiled, showing the few teeth he still had.

Then Ariel began to talk to God for the first of many times. She talked to him in Spanish, so none of us had a clue what she was saying. Only the occasional "God help me" gave it away.

And then I watched *Snow White* for the first time.

Well, *watching* is a misnomer. I didn't even make it to the dwarves before I fell asleep. In lockup, I was usually long gone by that time of night, and I guess I couldn't fight the heaviness of my eyelids.

I wasn't the only one who struggled with sleep. When I finally woke up, it was because Jen was picking Ally up off my lap. She kind of flopped over and let out a helpless moan, as if that was her only method of defiance.

I didn't immediately let them know I was awake, but just sat there for a moment. Once I thought Jen was out of the room, I opened my eyes and sat up straight. To my surprise, everyone but Butler Charles was gone. Charles had his head laid back, mouth gaped open, and was snoring loudly.

"Charles," I whispered.

He didn't stir.

I was about to nudge him when I felt a hand on my shoulder. I nearly jumped out of my skin.

I could tell Jen was trying not to laugh, but she couldn't hide it. "I'm sorry. I didn't mean to scare you."

"It's okay," I answered.

"Brandon told me to leave you, but I thought you'd be uncomfortable down here."

It was a nice gesture, but Jen clearly had no idea how hard the beds in juvie were.

"Thanks," I said. "But what about Charles?"

"Oh, he'll be fine," she answered. "He usually does this a few times a week, anyways. I'll get him a pillow. And believe it or not, we find Ariel zonked out from time to time with the TV still on. I guess their rooms are too far for them to make it before they fall asleep."

"Wait, they actually live here?" I didn't know those types of arrangements still existed.

"Yeah, they do." She put a pillow under Charles' head, which only stopped his snoring temporarily. She turned back to me. "Well, I hope your first day with us was good. And I hope you forgive Brandon. He doesn't know how to act around you."

"Well, he could start by acting like the guy I met yesterday."

"But the day was good besides that?"

"It was fine," I answered through a yawn. "I guess I'm gonna go to bed." I didn't want to prolong the conversation. I also didn't want to give her more lee-way in defending her rude husband.

"Yeah, you probably should," she replied. "And so should I."

Jen walked up the stairs with me, then we parted ways. I watched her walk all the way to the opposite end of the hallway, past the second set of stairs. She went into the furthest door on that side of the hall. That's when I came to another realization of why I didn't belong in this place. Not only did Brandon feel disgusted that his daughter had sat on my lap, but he was so disgusted with me that he made sure my room was the furthest from theirs. My suspicion was that I was probably the only person in this house roomed on this side of the staircases.

But what did I expect? Well, I guess I actually had no expectations at all. I have to keep reminding myself that just yesterday I was in a locked room with no control over my life.

Honestly, though, how much control could I possibly have if I stayed here?

***

And so my first day as a spoiled rich kid was over. Unfortunately, my nap has left me wide awake now. I'm staring at those freaking ivory inlays in that clock again. I don't know why I want to rip them out so bad.

It's noisier tonight than it was last night. I just looked out the window. The traffic is heavy. I suppose that's just New York on a Saturday night. I saw a lot of people walking, too, some hollering and screaming, some staggering drunk. Some looked like they were heading home, but others seemed to be just starting their nights.

I guess I better put my brand new clothes away. Oh, wait, I forgot to mention something. When I got back from shopping with Jen, I found a brand new laptop on my bed. I'm not sure if it was Brandon or Jen's idea, but, either way, this family is definitely sweetening the pot. Now all I need is a mini-fridge stocked with booze and I'll be all set.

I should have thanked them tonight. But there's always tomorrow, I guess. I wonder what tomorrow will bring. How much more can I get out of them before I tell them I don't want to stay?

I guess that's the thief in me talking.

Chapter 4

August 14, 2013

I have come to the conclusion that Brandon is a ghost in this house. I've been told that he has "been around" or "he came home late," but I've only seen him once in nearly a week. And that was just by chance. Two nights ago, I happened to see him going into his room from across the hall very late.

I get it. He's a famous financial guru. But seriously, is it just me, or is it kind of strange that a near-celebrity would bring his criminal brother home to live with him in his mansion with his wife and daughter, and then be out of the picture most of the time? He's either stupid or extremely trusting.

Stranger still is my own slow acclimation to his success. I don't much remember the Brandon of my childhood. That's because he was never around, but it's still hard to reckon with his transition from dysfunctional family escapee to multimillionaire. I've thought about it a lot and I've come to the conclusion he's had to have some shady business deals or something. I just can't reconcile the teenager I knew with the man I'm seeing. Well, not actually seeing as of late. I can't say I like how unfair it seems, that he could have made so much of himself in so little time, while in the same span I've made so little of myself.

But that's all beside the point. I don't know if I'll ever be able to reconcile it completely. And, you know, it doesn't matter all that much. As soon as I get the chance, I'm going to tell him why I can't be here anymore. Why I can't live with them and call this place my home. It sounds easy, but for some reason I have a feeling I'll be met with strong opposition.

I've been extremely busy this past week doing a whole bunch of pointless nothings. I know it sounds like a dream. I get fed three times a day. I have free run of a mansion. The housekeeper is pretty much at my beck and call. But it's not a dream in the least. It's a recipe for utter boredom.

I remember as a kid when some of my teachers would say they were ready to come back and teach because they got bored over the summer. And I remember thinking how stupid that sounded. But I'm starting to understand it now, in part at least.

Back before I was locked up, I always had something to do. I was as busy as they came, forging my empire of dishonest labors. But now that I don't have that option, I'm bewildered by the freedom I have to do whatever. Whenever. And my family—I guess I can call them that since we're related—they haven't helped much. It's like they want me to go out on my own and do what a normal eighteen-year-old would do. But I'm not a normal eighteen-year-old. I don't know what it is to be a teenager. I've been an adult for the past five years. I've had to be.

Most of my days here have started off about the same way. I wake up very early. For some reason my body just doesn't seem to allow me to sleep in. It's extremely annoying, but I've decided not to fight with nature.

Breakfast has been the one constant in the Lane household. Every day at seven a.m., Jen and Ally wait for me at the little table by the bay window. I've learned that Jen really is quite the cook. Breakfast is always different and always delicious. Ally sits closest to the window and saves a seat for her imaginary friend, Wilbur. I haven't been able to quite figure out what Wilbur actually looks like, but I've been told that he greatly dislikes being sat on and that he thinks that I weigh a ton. Needless to say, I sit in the chair across from Wilbur now, the one closest to the kitchen. Jen always sits facing the window because Ally says she likes to see her mommy's face lit up by the sun.

And, truthfully, that is the most interaction I get with them. About twenty minutes of conversation before Ally goes off to pre-school with Ariel and Jen leaves for work. In case I forgot to mention, Jen is a realtor for some high-class real estate company. So not only is Brandon infinitely rich on his own, his wife gets commissions on multi-million dollar homes. I guess that little amount of work constitutes being "part-time work" in her mind.

Most of our morning conversations consist of how Ally is doing in school, which she quite dislikes. I guess she attends some private school that goes year round, but Ally is always ready to voice her opinion on the matter. Her favorite line is usually some variation on how she wants to be like normal kids and have the summer off. To which she always adds, "It's not fair. And Wilbur agrees, don't you, Wilbur?"

And I'm expected to play along. That's because—as I'm often told—Wilbur and I are best friends. Unfortunately, I don't know how to play along, so I generally just stay quiet and eat as much as I can. Did I mention how wonderful the food is? Today I had about a pound of French toast. Thankfully, Jen is kind enough to not force me into any of the conversations and is quick to grab Ally's attention when my awkwardness becomes obvious.

But the last few days, well, I feel like I've come out of my shell, at least a little. I talked to Wilbur for the first time the other day, about which Ally seemed absolutely overjoyed. I think I'll make it a point to at least say "hi" to my faceless friend at breakfast because I've noticed the mood of my days tends to be directed by the mood of my niece. On Tuesday, she was not happy, and that day seemed to be the longest, most uneventful day of them all. Please note that I am not superstitious, but that doesn't mean I'm going to ignore clear correlations.

I've also noticed in the last few days that Jen has been asking me more questions. A few days ago, she asked me what I was going to do that day. In my sadistic humor, I told her I was going to kill my landlords and pillage their belongings. She didn't seem to find my answer humorous at all, but Ally laughed a little. Well, I don't think she quite understood what I said. Ever since then, Jen's been asking some variation of the same question, to which—lesson learned—I've responded in more of an adultish manner.

But this morning Jen looked at me in all seriousness and asked "So what do you plan on doing with your life?" It came out of nowhere. I didn't think through my answer. And now that I think about it, it was as good a chance as any to tell her my future did not include living here and forever accepting their handouts. Instead, I stupidly said, "I don't know," and we kind of left it at that. She didn't seem to mind my answer and quickly took another bite of her toast. I don't know if it was my lack of a clear answer or her quick dismissal that fueled the sudden uneasiness I felt. I just hope they don't think I plan to live like this indefinitely.

I know if Ally had her choice I'd stay here forever and be her grown-up playmate. I've given this little girl nothing to latch onto, yet she never ceases to tell me how happy she is that I'm living here, or how badly she wants me to play with her when we have a chance. Which isn't often because she has a schedule that leaves little time for play. My presence alone seems to be enough for her, which I must say is a good thing. I really have no redeeming qualities, so if her happiness was based on my actions or feelings, she'd hate me dearly.

In all honesty, it's a nice feeling to have unconditional friendship. I have a hunch that this is exactly what Brandon is trying to convey by allowing me to live here. But his method is not quite as effective as his daughter's.

But that's enough of my woeful story on wealthy living. It would be a lie if I told you that I've not found or done anything of my own desire or volition. It would also be a lie if I said that I hadn't enjoyed any of my time here.

Off the top of my head, I can think of two things that have caught my interest this past week. First, I found a way to use these criminal hands that didn't involve—you guessed it—crime. It was Wednesday morning when I woke up to the faint sounds of music. I could barely hear it in my room, but when I opened my door, I heard what sounded like a classical piano piece. It was a familiar song, but I couldn't put a title to it.

My first thought was *Who would be playing music at this hour?* But I decided to follow the sound, as it was at least something different from the usual dead silence that filled the place. I was nearly down the staircase when I first noticed that something sounded off in the music, as if some of the notes were being played wrong. By the time I reached the bottom step, the music stopped for a moment, then started again. That's when I realized that that the music was actually being played on a piano in the house.

I hadn't seen a piano, but I'd been told that Ally was taking lessons, and what wealthy child taking piano lessons didn't have an immaculate grand piano to practice on at home?

The sound came from the door opposite the living room. It was the one part of the house I had not yet been in, as the other side of the foyer seemed to have all of the amenities I needed, like the TV and a bathroom—and it connected to the kitchen.

I opened the door as slowly as I could to not make a sound and disturb the player. The music didn't stop. I snuck in and stopped immediately. It was hard to believe the size and beauty of the room I had entered. The ceilings were as high as the foyer's, meaning as high as the main floor and the balcony. But there was no upstairs in this room, only one large space that ran almost the entire depth of the house.

Like much of the mansion, it looked like an estate from times long past. Long drapes covered the tall windows on the front of the building. The walls weren't really walls at all, but bookshelf after bookshelf after bookshelf. The shelves were all filled to the brim with books. There was even one of those moving-ladder things, which I thought only existed in libraries on movies or TV shows.

And the ceiling was amazing. It was covered in large paintings in strange designs. There was a massive white pillar that descended from the middle of the ceiling to the hardwood floor. Around the pillar were several skylights where the morning sunshine came in and lit up the room. And there were chairs and sofas everywhere. It truly looked like an old library from some stately mansion from history past.

Against the far wall of the room was a small area where there was no furniture. That's where the big, black, grand piano stood facing the doorway. I could barely see blonde hair peeking over the top of it.

As I started to walk toward the piano, I noticed Butler Charles passed out on a brown leather sofa. Rarely did I see the old man not in a position of rest. Actually, I have never seen him working. That being said, he is the groundskeeper, and I have not yet seen the back yard.

I had nearly reached the piano when Ally noticed me. She smiled and kept playing. Her fingers moved so fast I couldn't keep up with them, and the sound they made was beautiful, save a few off notes here and there. I sat down beside her, and for the next few minutes she played, with just little hesitations as she turned the pages in front of her.

When she finished the piece, Charles suddenly woke up. Actually, he nearly jumped out of his seat and left the room through the door I had entered. I don't think he even noticed I was there.

"Do you like that song?" Ally asked me. There was still a hint of sleepiness in her young voice.

"I did. It sounded very familiar. What's it called?"

"Are you serious? It's the 'Well Tempered Clavier' by Bach!" she said, as if I should have known.

And for the next five minutes, I had a surreal experience. I received a lecture on classical music from a five-year-old who probably couldn't even spell the title of the song she had just played, nor the name of the composer, either.

I didn't hear half of what she said. She lost me with phrases like "the movements of Bach's music" and "the seventh measure of this piece," but I found humor in how adult she sounded. It was nothing like the way she acted at breakfast.

"You're not listening to me, are you?"

I didn't even try to lie. "Can you show me how to play?" For some reason, I felt intrigued by the instrument in front of me.

A huge smile came over Ally's face, but before she could say anything, the door opened. "It's time for breakfast." It was Jen.

"Aww, Mom! We were having fun!" Right before my eyes Ally went from adult back to child again.

"Well, fun will have to wait, young lady."

"Fun sucker!" I added, just for a reaction, even though I wholeheartedly agreed with Ally.

I didn't get much of a reaction, though. Jen just smiled then opened the door wide enough for Ally to walk through.

I followed.

But I have not given up on the piano. I decided that night to use my brand-new laptop for the first time. I found some tutorials online. They were about as confusing as Ally's lecture, but now, I can proudly say, in the last two days I've gained some insight on reading music. I have yet to make a beautiful sound on the piano—but, hey—you have to start somewhere.

***

So...switching gears drastically...I told you there were two things that have caught my interest this week. The first one, the piano, is at least a way to pass the time until I can finally talk to my brother and figure some things out. The second is not even in the same category. We'll get to that. This time, I have to take you back even further. To Sunday.

I can't say I dreamt of Disney Saturday night. I really can't say I even dreamed at all. Regardless, when I heard the knock on my door, followed by Ariel's broken English, waking up was the last thing I wanted to do. I knew it was early because the sun hadn't even begun to shine through my window. But Ariel was persistent and kept on knocking.

Finally I answered, "You can come in."

Like Jen had done when I was with Ally on Wednesday, Ariel just poked her head around the door. "Time go to church," she said.

At first, I thought I had misunderstood her. "What did you say?"

"Be. Ready. For. Church." She said it really slow, like it was my hearing and not her dialect that caused the confusion.

I heard the word *church* loud and clear this time. And I nearly laughed.

Ariel looked at me, her dark unibrow—okay, so they're not really connected, but close—furrowed in a look of confusion.

I was not about to start an argument with her. I realized her visit was not meant to question whether I felt like going, but to tell me very matter-of-factly that I *was* going.

Thirty minutes later, I found myself riding with the family—minus Brandon—in what Ally called their "church car." It was a black boat that looked like it belonged in Gotham City or with some rich mobster. There were two rows behind the front seats. I had to sit in the middle row between Butler Charles, who happened to be sleeping again, and Ariel, who carried a massive Bible, a purse, and another tote bag filled with something very heavy. I ended up with the heavy bag on my lap. Ariel said it was "Sunday school treats for kids."

Ally and Jen sat in the back. That means, as you may have concluded, there was a driver for our "church car." A trained driver, I might add, one who never spoke a word and never even looked back at us. I later learned his name was Andy. Ally sang what sounded like nursery songs the entire time, which was fine with me, as the singing partly drowned out Charles' snoring. Jen hummed along. There was little talking, except when Jen complimented my new outfit. I just *happened* to pick out one of the shirts she and I both liked when we were shopping.

Before I move on, let me just say this. Going to church is not the second interest I wanted to tell you about. As a matter of fact, I really don't want to talk about that mental place at all. It was everything I imagined it would be—well mostly. It was massive and full of dressed-up people, to which I felt immediately rebellious in my jeans and long-sleeved T.

First they sang weird songs, and then the pastor talked about God knows what. I'm sure only God himself could understand the weird stuff he was saying. It did have a slight, heavy-metal feel to it as he said things like "covered by the blood" and "the heavy chains of hatred." But that didn't make what he was saying any more appealing to me.

Jen seemed to eat it up, though. And I assumed Charles and Ariel did, too, but I never saw either of them the entire time we were there. Maybe there was a separate service for illegal aliens and a nap room for the elderly.

This is totally off the topic, but Jen looked gorgeous. She was wearing a very form-fitting, springish dress that came just above her knees. And her hair was in these strange braids that tangled around the back of her head and made this elaborate design. Did I mention her figure? How did my brother land her? It had to be the money. But I'm done with that. I mean, it has to be some type of sin to talk about your brother's wife like that, right?

Jen was kind enough to guide me through the service so I didn't look like too much of a fool in front of eight thousand people I didn't know. I found the church population in the little program thing they gave out at the front door.

The last thing they did during the service was pass a very large number of golden plates around. And people put money in them. I nonchalantly glanced over at the check that Jen had filled out. It was for two thousand dollars! I almost fell out of my chair. How's that for a hint at how rich my brother is?

Finally, it was over. Every presupposition I had about church had been affirmed. I was ready to walk out in no way changed by the experience.

But that's when it happened.

I was following the long line of people trudging toward the exit when I heard a very soft voice with a slight English accent behind me. I turned and met the gaze of two dark green eyes surrounded by freckles.

"Hello, how are you?"

"Hi," I replied. Somehow I managed to not answer the question.

She smiled, then walked past me and pushed her way through the crowd instead of moving with it like Jen and I were doing.

If Jen was the epitome of the word *beautiful*, then there are no words that can adequately describe this girl. She was shorter than Jen and had a thinner frame. Her hair was brown, but shorter and kind of spiky. It wasn't buzzed off like my hair, but it was definitely not the typical style of a respectable women.

But none of that really caught my attention as much as her clothes did. She was wearing a blue sweater and one of those plaid skirts like you see on Catholic schoolgirls, but this church was not Catholic. Anyway, the skirt was quite short for church. Her outfit was set off with a pair of red, low-top chucks. I also noticed a piercing in her left eyebrow and ears covered in studs.

I wasn't the only rebel in the audience.

I guess I was staring, because Jen grabbed my arm to get my attention. "I wouldn't even think about it," she said. "That's the pastor's daughter, Analeigh. She's trouble."

"But her accent?" I asked.

"Adopted at thirteen," Jen answered. "Just stay away. Please just trust—"

"She's trouble." I replied. "Got it."

But *trouble* was exactly where I belonged and exactly why I instantly became so intrigued with this

Analeigh girl, who seemed to disappear as quickly as she had appeared.

Needless to say, my first time at church turned out to be better than expected. I had something to look forward to next time. There was someone that seemed to fit in just about as well as I did. The only bad part was I'd have to wait a week just to try to see her again.

So far, my justification to seek this girl out is pretty weak if I must say so. *Maybe I can help her* is what I've been telling myself. But I'll be honest with you. It's a lie to convince myself that I'm not looking for another friend besides my five-year-old niece.

***

So there you have it. A painfully slow summary of my week. My ups and my downs and my in-betweens. I feel like this whole account has been no more interesting than the melodramatic diary entry of a depressed teenage girl. I apologize if that is the case. At least now you can see how boring my week truly has been. I've learned to read music and developed a stalker mentality.

I better wrap it up before Ariel comes in to turn down my bed. You can add *stubborn* to the long list of adjectives describing her. Every night like clockwork, she comes in and asks if I want it done, and every night I say no. But she seems to like what she does. If Butler Charles' workload is any indicator of what is expected of Ariel, then I'd say she has it pretty easy.

***

Here comes weekend number two. Wish me luck.

Chapter 5

August 15, 2013

J ust before midnight, I found myself pawing through the downstairs bathroom's medicine cabinet. I just couldn't sleep, and it was the perfect excuse to find some prescription pills. In juvie, drugs were an easy favor away. If I took any pills, it was few and far between, but sometimes a heavy dose of sleep aid was just what the doctor ordered.

Unfortunately, the downstairs bathroom was clearly set up for guests. There was some children's pain reliever and some different types of antibiotic ointments and antihistamines, but nothing of the therapeutic level I was looking for.

Defeated, I started back up the stairs, but as I set foot on the first step, I distinctly heard my name. It wasn't someone calling me, or even speaking to me at all. It was Brandon's voice coming from the living room.

I slunk down to the foyer door, trying to make as little noise as possible.

"I hope you're right," I heard Jen say.

I could almost see Brandon embracing her. "It'll be fine," I heard him say. "He may be angry, but it's for his own good. There's no need to dance around responsibility."

"It just might be better to wait awhile until he's comfortable," she said.

"That may never happen."

There was a long pause before Jen conceded. "I guess you're right."

By "he" I was assuming they meant me. What would make me angry? I had a strange feeling I was going to be asked to work, or do something to pull my weight around the house that I didn't even want to stay in. So much for the life of leisure.

Apparently I had come in at the end of the conversation because I heard both of them shuffling toward the door. My first reaction was to try to run up the stairs, but I knew there was no way to get up there fast enough without being seen. I didn't want to be caught.

So I froze, flat up against the wall. The door swung open and Jen was the first one through. She immediately went down the hall toward the kitchen without any suspicion on her part. Brandon, on the other hand, started to walk up the stairs across from me. He was still in a suit, apparently not long home from work. It only took him a few steps before he looked my way and caught me pressed against the lower wooden panels of the wall.

"How long have you been sitting there?"

I felt like a thief caught red-handed. "Long enough to know you were talking about me."

Brandon stood still but placed both hands on the railing. "Let me rephrase the question. What did you hear while you were spying on us?"

I pushed myself to my feet and started walking up the other staircase, across from him. "Not much. Except something about responsibility. Is there something you want to tell me?"

For a split second, Brandon looked a little amused. But his face quickly went flat. "Good. It's late and I'm not in the mood to talk tonight. But we'll talk later."

I was actually content with that answer. All I wanted was to get back to my room. I was embarrassed enough as it was, so I didn't want to prolong it. But I only made it a few steps before Brandon asked, "May I ask what you are doing down here this late at night?"

I could have asked him the same question, but I chose to stay brief with the conversation. "Just couldn't sleep," I answered.

"Okay," he said, "but I'm not keen on having you sneaking around my house at night. You wouldn't steal from us or do anything like that, would you?"

So much for brief.

"Actually," I responded angrily. "I was down here looking for drugs. I can't sleep, and a small dose of sleeping pills would have done the trick. So, yes, I would steal from you, hoping you didn't keep count of your prescriptions."

I expected some backlash, but Brandon didn't say anything right away. He walked up to my level, turned, looked across the foyer, and said "Good night. And, by the way, all you have to do is ask. I can get you some sleeping pills."

I was in fight mode now, but there was clearly nothing to fight about. So I didn't say anything. Defeated a second time, I started toward my room. Just as I grabbed the door handle, I heard Brandon say my name again. He was in his bedroom now, only his head sticking out past the door.

"Never mind," he said. Then he shut his door.

Though he couldn't see me, I flipped him off before going into my room for a sleepless night.

Chapter 6

August 17, 2013

Well, the explosion just happened. I can still feel the adrenaline blasting through my veins, and anger—pure, unadulterated anger—along with it. I could have killed him. In an alternate reality, I could see Brandon at the foot of my bed, bleeding out, begging for his life while I just watched him die. Fortunately—or, unfortunately, however you want to look at it—that wasn't my real reality.

Believe it or not, after a week of hiding, Brandon just walked into my room and said, "You start school on Monday." Again, not "how are you doing," or maybe just a cordial "hi." It was a command, not a question.

The words had barely left his mouth before I went off. And I mean, *I went off.* I'm not one hundred percent sure exactly what I said, but it was a curse-laden barrage of screams. Brandon just stood there, a blank stare on his now clean-shaven face, while I called him every name in the book and told him repeatedly that I was leaving.

Then, when I realized I wasn't getting enough of a reaction out of him, I stood up and began to yell at him at face level. We stood there, toe to toe, for about two seconds, when all of sudden he put his hands on my chest and pushed me onto the bed.

The blank stare was gone.

"Now you listen to me, you selfish punk!" he yelled, pointing his right index finger at me. "You're eighteen years old, you have no job, no education, no direction, and no money to do anything except shoot your life straight to hell. You are going to school because I'm giving you a second chance. And you are going to take it. You have no say in the matter."

I had to admit he was right. Which made me even angrier.

And he had plenty more to say. "Did you think I brought you here for free handouts and a life of leisure at my expense? I want to help you. But you have to let me help you."

"Like you helped Kim?" The words came out before I even had a chance to stop them.

Brandon's face immediately went blank again. "Just…you…," he muttered, trying to find words. "You're going to school, and that's it!"

"Who made you king?" I fired back.

"No one. Just let me help you."

I didn't respond.

Brandon turned around and left as fast as he had come in.

And just like that, it was over.

But for the last ten minutes or so, the conversation—or, rather, the yelling match—has been running over and over in my head. I've been thinking of the things I should have said, could have said, and wished I had said. But I keep coming up with the same conclusion.

I hate to say this, but Brandon was right. As much as I've wanted to leave this place, I have no resources, and no clear direction. And it makes me so angry! I'm so pissed off, I don't even want to write anymore. I'm pissed because I'm stuck here in my room, and now I can't even join them for the movie tonight. There's no way I can face him.

And I'm pissed because, as much as I don't want to admit it, I think this is exactly what I wanted to hear. Not the whole school thing. I will not be going to school no matter what he says. But the fact that I'm not leaving this place.

And you know what? I'm just pissed because I can be pissed.

Chapter 7

August 19, 2013

I hate admitting to a lie, but I know I said there was no way I was going back to school. Well, at the time, I really meant it.

But at 7:30 this morning, I stood in front of the dreaded institution. I wasn't ready to start my senior year of high school, though. The last time I stepped foot inside a school building, I was thirteen, and I had just finished the seventh grade. I was two weeks into the summer when my parents were killed. A week later, I was on my own. How's that for an educational career?

I know I'm only eighteen years old, but the kids around me all seemed so young. I felt so out of place. All I could think about was how much it was going to suck. When it comes to real life, I can hold my own. But when it comes to books? I know I'm completely inept.

At least Brandon was kind enough not to send me to some extravagant private school, where my tattooed, white-supremacist look would have me immediately shunned. The good news is that my hair is growing out now, so I'm starting to look somewhat less conspicuous.

The school, which is named after some dude I've never heard of, is a mammoth building that looks more like a prison camp than an educational facility. The walls were once brick red but have faded into more of a dull gray, and the windows actually have bars on them. The kids—I know they're my peers, but I still can't get past the fact of how much older I feel—seemed to reflect the despair of the building. Though I couldn't imagine they were any more displeased or anxious than I was.

Not knowing what else to do, I just followed the long line inside. Me, the jocks, the goths, the preps, the stoners, and every other imaginable shade of humanity.

Goal number one was to find the school office. Jen told me they would be able to help with whatever questions I had. At the time, I was embarrassed to tell her that I had no actual knowledge of how anything in a public high school actually worked. Once I was inside the building, I wished wholeheartedly that I had asked her every question that came to mind. I was a fish out of water with no sense of direction.

If not for my overwhelming anxiety, I would have been absolutely bitter. And I feel justified saying I had good reason. Brandon had given me no choice. Go to school or...yeah, go to school. Every part of me wanted to leave the house this morning, walk around the corner, and see if I could get back in through the back somehow. But I figured Brandon had connections—like all rich people do—so there was no way of getting out of it.

Even if school had been out of the picture, I don't think my day would have been all that great. I was already disappointed and quite frustrated. And I'm kind of ashamed to tell you why.

But here it goes.

As you know, I'd waited an entire week to try to find the pastor's daughter. But of course (just to add to my disappointment) she wasn't even at church yesterday. It was like I had built up this overwhelming anticipation and couldn't find a way to release it. I likened it to waiting for my last day at juvie, then realizing that I had the wrong day marked on my calendar and I still had to wait another week.

Okay, I know that was a terrible analogy. But like I said, I'm not very smart.

I just couldn't get her out of my head. I left the church thinking about her, I went to bed thinking about her, and I woke up thinking about her. Even as I walked through the school hall, amidst all the chaos and confusion, I couldn't stop thinking about her.

As I'm writing this, I'm thinking about her.

Inside the school, the anxiety was immediately heightened by my confusion and disorientation. High school is nothing like I imagined it to be. Everything I thought I knew came from TV shows and movies, but the shiny floors and freshly painted lockers, walls, and everything else in TV high schools did not exist in my reality. This place was a dump. Years upon years of irresponsible teenagers had taken its toll on the place. Rusty lockers. Dirty floors. Cracked windows.

By the time I found the office, I was already running behind…along with half the foreign and freshman population. I stood in line forever just to get my class schedule and find out my first class wasn't even in the same vicinity.

Needless to say, I was late to English. Luckily, Mr. Harrington, the resident dinosaur of the school, as I later learned, barely seemed coherent enough to notice me walk in. He gave Butler Charles a run for his money when it came to the "old" category. But Mr. Harrington, or Tom, as he asked us to call him, was a little more agile and much less sleepy than the butler.

But no less senile. Eight times he "forgot what he was about to say." Yes, I counted. It took the entire period for him just to tell us about the three major writing assignments. If only I could have shown him my trash bag full notebooks at home, he'd have been able to see how much I really didn't need this class.

Nor do I need chemistry, geometry, or political science. Unfortunately, I do need somewhere to sleep each night, so I guess I'm stuck in this school for now.

I felt even more stupid after each class. For one thing, I was ill-prepared for any first-day assignments. How was I to know I was supposed to bring things like a protractor or a compass, or some type of binder to hold the crap-load of paper that each teacher would be handing out? Nobody told me any of this. I mean, maybe I should have known, but forgive me for living on the outskirts of society for the past five years.

And then I got all of those pitiful stares as I walked from class to class, carrying my stack of papers and trying not to drop them all over the place. As famous as my brother is, I'm sure most of them knew I was the reject, the one that got rescued from a life of crime. From experience, I know information like this travels fast.

I also began to notice the groups of individuals pointing fingers and laughing as if I couldn't see them. Or maybe they didn't care. At least there was one thing in that awful place that fit the mold of the high school experience as I had imagined it. The ones that laughed at my expense were the ones I'm just going to call the dominant genes. You know what I mean. The blond cheerleaders with skirts that don't cover their underwear. The big, bulky jocks who date said skanks. Basically, the people who in another life would have happily shared my tattoos and cried. "Heil, Hitler," while others were being led to the slaughter.

But I consciously made an effort not to break anyone's teeth in on my first day. Not because I didn't want to, but because I wasn't ready to have another round with Brandon. Or have to explain to Ally what a suspension was. I just needed to stick to myself and stay clear of any deviant behavior. That was my new goal in life after all.

But the whole "stick to myself" mantra became meaningless in my chemistry class when I was forced to find a partner to do my labs with for the quarter. I did everything I could to find the most loserish, darkest, most introverted person in the room. First, I tried to partner up with the Marilyn Manson look-alike in the back corner, but one of his own stepped in before I could get there. Then there was the girl with braces, the one who clearly hadn't developed yet and wore the baggiest sweatshirt she could to hide that fact. But even she was quickly taken by the freakishly tall kid with acne, who was clearly in a dogfight with puberty himself.

Defeated, I went back to my desk and hoped that someone would be forced to sit beside me. I wasn't that lucky. Somehow, I had managed to be the odd one out.

"That's not right," Mr. Gregg, the chemistry teacher, said. "Jess, come up here and partner with Mr. Lane."

I turned around and saw someone I had missed. Either I was blind or she had to have come in late. This girl wore skin-tight black jeans and a white tank top…with a black bra on underneath. The tank was extremely see-through. No lack of confidence, that was for sure. And it was understandable. She had the same features as Jen. She was tall and slender with long blond hair. But unlike my brother's wife, she was a little heavy on the black eye shadow and lipstick. As she walked toward me from the back of the room, I couldn't help but be a little intimidated. She had that kind of presence.

"Thanks, Darin," she said to the teacher as she sat down beside me.

"It's Mr. Gregg, or sir, if you must." He gave her a meaningful stare, as if her lack of respect was expected. "Okay class, let's—"

"Hi, I'm Jess," she told me with a cheery but soft voice. Definitely not what I was expecting.

"I'm—"

"Alex Lane. The millionaire's charity case. Trust me, everyone knows who you are. There are no secrets here. Well, I mean, there are a few."

"That's comforting," I replied.

"Don't worry," she said, turning to face me. "I'm the girl that plays with fire and voodoo dolls. Or so I hear."

I was feeling a little more at ease. "So we're both freaks? Although I don't get that vibe from you."

"Yeah, well, appearances aren't everything, now, are they? I mean, that burning cross on your forearm would really offend some of the more religion-oriented folks in here."

I immediately felt the urge to cover my tattoo. I was about to respond, in fact, when Mr. Gregg cleared his throat.

"Are you two done talking?"

"We are now," I answered, which garnered a few laughs from the rest of class.

And then I got the stare. "Well, that's good, Mr. Lane. Now, class, here's a podcast from the great scientist...*blah blah blah*."

Well, that's about all I got out of chemistry that day. There was a whole bunch of odd looking tools in front of me. Goggles, glass vials, other weird things I had no idea how to use. Thankfully, I didn't have to. Those would come in a later class, so I could surely embarrass myself then.

After chemistry, I wondered whether or not I really wanted to join the rest of the school in the cafeteria for lunch. If everyone knew who I was, I could only imagine what could be waiting for me in there, especially if I was forced to sit alone.

"Hey, Alex, why don't you come sit with me and my friends?" Jess asked. Well, that was one problem solved. She stepped in front of me and began to walk backwards.

"You really want to be seen with me?" I asked her.

"It doesn't matter. They all look at me, anyways. You won't throw off my swagger, if that's what you mean."

"But I thought we were freaks," I said. "We shouldn't have friends, right? Maybe I should just eat alone."

She started to turn around. "Well, suit yourself."

"No, wait!" I said, a little too loud and desperate.

Jess started laughing. "I was totally kidding. I mean, seriously, no need to be so high strung."

All I could do was laugh at myself, and hope my embarrassment wasn't too noticeable.

"Come on," she said, walking beside me. "We can always use another outcast at our table."

The cafeteria was a madhouse. It was loud and it smelled like hordes of sweaty teenagers mixed with hospital food.

"Welcome to paradise," Jess said. She reached down and grabbed my hand.

As usual, my instinct was to pull away, but her grip was tight. She started walking, and pulled me with her.

"Not so high strung, remember? I know I'm a girl, but it's okay to touch me."

I had no words to respond with. I was beyond uncomfortable, so I decided I might as well just go with the flow and see where it took me.

Jess guided me through the masses, pushing through people without apology. We attracted a lot of stares, though. I saw so many eyes looking at me, and people's smiles as they made comments under their breath.

If only all the comments had been quiet.

We made it to nearly the middle of the cafeteria, when a large dominant gene letter jacket walked up to Jess and stopped directly in front of her. He had *jerk* written all over his face, as did the table of letter jackets behind him.

"Well, well, well," he said in a loud voice, clearly trying to get the attention of the entire room. "What do we have here?"

"Get out of our way, Levi." Jess tried to go around him, but the big goon stayed in front of her.

"Not so fast, Gothika. What are you doing with this juvenile delinquent?"

By now, the cafeteria was silent.

I was doing everything I could not to get involved. *Don't get suspended, don't get suspended, don't get suspended*, I kept telling myself.

"It's none of your business," Jess said. She released my hand, and pushed him hard on the chest.

He didn't move. This Levi kid was quite the chunk of muscle. He stood at least half a foot taller than me (I'm just over six feet tall, in case you wanted to know.) And I bet he had at least fifty pounds on me, too. I'm pretty lean and strong (I worked out a lot in juvie), but this dude looked like he spent half his life in the gym.

Not that I feared muscle in the least. That was my problem. I feared no man, which could only mean my suspension from high school was getting ever nearer.

"No need to get out the claws, Jess," he said. "I just asked you a question."

"And I answered it," she spat back. "It's too bad your brain is even smaller than your manhood. Then maybe you would have known that."

The cafeteria burst into laughter.

"You would know the size now, wouldn't you, you little wh—"

"Just shut your mouth!" I yelled, stepping in front of Jess. I'd had enough dumb jock for the day. Not that it takes much to set me off in the first place.

Jess grabbed my arm and tried to pull me back. "Alex, it's okay. I can handle—"

"No," Levi said. "Let's hear out our resident criminal," Levi said, his smile growing even larger.

And now I was in the spotlight, exactly where I didn't want to be. And I had nothing to say.

"That's what I thought," Levi said. "You might as well let the little princess do all of the talking."

Now I could talk. "You might as well just listen to me and shut your mouth," I responded. "Before I wipe that stupid smile off your face."

The whole table of letter jackets stood up.

"What, you really think you can stand up to me and walk out of here without a busted up face?"

I didn't have to wipe away the smile. Levi looked really angry now.

"Yes, I think I can." Actually, I knew I could. I had every confidence that I would lay that giant oaf out. "And when I'm done with you, I'd be happy to do the same to all of your boyfriends behind you."

Of course that set off the chants of "Fight, fight, fight!" It filled the cafeteria.

Jess pulled me back a step. "Alex, don't do it."

Levi took off his jacket.

Well, if I was sure of one thing, it was that I couldn't think of a better reason to get kicked out of school on my first day than to beat the crap out of the idiot in front of me.

I felt the adrenaline start to take over. The sound of the chanting began to fade until it was barely audible. Some new part of me was trying to remind me of the oath I took when I got out of juvie, that is, not to do criminal things anymore. The old part of me kept saying that having a fight at school was not considered a crime. The old part was winning the battle.

And then things happened both very quickly and yet slowly at the same time. I know, that doesn't make any sense at all. But I saw Levi pull his right arm back for the first blow. And I was ready to respond.

I was three steps ahead of him. First, I would move out of the way just in time, and let his momentum carry him past me. Second, I'd kick the back of his right leg, just behind the knee, which would force him to his knees. And, third, an elbow to his jaw to knock him out.

I was already thinking about his friends, and how they would be a much bigger challenge.

Unfortunately, none of my planning came to fruition.

Because at that moment I saw her. Just over Levi's left shoulder stood the pastor's daughter. Her green eyes met mine, and I was frozen. I could tell she was yelling, but I had no idea what she was saying.

And you know, I may have even smiled at her. At least that's how I remember it. Well, that's actually the last thing I remember, before I felt a crushing pain in my left temple.

And then everything went black.

***

I remember briefly waking up and feeling the pain that filled my head. Not one of those little pains that stick to one place, but all over. I knew I'd been knocked out. It wasn't the first time that's happened to me.

Then I heard the school nurse saying, "That's what you get for letting just anybody come to this school." I didn't actually know it was the nurse at the time, but I put two and two together later on.

And then it's flashes of memory. I know I walked down a hall that didn't have very many people in it. And I remember going through a door with words on the glass window. Everything else is hazy, almost like a dream.

Levi must have had a mean right hook.

And then I knew I was sitting on an awful-looking brown sofa. In front of me was the door with words on it. It was actually two stickers that said *Principal* and *Vice Principal.*

I sat there for quite some time, reeling from the pain of the headache, what I believe had turned into a migraine. It's hard to believe the nurse just let me go. This school was a dump. My vision still wasn't up to par. I couldn't see much peripherally.

That's why I didn't see him sitting beside me. When I actually felt the brush of an arm, I realized I wasn't alone.

I turned to see a tall, muscular guy that looked like Jess' twin sitting beside me. He had short blonde hair. Like Jess, he wore very tight black jeans and a tank top, only his was dark green. He was covered with tattoos—and I mean *covered*—and piercings galore.

"Did you get knocked out, too?" I asked, trying to smile.

He returned the smile. "No," he said. "I tried to do the knocking out. I wasn't as successful, though." His voice was extremely high pitched and feminine, as were his hand gestures. It seemed like everyone I'd met today didn't fit their appearance.

I looked him over. "You don't look like one of those meatheads."

"Oh, I'm not, believe you me. I was after Levi. I got him a few times, but I couldn't land the haymaker like he got you with."

"Wait." I had to get the story straight. It wasn't making sense. "What happened?"

59

"Well," he answered, crossing his legs like a woman. That was definitely something I'd never seen a goth do. "You really weren't part of it, except for getting hit. But I needed an excuse to punch Levi, anyway, so thanks. That moron deserved it."

"But why were you helping me?" I felt a little creeped out that this clearly gay goth was defending me. I didn't think I put off as such, but maybe my stint in juvie gave the wrong impression.

He must have seen the look on my face, or maybe he just knew by the tone in my voice why I was asking that question. "Don't worry," he said with a laugh, "I'm not gay if that's what you're thinking."

I must have sighed audibly, because he kept laughing. And then, contrary to his answer, he laid his hand on my leg.

I pulled my leg away. "I'm sorry," I said. "It's just your voice. And the way you present yourself. I thought—"

"You thought what everyone else thinks," he cut in. "No need for apologies. I'm what you would call a metrosexual. Just with a knack for the dark, as you can tell. Stereotypes will getcha. You know what people will say after this? That I was just trying to be macho as a cover. And I suppose if I ever have a girlfriend, that will be a cover, too."

I'm not going to lie. That's exactly what I would have thought. Juvenile, maybe, but I think it's just easier to fit people into nice little categories. Although that's never really successful.

He smiled again. "My name is Thomas, by the way. Nice to meet you."

I shook his hand. "My name is—"

"Alex. I know. The millionaire's—"

"—charity case," I finished. "I've heard that before."

We both laughed. By then, my headache was starting to subside, if only a little. "So, I still don't know why you defended me."

"Well, it was nothing," Thomas answered, putting his right hand over his heart. "But Analeigh and Jess were so worried—"

"Wait!" I couldn't believe it. "You know Analeigh?"

"Yes," he responded. "And Jess does, too. You were coming to sit at our table when that idiot decided to make his presence known. Like he does at least ten times every year."

So I really had seen her before the blackout.

"Are you okay?" Thomas asked. I must have had a dazed look or something.

"Yeah, I'm fine. I've just been trying to find Analeigh for the past week."

"Well, you found her. And her boyfriend." Thomas chuckled.

"Wait! Her boyfriend?"

"Yeah, Levi and her have been dating for a while. For the life of me, I don't know why."

I couldn't believe it either. "But why would she—"

I was interrupted by a door opening. Levi walked out. His face was busted up, bruised, and bleeding.

"How you feeling, sweetheart?" Thomas asked, starting to stand up.

Levi jumped a little. "Freaks," was all he muttered, before he went out the main door.

"You come back and see us," Thomas called after him.

"Thomas!" a voice yelled from the room that Levi had just come out of. "Get in here!" It was Principal Covington. I would be meeting him next.

"Well," Thomas said, giving me a military salute. "I don't think Levi will be bothering you anymore. And we'll be seeing much more of each other in the future. After our suspensions, of course."

I didn't know if that was good or bad. But either way, he had connections to Analeigh. Although now, knowing that she was dating the loser that had knocked me out, I wasn't so sure I was as interested in meeting her.

But it didn't look like I'd have a choice.

***

I had my turn with Principal Covington and was told exactly what I was expecting to hear. I was suspended for the remainder of the week.

"Mr. Lane," he said, "this isn't going to happen again. Your brother had to pull a few strings just to get you in at senior level classes. You should have been a freshman. So don't blow it."

I was dismissed and found Jen waiting out front for me. "I don't even want to know what happened," she said. "It's over now. I hope you learned your lesson."

I didn't say anything. It was strange to get such direct parental guidance from someone who probably hadn't even been out of high school for ten years herself.

She didn't say much of anything else on the ride back. I wasn't sure why, that is, until I walked into the house. Brandon was sitting on the lowest step of the right staircase. He was wearing a suit and had clearly just come from work. He stood up.

I didn't even attempt to speak. I was prepared to receive my judgment.

But he smiled as he walked over to me. "That's quite the shiner."

"Quite the headache as well," I responded, unsure what to make of his comment.

Brandon looked uncomfortable as he put his hand on my shoulder. "Alex, I'm not going to get mad at you for taking a punch or defending the honor of some girl—what was her name?"

"Jess."

"Yeah. Her. But I would have been really angry had you done what I think you are fully capable of doing. You were going to hurt those boys, weren't you?"

How did he know all of this? *Connections, connections, connections*, I thought.

I must have given him a strange look, because he answered my thoughts. "I've talked to Principal Covington. He told me what happened."

"So he told you I didn't do anything wrong?"

"Yes." He finally released my shoulder. "He told me you threatened to hurt them, though. My question is, would you have done it?"

"Without question."

Brandon's smile went away. "That's what I thought. And that's what scares me. But you didn't. And that's really what is important."

"But I could have, you know."

Brandon looked me squarely in the eyes. "Yes, I know. But you're not going to. Right?"

I thought maybe I was getting some Jedi mind trick. Or maybe it was just a trick question. "No," I replied.

"Good. Unfortunately, the good old principal still wanted to set an example with you, so I couldn't get you out of being suspended.

"It sounds like you've already done enough for me." I said.

Brandon clearly didn't get my sarcasm. "Well, that's okay, it's no problem—"

"No," I interrupted. "You haven't done me any favors."

When he didn't respond, Jen gave a loud sigh, I suppose to cut the tension. "Okay, boys, let's just end it at that. Since we're both home early, I'll have Ariel help me cook up a nice early dinner tonight."

Brandon was the one to end our stare down, to which I was relieved. "Okay, hunny." He pulled her close to him and kissed her on the forehead. "I'll get cleaned up."

"Okay!" Jen said. Her voice was way too bubbly for the current situation. "I suggest you do the same, Alex. Dinner's at five."

I didn't know what it meant to get cleaned up for dinner, so I just sat in my room for a couple hours. More surprising than Brandon's lack of anger was the cell phone sitting on my bed. And it wasn't the cheap little flip-phone things I remember using before. It was much nicer. Jen had left a note beside it that said *Unlimited minutes and data. Have fun!*

I had just gotten suspended, and they were treating me like I was a royal guest. Maybe Brandon figured positive reinforcement might work better than negative reinforcement with me. Or maybe they were just nicer than I gave them credit for.

I got through the awkward "thank you" as soon as I could at dinner.

"We'd rather have you calling us than Principal Covington," Jen said.

I followed up that awkward exchange by getting called out for eating before praying.

"No food until it is blessed!" Ally said.

Everyone laughed as I told them I was sorry.

Brandon *blessed* the food. It took an awfully long time.

But it was worth the wait. It was absolutely delicious. Chicken with mashed potatoes, corn, and some cheesecake dessert that was to die for. I ate more than my fill.

Everyone was there except Butler Charles. "He goes on vacation once every month in Syracuse," Jen told me. "He's usually only gone a few days."

Brandon was in a good mood still, which may have been due to the amount of wine he drank during the meal. Jen capped him off at four glasses. He told us stories about his day, how he nearly managed to lose a seven-million-dollar account, before he spilled his coffee all over his shirt.

"It's a good thing you always keep extras," Ally declared.

"Always be prepared," Brandon told her.

"Right."

Ariel excused herself first, saying another prayer—at least I think that's what it was—as she stood up. All I got out of it was, "Thank-you-Jesus."

And that was about it.

If you take away my humiliation and the pounding headache, it was a fairly good day. Well, at least it ended fairly well.

It was actually one of those days that're hard to categorize. It felt more like two days wrapped up into one. But that was probably because of my forced nap in the middle. The day came with both disappointment and relief. For one, I seemed to have made a friend or two without even trying. But it sucks that I won't be seeing them anytime soon due to my suspension.

Yes, I said it would suck being out of school. I'll probably never say that again.

And, two, maybe Brandon is starting to come around. Unfortunately, he has about eighteen years of hell to make up for.

But I can't really complain. I didn't kill anybody today. And that's always a plus.

Chapter 8

August 20, 2013

Only two turns. That's all it took to reach from where I was sitting, which happened to be the bottom step of the mansion, to where I was arrested just under two years ago. The place couldn't have been more than two miles away. Until today, it had never really occurred to me that one of the lowest points in my life (of which I have had many) happened so close to where my brother and his family called home.

I had to wonder…did my name come on the news that night? Was Brandon shocked that after three years apart, with no contact whatsoever, we were actually living so close together? It's all speculation, of course, including the idea that Brandon actually lived in this house at that time, but I can only imagine his surprise.

It was just about as surprising as Brandon becoming a millionaire in such a short span of years. But that's another point altogether.

I sat on that bottom step for hours, facing south, wondering how long it would take me to reach that spot. The spot where I handed over my last hit of heroin. Where I put a gun in an undercover cop's mouth and was ready to pull the trigger before his friends surrounded me. And where the scar over my left eye originated, after said friends pounded my face into the cement while handcuffing me.

To this day, I only remember one sentence. One of the cops jokingly told his partner, "After years of crime, the great Alex Lane is sitting in the back of my car and bleeding all over it." At the time, I was swinging in and out of consciousness, but I do remember the gross amount of blood all over me.

I imagine some newspaper headlines were about the same.

Those were the days—the days I can't imagine going back to, yet feel a constant pull toward. I was a superstar, but for all the wrong reasons. I think it's easier finding fame doing wrong than doing right. But that's quite a proclamation from someone who's never really done anything right in his whole life.

That being said, the problem of figuring out how long it would take to get from the point I was sitting at to the point of my arrest seems rather insignificant in the whole scope of things.

And, honestly, I feel rather insignificant sitting on the steps of a modern-day palace, staring aimlessly down a road once traveled, wondering how to run back to a garbage hole that I so luckily crawled out of. Or, in more precise terms, was drug out of.

Chapter 9

August 24, 2013

Another week stuck in the mansion. But don't get me wrong, I've found ways to entertain myself. I've almost learned a song—"Twinkle Twinkle Little Star"—on the piano. When she heard it, Ally immediately graduated me to her intermediate piano primer. What can I say, I'm a musical virtuoso. I have no idea what that actually means, but it sounds good.

I bet I've put in at least six hours a day on the piano. My biggest fan is Butler Charles. The old man walks in just to listen, then, two hours later he's waking up, disoriented and wondering how he got there. I don't know how many times I've seen him wake up in a daze, absolutely confused, before lying back down again. I doubt his work is ever done. I can't imagine it ever started in the first place.

My first concert was on Thursday. After Jen picked Ally up from school, they heard me playing in the library—well, that's what I call the big room full of books. They all call it the den, but that just doesn't sound right to me. I ended up playing for the whole household, minus Brandon, for at least thirty minutes.

Ally keeps telling me how great I am. But I didn't really think much of her praise until Jen told me it took most people months to learn what I had picked up in a week and a half. I don't know why, but piano playing just seems to come easy to me. Maybe it's the fact that I find it so relaxing.

Much to Ally's liking, we had a lot of time to play this week. For some reason, she only had half days on

Thursday and Friday. Something about an annual teacher's meeting. You know, private school stuff.

All Ally wanted to do was play hide-and-go-seek. So we played for countless hours. Except I was only allowed to hide in certain rooms because it wasn't fair if I used the whole house. Needless to say, I was the seeker the majority of the time.

And Ally is quite the hider.

She made it a little easier on me by jumping out of her hiding spot every time I came close. I think she has a fear of being found. I don't know why. Once I was within a few feet of wherever she was hiding, she always jumped out and wrapped her arms around my waist.

Ariel didn't like us much those two days. I'm not sure why, but I got strange glares from her every time I came out of a room with Ally slung over my shoulder. She went into every room that we came out of. I suspect it was to make sure everything was put back in its place. I didn't see the point since half the rooms were never even used.

During our games, I did come to a conclusion on one thing: I was right about room placement. My bedroom is the only one in use on the left side of the staircases. Everyone else lives on the opposite side of the second story hall. So as much as this family tries to make it seem like I fit in perfectly, they sure as heck aren't going to share a bathroom or even the same side of the upstairs with me. I just wondered if they feel the same now, after a few weeks.

As much as I want to think they feel differently, I'm a realist. And a pessimist. That's because life usually tends toward the negative. At least in my life it does. But things seem to be looking up now. It makes me wonder how long this can last.

All good things must come to an end. Right?

＊

This morning, I heard the doorbell ringing at the crack of dawn. Well, it probably wasn't that early, but it woke me up on a Saturday morning. I didn't really think anything of it at the time. I just rolled back over in bed. I was just about ready to fall back to sleep when I heard a knock on my door.

"I'm sleeping, Ariel," I mumbled.

"It's not Ariel, it's Jen. And some girl is at the front door for you."

I acted like I was still mostly asleep, but I couldn't have been more awake. "And what does this girl look like?" I asked in an overly groggy tone. I was already up and putting on pants. I didn't even mess with a shirt.

"Well, she looks kind of dark," Jen said. "And, ummm…she's wearing black, and—"

I opened my door. "What color is her hair?"

Jen was in her bathrobe, and her hair was put up in a ponytail and extremely frizzy. "She's blonde. She'd be really cute with a little less eye shadow and some color in her outfit," she said, finishing her sentence through a yawn.

"You look awful," I said.

Jen was taken aback at first, but then she smiled. "You suck." She turned around and started walking back to her room. "And tell your girlfriend it's way too early on a Saturday."

I started down the stairs. "Vampires don't sleep," I yelled. "The question is how's she handling the light?"

I heard Jen chuckle before her bedroom door closed.

Surprisingly, when I went downstairs, I saw Brandon come through the living room door and walk toward the kitchen. He had the newspaper in his hand. He nodded his head. I guess that was his version of "good morning."

I thought I'd find Jess—at least, that was the only dark, blonde-haired girl I knew—standing in the foyer, but there was no one there. I looked down the hall toward where Brandon had gone. She wasn't there, either.

I couldn't imagine her not being invited in.

So I opened the front door, and there she was, standing at the bottom of the steps with her arms crossed. She had black jeans on again, and military style boots that went up to her knees. And confidently, she wore a button-down, white and black, polka dotted shirt, which was nearly unbuttoned all the way down, with what must have been her signature black bra showing.

"Where's your shirt?" she asked, her lips forming into a smile.

"Where's yours?"

Her smile got wider. "At least I have something worth looking at."

I opened the door wider and flexed my abs. "As do I."

Jess uncrossed her arms and started laughing. "Well played, sir. And holy crap! There's, like, eight of them. I'd almost ask to touch them, but you haven't even bought me a drink yet. "

I felt the sudden urge to cover myself up. "Thanks. Did Jen not invite you in?"

"She did, but I told her I'd just wait out here." She had a look on her face like that was normal.

"Well...," I said, "do you want to come in?"

"No. It's nice enough out here." She sat down on the bottom step.

"Well...okay." I shut the door behind me and walked down the steps. I sat at the same level, but a few feet away.

Jess started laughing again. "I'm sorry, but you are freaking hot, well, except for that black eye. You should show off what you got a little."

"I'm not you," I said, rather insensitively.

Jess stopped laughing. Her smile turned into a scowl. "What's that supposed to mean?"

I instantly wished I hadn't said it. "I mean…uhh…" There was no way I was digging myself out. "I'm sorry, I just—"

She burst into laughter again. "I'm just kidding. Man, you really are that high strung all the time, aren't you?"

It seemed like every time I was with this girl, I ended up laughing at myself.

She leaned against the railing and started to button up her shirt. I watched her, feeling very uncomfortable, very unsure of what to say. When she was three quarters of the way buttoned up, she put her hands out and struck a pose. "Better?"

"Modesty suits you," I answered, although the shirt was quite sheer, and having it buttoned up didn't really hide much of anything. "So why are you here?"

She didn't answer immediately. I saw a blush starting on her cheeks. "Ah," she muttered. "Question of the hour." She pulled her legs up to her chest, and rested her chin on her knees. She started to chew her bottom lip. For the first time since we met, her demeanor matched her soft voice. She seemed more like a teenager. Not quite so intimidating.

"Well…I'm not really good at this, but…" She put her legs down and scooted over closer to me, then leaned in and kissed my cheek. When she pulled back, her face was as red as the bricks on the wall behind her. She covered her face with her hands and started laughing.

"What was that for?" I managed to ask. I imagined my face was as red as hers. But I wasn't laughing.

After a moment of what can only be described as giggling, Jess looked up. "I just wanted to thank you. I've always told Analeigh, if some guy ever stood up for me like that, I'd kiss him right there on the spot. But, unfortunately, you weren't quite up to par for a kiss right then."

I heard everything she said, but Analeigh's name seemed louder than anything else. I immediately remembered seeing her coming toward me, saying something…that was just before I saw black. And then for some reason, I pictured her coming over and giving Levi a hug while I was lying on the cafeteria floor, knocked out cold.

"Okay," Jess said, "at least say something. I'm dying here." Her face hadn't gotten any less red. I could tell it took everything in her to look me in the eyes.

"You don't need to thank me," I replied. "If you want the honest truth, it was more out of annoyance than anything else. I'm not a hero. I never have been and probably never will be."

I imagine if I had been a little less honest I could have gotten more than just a kiss. But I wasn't interested.

Jess seemed a little less giddy after I answered. "Well," she said, "either way, thank you."

"You're welcome."

She abruptly stood up and started to walk away. No goodbye or anything.

"That's it? You came all the way over here just to do that?" I yelled after her. "And at this time on a Saturday morning?"

She didn't even turn around. "Yes, I did. But don't worry, I'll be seeing you soon. And Thomas told me to tell you hi." She waved backwards over her head.

Of course he did, I thought. The gay guy that isn't even gay. Or so he claims.

I sat there until Jess had walked around the corner. I wasn't sure what to think of what had just happened. But I knew one thing: Jess was one weird girl, which in turn, made her someone that I wanted to get to know better.

Then my thoughts immediately turned back to sleeping. But there was one problem. When I tried to open the front door, I realized I had locked myself out.

You've got to be kidding me, I thought.

I reluctantly started knocking on the door. The first two times were a bust. But on the third time, the handle moved and the door opened. Jen looked about the same as she had earlier. "Did I mention that you suck," was all she said. Then she turned and started walking back to the stairs.

"Thank you," I said. "And you don't look *that* awful."

She shook her head, but didn't turn around. "Nice try. Now go back to bed. And I'll see you at a decent hour."

At that moment, the library door opened and Ariel stormed through. "Who's knocking the door? Something wrong?" She was breathing heavily, probably from running the length of the den.

"Impeccable timing, Ariel," I said. Then I started laughing.

Chapter 10

August 25, 2013

Church was, well, church. First there was the standing—an obnoxiously long amount of time standing I might add—and pretending to sing some strange songs about salvation and other useless religious themes. That was followed by an even longer amount of time sitting while listening to the monotonous pastor blabber on and on about how my soul needed to be saved. Between you and me, I don't think there is anything that can save my soul.

"Just try to listen," Jen told me.

I wanted to tell her I'd listened to every word, every week. And *nothing*. It was a waste of time.

"Brandon's the lucky one," I'd told her earlier this morning as I climbed into the car, barely awake. "He somehow manages to get out of this every week."

"Not by choice," she responded. "He would do anything to be here."

Not *anything*, I wanted to remind her. Brandon's excuse for missing life was *work*. How rich did the guy have to be to realize that money isn't all there is to living? Even I, one who has cheated, lied, and stolen to obtain wealth, knew that.

The excruciating service finally ended, and once again I found myself moving slowly in the long line of people who were trying to get out.

Jen was right behind me. "That wasn't so bad, now, was it?" she said.

"It was fine," I lied.

As I had done the last few weeks, I waited at the front door of the church while Jen gathered up the rest of the family, which seemed to take as long as the church service had. A few people said hi as they passed me, but most of them seemed to be avoiding me like the plague. I'd heard from juvie ministers that churches were the most inviting places in the world for convicts like me. Well, I wasn't feeling invited at all.

Granted, I didn't try all that hard to break out of my shell either.

A minute later, I spotted Jen and Ally walking toward me, hand in hand. Ariel was right behind them, lugging her usual assortment of crap. I suspected Butler Charles was coming, too, but he always took a heck of a lot longer to make his way to the door.

Ally waved when she saw me. She looked adorable in a brand new red dress and pig tails. I can't believe I just said "adorable." Is this little angel making me soft?

I started to wave, but then I heard my name coming from the opposite direction. I turned around just in time for Jess to throw her arms around me. "Good morning, stranger!" She had to be the most touchy-feely goth/punk princess I had ever met.

She let go, probably because she realized I wasn't hugging her back.

"Wow, you dress up nice," I said.

She looked more religion-friendly in a long black shirt that went nearly to her knees with black tights underneath. She had the same boots on.

"I don't slut it up all the time," she responded with as much, if not more, sarcasm than I had given her.

Then Thomas walked up and leaned on Jess's shoulder. "Hey, Alex." He had dressed up, too. A black sports jacket over a black tank top with black jeans that had been cut off about three quarter length. And (you guessed it) black boots. He set off the outfit with a newly shaved mohawk.

With these two here, I didn't feel so out of place. "You look great too," I told him.

Thomas struck a pose. "Well, thank you!"

At that moment, Jen and Ally stepped up behind me. "Hi," Jen said. "Alex, are these your friends?" How motherly. Right?

I did the polite thing. "Jen, Ally, this is Thomas. And, Jen, you've met Jess of course."

"Hello," my friends said at the same time as Thomas also saluted.

Ally looked up at them. "You both look scary."

They laughed, but Jen quickly pulled her daughter closer to her. "I'm sorry, but I think that's our cue to leave."

"Do you mind if we borrow Alex for a while?" Jess asked. "We'll bring him home before bedtime." Thomas chuckled.

"Okay," Jen said, "I try to have him tucked in by nine."

I mouthed the words *you suck* to Jen. She smiled and mouthed the word *Payback.*

I waited until Butler Charles finally caught up with the rest of the family before I turned to my new friends. That's when I saw Analeigh leaning against the church wall beside Jess.

"Hello," she said in her beautiful accent. This girl seemed more beautiful than I even remembered. Her short hair was a little spikier than the last time, but her green eyes looked just the same—mesmerizing. And her smile...crap, she has a wonderful smile.

"I'm Analeigh," she said. "But you can call me Ana."

"And I'm—"

"—the charity case."

I should have been tired of hearing that, but for some reason, I didn't mind it coming from her. "But you can call me Alex," I managed to say.

She smiled a little more. "He's a funny one, Jess."

"I told you," Jess said. She stepped beside me and hooked my right arm with both of hers. "Cute, too. Right?"

"Absolutely adorable!" Analeigh—now just Ana— agreed. "I think we will keep him. Thomas, let's take your car and show our friend a little fun, shall we?"

I was sure my face was brick red.

***

Thomas' car was a 1992 Jeep Wrangler. We left the top at the church, much to his chagrin. The girls thought it was too nice a day to be closed in, or *fettered*, as Jess aptly put it.

It really was a beautiful day. I don't claim to know much about the weather, but a sunny day in August is rarely as mild as the high 70s. (I only know the temperature because I heard two elderly ladies talking about it in the pew in front of us during the service.) There were only a few clouds in the sky, those big, fluffy ones that only seem to occur in the summer. There was also a strong breeze, which was an added bonus.

And there was Ana. I sat behind Thomas in the back seat with Jess, where I had a perfect view of this beautiful girl. She had her legs propped up on the dashboard, her skirt barely covering anything as it was blown back by the wind. She had her eyes closed, too. We were listening to some indie folk song pounding out at a nearly painful decibel level. And I found myself lusting after her. This was not the sweet, innocent love-at-first-sight kind of feeling. This was a desire that made me feel disgusted with myself.

Let me explain that last statement.

Analeigh is only sixteen years old. She's a sophomore. That made me a pervert at that moment. I'm not exactly sure how she ended up with this senior group, but I have my suspicions that her big-ape boyfriend may have had something to do with that. A pervert himself. But I'm not getting started on that right now.

Because it doesn't matter. I just couldn't take my eyes off of her. That is, until her eyes opened and she looked at me. I know she caught me staring, because she immediately put her legs down and turned in her seat.

I wasn't really embarrassed.

We drove through several miles of New York traffic, turn after turn, seemingly driving to nowhere—well, nowhere fast. I really didn't care. I was out of the mansion for once, and it was kind of liberating. We were going away from the city, north into the Bronx. I wasn't sure where the good time was going to be on this side of town.

I also didn't recognize any of the songs Thomas played. Where was the screamo punk music? When I looked around at these kids singing their hearts out and having a good time to music where banjos and violins were the leading instruments, I realized that it was impossible to judge these people by the way they looked. In theory at least. I had been wrong about Jess. I had even been wrong about Thomas. The jury may have still been out on Ana, but it was definitely leaning strongly in the same direction.

"Come on," Jess yelled over the music, "sing with us!"

"I don't know the—"

"What?!" she yelled even louder.

"I. Don't. Know. The. Song."

"What? You're kidding me?" Ana screamed as she turned around and got up on her knees and wrapped her arms around the headrest. "How can you not know this song?"

79

I shrugged my shoulders. "Incarceration?" I'm not sure if it was loud enough for her to hear me.

"Well we've got a lot to show you then!" she yelled.

And for the next two or three minutes they all belted it out, Thomas, too. It wasn't that memorable, except for the repeated "heys" and "hos," to which Jess screamed while pretending to hold a microphone. Thomas and Ana were laughing hysterically.

And I was laughing, too.

The song was barely over when we apparently reached our destination. Thomas turned the music down. "Home sweet home," he said.

The exact location meant nothing to me, but I'd been in this area before. It was an industrial park. In another life, I'd frequented a few spots down the street to make a little cash, but I'd never ventured up this far.

"Have you ever been around here?" Ana asked, still facing the back seat.

"Never," I lied.

"Well…" She paused to turn around and put her seat belt back on. "well…it's not much, but it's our place." She turned her head and looked at me very meaningfully. "Have you ever had a place like that?"

"No, I haven't." My brother's mansion was the closest thing I'd ever had to a home, but I spared them the details. Nobody wants to hear my sob story. And I didn't want to kill the mood anyways.

"That's a shame," Ana said.

Thomas was turning into a parking lot that looked destined to be abandoned. As did the small building it was attached to. It looked like a miniature warehouse that hadn't seen use in quite some time. The façade of the building was a dull gray sheet metal. About halfway up the front wall was a line of windows, some of which had been broken out, others spray painted black. There were a few other cars in the parking lot, and I thought I saw some light coming through one of the windows at the far left of the building.

"We have a friend named Hannah whose father owns about half of the factories around here. All this land is his." Jess pointed at a row of much larger buildings that were clearly still in use. "But this little gem is no longer needed. So it just sits here, and we've kind of commandeered it."

"Well, the rest of the school has," Ana added.

I had no idea what they meant, but I didn't ask any questions. I'd find out soon enough.

And let me tell you, I couldn't have been more surprised. From the looks of the place, I would have never guessed it could have been used in any way profitable. Well, my pessimism really seems to be taking a beating lately.

When they opened the tall metal door, I thought I was walking into some kind of club lounge. It was all one room with a cement floor and the skeletal look of an industrial building. But all around on the floor were couches and chairs, all different shapes and sizes. There were paintings and pictures hanging on the walls in no real pattern. And there were a lot of lights, mostly dim, some with different colored bulbs. In the back was a pool table, and to the left of it, some old arcade games. And there were other people. Not people that looked like us, but normal individuals.

Thomas did a bow. "Welcome, friend."

"What is this?" I managed to ask.

Jess pulled me in by the arm. "This is our place, like Ana told you in the car."

"And this is Hannah," Ana said, as a short Asian girl with a blue sweater, khakis, and big black glasses walked up to me.

"Hello." She had no accent at all. Hannah put her hand out to shake mine.

I shook it. "Hi." That seems to have become my normal greeting.

"I'm going to get a beer," Jess said. "Hannah can tell you a little more about this place."

"I'm with you," Thomas said, and they left me with this girl who had to be even younger than Ana.

"Get me one," Ana yelled after them as she plopped down on a nearby sofa.

Hannah smiled at me, baring all her teeth. "I know, your first thought is 'who is this nerdy little oriental girl in front of me?'"

She was right. See, the whole judgment thing was still there in theory, if not in practice.

"My full name is Hannah Yu Na," she said, "and I'm a third generation, so I'm as American as American can get. And I'm a senior, despite my generally young appearance. I'm the president of the chess club and I'm on the math team. And I—"

Ana cleared her throat. "How about the important stuff?" She patted the couch beside her, signaling us to sit down.

I mouthed a *thank you* to Ana and sat in the middle of the yellow sofa, with Ana on one side and Hannah much too close on the other.

I was still very confused. "Okay," I said, "so please explain this place."

"It's easy," Hannah answered. "It's just a hangout. I have the money to dress up the place, and now we hang out here."

"But how do you know Jess, and Thomas, and—"

"Right," Hannah interrupted. "Because I'm the nerdy Asian, and they're the punk princesses. Don't tell Thomas I called him that." She whispered the last part.

"Oh, he knows." Ana chuckled.

I didn't want to respond. She painted my stereotypes perfectly.

"It's okay," she said. "And it's understandable. But we've been friends forever. I happen to be rich, and my father has this place he doesn't use, so the four of us thought we'd turn it around and put it to use."

"And all the people?" There were at least ten other kids scattered around the room.

"Just people from school," Ana said. "At school, you have your cliques and your social racisms, but you'd be surprised at the people that come through those doors. We leave them open to anyone. Unless somebody acts stupid."

Like Levi, I thought.

I had several other questions, but I decided to let them rest for now. This place was rather nice for a bunch of high schoolers. Wealthy connections do come in handy. I would know.

Jess and Thomas returned, both of them forcing themselves on the couch that was clearly meant for no more than three people. I was pushed much closer to Ana, but she quickly scooted up to the armrest.

Thomas passed out the beers, but I waved mine away. "I don't drink."

"Seriously?" Jess asked.

"No. Yes. I made a promise to myself after I got out of juvie."

"Then you don't smoke either?" Hannah asked.

"Nope."

"That's too bad. My boyfriend over there has connections to the good stuff." She pointed at a kid in blue jeans and a T-shirt who was entertaining a group of other guys. "His name is Reuben. As you can tell, he's kind of a clown."

As soon as she said "clown," Reuben fell backwards onto an orange couch and flipped it on its back.

"And by good stuff, you mean…?"

"Marijuana. Mary Jane. Weed. Whatever you want to call it. You're missing out." Hannah looked me over like I was an outcast.

I looked at her, then looked at this Reuben kid, and I just couldn't make the connection. They had to have been the oddest couple I've ever seen. They definitely gave Ana and Levi a run for their money.

"Well, that means more for us," Thomas said. He had beers in both hands (his and mine) and he raised both. "Cheers."

I was probably the only person in the room attempting to be sober, but you can't stop a contact high. Though none of my new friends smoked anything near me, it seemed like everyone else was lighting up constantly, especially Reuben's group. I may have made it look easy, but I was dying inside. I could taste the cigarette smoke and the beer, and I longed for both. But I didn't let my salivation for either substance rule me.

I don't know if the rest of them just weren't doing it because I wasn't, but the smoke-filled room—plus copious amounts of liquor—made for quite an interesting afternoon.

It couldn't have been any later than three o'clock when the dancing started. Thomas manned a large stereo by the arcades while the girls started dancing in a large open area in the middle of the building. I didn't know any of the songs, but I enjoyed watching them dancing without any inhibitions. Some of the others around the room joined in, but no one really said anything to me.

Only the toasted drug dealer introduced himself. "Hi. I'm Reuben." He offered me a joint.

I shook my head, and he walked away to join the dancing.

Although, as Ana pointed out, the cliques co-existed here, I don't think any barriers had been broken down, per se. Except for Hannah and my group, it seemed like they all stayed to themselves, even on the dance floor.

Even though Jess tried to get me up several times, I didn't join in on the fun. I just watched, and laughed and laughed and laughed some more. I honestly don't think I've laughed that hard in my life. But watching them all make fools of themselves was hysterical.

They really had a way of making me feel comfortable, even if I was dying of temptation with the half-smoked joints and nearly full beer bottles lying all around me.

I don't know how long the party went on, but we moved to the pool table at one point, and then to the arcade games. In between, there was more dancing, then lounging. Then dancing. Then more games.

But not much conversation.

It all came to halt when the door opened, and a group of letter jackets—led by my best friend Levi— walked in. They were already yelling and acting like fools. Not any different than anyone that was already here, but none of these people had *jerk* written on their foreheads, either.

I guess Ana wasn't lying. Anyone was allowed in here.

Thomas sat down beside me. "Don't worry," he said. "They're just here to have some fun. They come in occasionally."

"I'm not worried."

They looked like they'd been drinking already. Drinking a lot. Some of them were stumbling into the furniture.

"Here's what's going to happen," Thomas continued. "The really tall one that looks like the Hulk—"

"Which one?"

"The one behind Levi." He pointed at a very bulky kid with a comb over. "His name is James. He'll be drunk and he'll challenge someone to an arm wrestling match. And someone will be stupid enough to do it and will lose royally. Happens every time they're here. Well, most of the time."

The party was quieter by the time the group made it to the pool table, which was just past the dance area. Only a few people lingered, including me, Jess, Thomas, and Ana. Even Reuben and Hannah went and sat somewhere else. Well, Hannah practically carried Reuben away.

As Levi passed Thomas and me, he didn't even glance at us.

Thomas was right. The big bone-head, James, took off his jacket and threw it on the pool table. "Okay," he yelled, "who's man enough to take me on this week?" He was staggering drunk, but I don't think it mattered. His arms were probably twice the size of the average male arm in the room.

"Come on!" some of the other letter jackets called.

I watched as Ana walked up to Levi and put her arms around him. He hugged her and they stood together, his arm slung over her shoulder.

I can't tell you how mad that made me. I'd been hanging out with her all day, and she never once even tried to apologize for him hitting me. He freaking knocked me out. Instead, she just smiled at him as if nothing had happened.

"It's a mystery," Thomas said, acknowledging what I felt at that moment.

"Come on," Levi yelled. "Anyone?"

Ana just smiled, but she didn't join in with the chorus of challenges.

By then, James had his shirt off and was flexing his muscles in body-builder poses.

But no one took up the challenge.

"Most of the time," Jess whispered, "somebody just does it to shut them up. She draped herself across our laps and Thomas started playing with her hair.

I felt it *was* time to shut James up. And, once again, you see how easy it is for me to put myself where I probably don't belong. But there were no threats of suspension this time.

"I'll do it," I said.

I wasn't loud enough. Everyone looked around.

I raised my hand like I was in class. "I said I'll do it."

"Seriously, Alex, you don't have to." Thomas tried to express concern, but he and Jess both looked rather excited.

"There we go," James hollered, flexing his biceps.

I pushed Jess's legs off mine, stood up, and sauntered to the pool table while the letter jackets began taunting me with oohs and aahs. The rest of the kids seemed to be following me. They didn't want to take part in the arm wrestling, but they sure wanted to watch.

"So," said Levi, "you want to get made a fool again."

I ignored him. But I noticed how uncomfortable Ana looked.

I stepped up to James...and let me just say this: he was a big fella. But if you remember, I have never feared any man. And at that moment, it was no different. I had every intention of winning.

James looked down at me and bumped my chest with his.

"Where at?" I asked, bumping him back.

Levi answered for him. "On the floor."

James immediately fell to the floor and did a reverse pushup to his stomach. The noise level was getting louder. Everyone was getting anxious.

I got down on my stomach with much less flashiness.

At the same time, Levi left Ana and crouched down beside us. He grabbed both of our right hands and put them together. "You both ready?"

I nodded my head. James just yelled curses at me.

"Okay," Levi said. "Get on your mark. Get ready. Go!"

I know what you're thinking right now. He had the muscle, I had the will. But the muscle wins. Before I even got off the couch, I knew it was going to be a hard win. Or quite possibly, he could have broken my arm. Because I'm stubborn.

But it wasn't even a challenge. I was too strong and quick. By the time I even felt any pressure, the baboon's arm was on the ground. The room went quiet. James had a look of pure shock on his face.

I just smiled.

"I want a rematch!" he finally yelled.

Then Thomas and Jess started hollering, followed by everyone else in the room. Well, not everyone. James' friends had the same surprised look on their faces that he had.

But it wasn't James that I cared about. I wanted to see the look on Levi's face. When I looked up at him, he had that "I want to kill you" expression. And I suppose, I had that "go ahead and try" look.

"Come on, James," Levi said. "We're out."

"Rematch!" James yelled.

I was already standing up.

"Shut up!" Levi yelled. "You lost, let's go." He barely even hugged Ana before he left, which pissed me off even more. He and his friends staggered out, leaving as fast as they had arrived.

But I didn't have time to think about it. When the door closed, everyone gathered around me.

"That was awesome!" Jess cheered.

And then I got a bunch of the same sentiments from the others, some from kids I didn't even know. When they raised their beer bottles and cheered some more, I started feeling claustrophobic.

And the party continued.

***

By the time it started getting dark outside, I needed a break. It was like I was overstimulated. I just wasn't used to this much socialization, especially in one day. Not that I wasn't having fun, though, because this was probably the most fun I've ever had. But it was just a little overwhelming after a while.

So I excused myself and went outside for some fresh air—some air that didn't smell like pot. After being in there it was hard to believe it was still Sunday. Harder still to believe was the fact that some of those kids were at church with me this morning.

I sat on the back of Thomas' jeep and just decompressed for a moment.

The New York skyline in the distance was beautiful, and the sounds of the city were music to my ears. I never realized how much I'd missed the city. A year and a half away was a long time. And being in the mansion didn't give me the opportunity to see much of the part of the city I'd left behind when I went to the detention center.

Or maybe it was just me. You know, since I've been living in this mansion with my new family, I've not once even ventured into the backyard. Ally told me Butler Charles did wonders out there, but I've never had even the slightest inclination to check it out. I've been walling myself in, that's for sure.

So maybe meeting all of these weird kids is exactly what I need to start living again.

Maybe *they* were the normal ones.

I might have had an epiphany right then. I don't really know what that means, but it sounds cool.

I lay down across the back of the jeep and just stared up at the stars that were coming out, at least the ones that were visible through the city lights. And I suddenly felt exhausted. I closed my eyes. As comfortable as it was, I might have fallen asleep, except—

"Too much for one night?"

I looked up to see Jess standing over me. "I know," she said. "We're a lot to handle all at once."

I sat up so she could have room to sit beside me.

"No," I told her. "I think I'm just a little lost in this world. It's hard to fit in when you've never actually been a part of it in the first place."

"A part of what?"

"Normal people's lives." I'd never known normal.

She laughed and climbed up beside me. "Well, if we're normal, then you must really be out there."

I didn't laugh. She was saying exactly what I was feeling.

She suddenly understood. "I'm sorry."

We sat there for the next five minutes or so, admiring distant Manhattan together. Jess rested her head on my shoulder. We were completely silent until she started to giggle.

"What?" I asked.

She raised her head. "I just saw James' face in my head. He's probably going to cry himself to sleep tonight." She stopped giggling and gave me a serious look. "Did you really know you could beat him?

"Absolutely," I answered. "See, I have this problem. It's called *no fear*. It serves me well most of the time, but it can also get me into a lot of trouble."

"Like with Levi?"

"Yeah, like with Levi. And now I have to go back to school tomorrow and face everyone, everyone that watched me get knocked out last week."

She grabbed my hand. "Hey, but now you have *us*. And we stick up for our own."

That did make me feel a little more at ease. But it also brought a question to my mind. A question I've been mulling over for a week. "Then how do you stick up for Ana when she's dating that idiot?"

Jess sighed. She didn't seem to want to talk about it.

"Come on!" I said. "He smashed my face."

She sighed again, even heavier. Then she looked back as if to make sure no one else was around. "Well, there's just something you have to learn about her..." I didn't realize I was going to get a lengthy discussion off of such a simple question, but I must say, I learned a lot about Analeigh right then.

"...Ana may be the leader of the pack, so to speak, but she clearly has her own issues. She'd probably kill me for saying this, but you'd find out soon enough."

Just get to the point, I thought.

"I know she seems so put together and in charge," Jess continued. "And that's why she is basically the natural leader. But here's her problem. Ana has absolutely no self-worth. Like, seriously, she's always thought very little of herself, ever since I've known her, even though she's so smart and beautiful. At first, when we were in middle school, it came in the form of cutting..."

I immediately thought of Jen.

"...but since high school, she's been throwing herself at every available piece of meat that will have her.

She's slept with more guys than I can count. And they all just use her. It's miserable to watch."

"So how do you let her do that to herself?" I asked. If they were truly her friends, they should be trying to stop her.

"Trust me," Jess said. "We've tried. But the best thing we can do is love her. Don't get me wrong, we still try to convince her otherwise from time to time."

It didn't make sense to me. She was such a beautiful girl. And she really did seem so smart and capable. The more I thought about it, the more pissed off I became at Levi. The phrase *using her* kept popping into my head.

When I didn't respond, Jess finished by telling me she didn't want to say anymore because Ana could give "quite the hysterics."

"That's fine," I said. "I think I've learned enough for one night."

"Thomas said you told him you had been looking for Ana. Why's that?"

I had forgotten telling him that. "I don't know. She just said hi to me at church, and, well, I don't know."

"Sounds like a little bit of a crush to me."

I couldn't disagree.

Jess laid her head back on my shoulder. "Don't worry, I won't tell."

We eventually went back inside. But only briefly. I guess everyone else had had enough, too. Ana and Jess grabbed a ride with Hannah. I guess they all lived in the same neighborhood. I went back to the church with Thomas to put the top back on his jeep, then he drove me home.

As fun as the night was, I couldn't have been more ready to get back to the mansion. It was only eight o'clock, but I was exhausted. And as you can see, I had a lot to write about.

"I'll see you tomorrow," Thomas said as I hopped out of his jeep. "Toodles!"

"Good night," I responded, holding in a laugh. His femininity would never cease to amaze me.

"And sweet dreams, hunny," he hollered as he drove off.

It was quiet in the homestead, which was the usual on a Sunday night. Ally was already asleep by about eight thirty, and Brandon and Jen were usually in their room by now, doing who knows what.

I went straight to my room and crashed on my bed.

But only briefly. I fetched the pen and paper—well, not literally, as you know, I've graduated to a laptop now—and I've been writing ever since.

Lucky you. Right?

But now, I truly must say it's beyond my bedtime. I've got to get a little sleep before school tomorrow.

Not to mention, I've got to sleep off this second-hand high.

Chapter 11

August 26, 2013

I am not exactly sure how late it was, but I knew it was well into the night. The rap on my door was barely audible. I have no idea how it woke me. I do know that I was having a pleasant dream, though the content of said dream was instantaneously gone.

The knock was quiet, so I immediately dismissed it as coming from Ariel. There was no quietness when it came to the housekeeper. Not expecting Ariel to be at my door was an instant relief, as my growing annoyance with her didn't need any help. Sluggishly, I drug myself out of bed and staggered to the door. I laid my head on the wooden frame, just as another quiet rap sent vibrations through the wood.

"Who is it?"

There was no answer.

Clearing my throat, I tried again. "Who is it?"

No answer again.

I was about ready to call the whole thing a mind-trick of my own making, but I opened the door just in case. I immediately felt her arms reaching around my waist. Had I not been both larger and stronger than her, I would probably have fallen over.

Ally was crying hysterically. I had no idea what to do.

First I pried her arms away. "What's wrong?" I asked her.

But there was no stop to the sobbing. She reached for me again, but I sidestepped her.

"Ally, seriously, what's wrong?"

Another awkward dance, and more tears.

So I did the only thing I could do. I sat down beside her on the floor. And I waited. As uncomfortable as it was, I couldn't think of any other viable option. She draped her arms around my neck and cried for at least ten more minutes.

Many thoughts traveled through my mind as she cried for what seemed like forever. They were mostly a collection of "I'm-not-prepared-for-this" and "what-do-I-do?"

The last time I'd seen a young girl cry so much was after my sister Kim came away from one of our father's many forms of abuse. She had always tried to hide it from me, but she couldn't keep me from hearing what was going on in that little, run-down house we grew up in. I didn't know what to do then, and I didn't know what to do now.

Ally finally toppled over onto my lap. She was quiet. And it felt like nighttime again.

I didn't say anything right away. What could I say? I was adequately unprepared to answer any questions she might ask. Nor could I ask questions she would be able to answer. But I didn't want to sit there all night.

Finally, and for the third time, I asked the obvious. "What's wrong?"

This time, no sobbing followed. Ally raised her head, her beautiful blue eyes filled with tears and reflecting the moonlight from my window in no way that I can truly describe.

"Mommy and Daddy are fighting."

How could I respond to that? What comfort could I give her? I had no control over her parents.

But I immediately wondered if the fighting had anything to do with me. I said nothing for several minutes, as I thought about how to get my niece back to her room without her asking me a crap-load of questions about relationships, something I had very little knowledge of.

"Daddy's always gone," she suddenly said before I could formulate a response to her first statement.

"What do you want me to do about it?" I asked. I know, this sounds even more insensitive now as I read it again. But I needed an answer from her because I was really lost on the whole thing. I could give her no sense of resolution. And you can't just tell a five-year-old that life sucks and there's no way to fix it.

"I just want to sleep with you tonight," she said. "I don't want to hear them fighting anymore."

What immediately came into my mind was the way Brandon looked at me the first time Ally sat on my lap. How disgusted he looked. How pissed off would he be now?

But how could I say no? If it meant I didn't have to comfort her with my words, then this was the only option I had.

"Okay," I answered. "Go grab my pillow and some blankets."

"We can't sleep in the bed?"

"No. We have to sleep here, with the door open. Just trust me on that."

Ally grinned. I could do no wrong. I could have made a hammock between the two staircases and dangled her twenty feet over the foyer, and she wouldn't have minded. She loved me unconditionally. She just wanted to be with her uncle and away from the nightmare of her arguing parents.

Ally slept very soundly, sprawled out on my lap in a pile of blankets and pillows. I didn't sleep much at all.

The immediate crisis averted, I couldn't help but wonder how such a well-off family could have any problems worth arguing about. They were rich. They had their God. They had each other. It was as perfect a family as my unknowledgeable mind could conjure up.

But the phrase "Daddy's always gone" kept popping into my head. I had something in common with Ally. Until now, her father had always been absent in my life, too. He was never around when I was a kid, and he's not around now.

Maybe he hasn't changed as much as I thought.

Chapter 12

August 28, 2013

My initial thought came out as a string of curses followed by a flat-out no. There was no way I was riding on the top of that thing. It looked like a dilapidated storage unit sitting on rusted clock gears. And the sounds it made were like the screeching of a dying animal.

"I don't think I can do that," I said, trying not to give away any hint of fear. I was not afraid of people, but this thing was not a person. It looked like a death trap.

"The great and fearless Alex Lane, huh?" Jess threw her arm over my shoulder. "And we thought you were better than that."

"Are you freaking kidding me?" I responded. "I'd rather have a gun in my face than ride on that. The gun's at least familiar."

Thomas was standing on the other side of me, laughing harder with each one of my refusals. Hannah and Reuben were about twenty feet away, leaning on another rail car, nearly obscured by the cloud from Reuben's Marlboro reds. Neither of them were half as interested in my plight as Jess and Thomas were.

I should have known as soon as Jess called it an "initiation" that it wasn't going to be easy.

"Hey, we've all done it," Thomas had said as we drove to this nondescript manufacturing plant in the middle of industrial slumville. "It's actually super-fun, if you ask me."

Of course they didn't give me any details about the task ahead until I was standing in that exact spot and staring my imminent death in the face. Jess nonchalantly pointed to the behemoth and laughed. "It's only a rail car. You get to ride it while it moves between the two factories it supplies. It's automated. So no one is going to see you."

Twenty minutes later, I was still firm. I wasn't going to do it.

"It really is fun," Reuben calmly added while Thomas was describing the initiation, a ride they all swore they'd taken many times. Of course, *everything* is fun when you're stoned out of your mind. And I know for a fact that falling down is also a lot less painful in that state of mind.

There were several points during the conversation when I nearly had the courage to do it. But my better judgment won out every time. A chorus of *boos* and whines followed each of my nos. My new friends were persistent, though, so I waited for the next car to come, an exact replica of the last one. Back and forth I talked myself into it before talking myself right back out.

"I'm telling you Alex," Jess said. "Once you do it, you'll see that this whole scaredy-cat thing is just ridiculous."

"Well Jess, after you."

"I'm not the one being initiated into the group here," she said.

Thomas did his best to sound sincere. "I promise, we'll all do it, too, if you do it first."

The next car was coming. It was behind us, but I could hear the awful sounds of rusty metal on rusty metal. It did nothing to calm my anxiety.

"You promise I'm not gonna die?" I asked for the millionth time.

"I can't promise you anything," Jess retorted. "It would be a shame, though, if our friendship started with you dead in this dump."

"That's reassuring," I responded. "I can't believe getting punched in the face for you wasn't enough of an initiation."

"No threat of death in that," Thomas said. "That only got you here. Consider that a blessing in itself."

I nervously laughed. "Yeah, a blessing. It would be a blessing to see one of you up there, doing it first."

Jess laid her head on my shoulder. "Yes, it would be, but—"

"Well, there you go," Thomas interrupted, pointing to the car that had just passed us. "I guess somebody was tired of hearing you cry like a baby."

Ana was standing on top of the newest piece of moving scrap metal. She had her arms stretched out like wings, like she was going to fly away once the car began to move. And as nervous as I was, seeing her looking so eager to ride away made me feel worse.

She smiled down on us. She wasn't even facing in the direction the car would be moving. "I pretend I can fly," she yelled. "And then there's nothing to fear. It becomes a dream, a new reality, an escape from the hell we live in."

Now it was Thomas' turn to throw his arm around my neck. "You see her? That's a woman who's not afraid of some piece of crap train car."

"And she'll be the only one having fun in about two seconds," Jess added. "Once you do it, you'll see what you're missing out on."

The car started to move, and Ana's smile grew even wider. Her eyes were closed. She looked like she was dreaming.

I was enthralled. The screaming of the rusted wheels momentarily grabbed my attention, but the beauty of her, standing tall above the world—above us—quickly pulled me right back in. I don't remember hearing another sound for several minutes.

I imagined she was some type of goddess, a woman that I could never in my life be with. The calm, blissful expression on her face proved that she was on a completely different plane than I was. We were nowhere near the same realm.

By the time the rail car reached full speed, Ana's plaid dress was nearly up to her chest. She wore black leggings that came almost up to her navel and covered the more intimate parts of her. But at that moment, I don't think she cared what was showing. She was dreaming.

She was flying.

It only lasted a few minutes before the automated car began to slow down. Ana was a lot smaller now as she'd traveled at least a few hundred yards. But I could still see how invigorated she looked. Like she'd just had the best day of her life.

I was still in my trance, but Jess shouted at me. "That's how it's done!"

And Thomas squeezed my shoulder. "See? Not so bad at all."

At that moment, I felt emboldened.

"Who's next?" Ana yelled as soon as her boots hit the ground.

Jess looked at me with a *so...how about now* expression.

I shrugged Thomas' arm off of me. "Okay! Where's the next freaking car? I'm ready."

By their reaction, you would have thought I'd just given them part of my brother's fortune.

Chapter 13

September 1, 2013

J ess and Ana invited themselves to movie night. I had no say in the matter. The word *strange* doesn't even begin to describe it. Picture this: I'm holding Ally on my lap. There's a rebel chick on either side of me, Butler Charles is snoring loudly, Ariel is talking to God, and Jen and Brandon look as uncomfortable as I've ever seen them.

The picture of dysfunction.

And just imagine if Thomas would have been able to make it. Brandon wouldn't have known what to make of him.

But after all was said and done—and as awkward as it was—it didn't turn out that bad. I think my family was surprised at the politeness and pleasant conversational skills of my friends. Ally absolutely loved them. After they left, Jen commented how nice they were. Not that I'm keeping count, but score one for criminal Alex Lane in the becoming-normal column.

Okay, now let me get you caught up with the rest of the week.

I didn't realize how hard it would be to make up for a week's worth of schoolwork. School sucks, plain and simple. My math class is a bear, even though Hannah and Reuben have been helping me a lot. I imagined Hannah would be smart—I know, Asian stereotype—but I never thought the resident stoner would be, too. But I'm pretty sure Reuben is even smarter than his girlfriend. And freaking hilarious too. He has the most sarcastic sense of humor of anyone I've ever met. And he tells me his brother Christopher is even more sarcastic and even funnier. But I've not had the opportunity to meet Christopher yet.

It may be hard to believe, but my favorite class so far is chemistry. It helps that Jess is my lab partner, but it's also fun to watch James' dull brain try to grasp the concepts. There's no way he'll ever get it, but Mr. Gregg will probably pass him just because he's a star on the football team or because he can't imagine the thought of hearing James' same dumb questions next year.

Outside of class, I've been spending most of my time with Jess and Ana. Thomas works most evenings, so I don't see him as much. But we've frequented the Coffee Shop—yes, it's actually called that—where he works, and he's been more than willing to hook us up free of charge. Whenever his manager isn't looking, of course. The first time I went in, Thomas strolled over to our table and pointed to this older gentleman behind the counter.

"That's my boss," he said. "Mike, the owner/manager. He's a coffee connoisseur and a real stuck-up jerk. Here, drink his coffee on me." And he handed me a cup of coffee.

The Coffee Shop is where we've been spending most of our time. Hannah and Reuben usually stop by for an hour or so, and they eventually end up helping me with my homework the entire time, though they don't seem to mind. That is, if they're not awkwardly making out in front of us. I've gotten used to it, but it took me a few days. They have absolutely no problem with public displays of affection.

After a few hours, it usually ends up just being Jess and me working on our chemistry or just messing around. Ana hangs with us right after school, but she usually leaves early to chill with Levi. *Chill* is the code word for *Levi needs to get lucky.*

It's frustrating every time she says "chill," but I've learned to ignore it. At least I try to.

But it also sucks because Ana is freaking smart. She's only a sophomore, but she fills in any of the gaps in chemistry when Hannah and Reuben can't.

I know I should just try to do my own homework. That do-good philosophy sounds good and responsible, but I know implementing it would most certainly lead to my academic failure.

On Friday night, Jess and I decided we'd wait for Thomas to get off work and then go to the warehouse. As cool as Hannah's property is, I guess it doesn't get a whole lot of use during the week. It's more of a weekend spot. I don't know why, but then I don't make the rules.

***

That night, Ana had already left to *chill* with Levi, and Hannah had just called Jess to let us know that she and Reuben were already there. As I was putting my books into my backpack, I noticed Jess was acting strange, almost like she was nervous. I actually kind of noticed it earlier in the day, but it seemed to get stronger when we were alone. I told myself to let it go. I wasn't sure if I was ready to ask her what was wrong. I don't think I was prepared to deal with her answer if something was bothering her.

I looked at my phone, just hoping it was close to the end of Thomas' shift. He still had fifteen minutes.

"Alex?"

I wasn't ready, but I guess it was time to be a real friend if need be.

I put my backpack down. "Okay," I said, "what's bothering you? You've been acting strange all day."

Jess seemed put off by that. Then a smirk came across her lips. "I have, huh?" But she still looked nervous.

"Well, if you're pregnant," I told her, "I don't know what to tell you." I was talking loud on purpose, maybe too loud, as some of the other patrons gave me strange looks.

Jess started laughing. I did, too.

"I can't believe you said that out loud," she cackled. "That's how rumors get started, you know?"

"Sorry." I was laughing so hard I could hardly talk.

It took a moment for us to stop laughing, as the more we tried to be quiet, the louder we were.

But then Jess turned serious again.

My laugh died slower, and I looked at her curiously. "Really, what is it?"

"Well," she said, "it's just this thing...I thought, maybe..." She couldn't seem to find the words. It was incredibly painful to listen to. She was squirming in her chair, even worse than when she thanked me after my knockout punch. "Well, I thought maybe we could, you know..."

I had no idea what that 'you know' meant.

"...we could...uhhmmm."

Thomas plopped down beside her and threw an arm around her shoulders. Pulling her close, he translated for me. "She wants to know if you'll go to the Homecoming Dance with her. How about it?"

I didn't know what to say. I didn't even know there was such a dance. I immediately felt my hands get clammy. The hairs on the back of my neck stood up.

Jess seemed relieved. She smiled. "Yeah...so how about it?"

"We actually go to dances?" I asked, still completely unsure if this was something I wanted to be a part of.

"What, did you think we sat at home and did séances or something?" Thomas let go of her. "No voodoo dolls, either."

"And we don't have to try and be freaks *all the time*. So...?" Jess asked again, still obviously nervous.

"Fine," I said. "I'll go."

Jess wrinkled her nose at my less than enthusiastic answer, but before she could say anything, I reached across the table and grabbed her hand. "Jessica Lynn Gray, I'd love to go to the dance with you."

The statement was out of my character, and wasn't quite true, but if I was going to a dance, at least with Jess, it would be fun.

She squeezed my hand and smiled. "Awesome"

Thomas slid out of the booth. "Well, while you two plan your wedding, I'm going to the warehouse to get drunk. With or without you."

Jess and I laughed.

"Just think, Jess," I said as I slid out of the booth. "Thomas will make *such* a pretty flower girl."

"With a pretty dress!"

"Have fun walking," Thomas said. He was nearly out the door.

***

We had barely stepped into the warehouse when Hannah yelled, "Did he say yes?"

Jess looked embarrassed, and I'm sure I did, too.

"Of course he did," Thomas answered. "One look at that pretty face, and he couldn't resist." He put his arm around Jess again, and they walked through the room together.

Contrary to what I expected, there was little boozing or smoking that night. For which I was thankful. I really didn't want the temptation again. The last time I was there, my throat had ached for alcohol and smoke.

Little smoking…well, that excluded Reuben. He lit up constantly, but he didn't act any different than usual. That helped me conclude that he was high a majority of the time.

There weren't near as many kids there, either. A few of Reuben's friends were playing pool, but other than that, we pretty much had the place to ourselves. We mostly just sat there and talked about a great many things, from politics to school to weekend plans to who was going with who to the dance. There were no surprises in the latter category until Hannah asked Thomas who he was going with.

And of course, Thomas couldn't make it easy. He had to make a game out of it. At first, I thought he was covering up the fact that he didn't have a date, but with each new clue, I could sense that he was telling the truth. I'd learned what lies looked like on the street.

His clues were very vague at first, especially to me, as I didn't really know anybody at school.

After about twenty clues and a thousand wrong guesses, Thomas rolled his eyes. "Come on, people! It's really not that hard." He stood up and started pacing. He rubbed his chin, as if he was getting ready to expound on some great philosophical truth. "Okay, next clue. Hmmm…she was the belle of the ball."

My friends all looked at each other, and I could see a realization on their faces. Reuben actually choked as he took a drag.

"You're kidding me!" Jess stood up and grabbed Thomas on the shoulders. "Tell me you're kidding."

Thomas smiled. "The one and only."

They all knew, but I still didn't have a clue. "Okay. Can someone fill me in?"

Reuben was the first to answer. "He's freakin' going to the dance with last year's homecoming queen, Samantha Wreams!"

I didn't know many people, but it was impossible not to know who Samantha—Sam—was. She was the president of about half the clubs in the school and her picture was plastered all over the school walls. She was rich and very pretty. One of the cheerleading captains. She had state trophies in about every sport she played in. Of course that meant every guy in the school wanted her.

Thomas sat back down and put his hands behind his head. "Yep, I landed the most popular and hottest chick in the school."

"Because she's tired of disgusting boys and she thinks you're gay," Hannah said in a matter-of-fact tone.

Her comment didn't faze Thomas at all. "Or because I'm actually just her type."

"Dude," Reuben said, "you're a freak! She's high class man-eater. Did you have to pay her? Because you know every man with something between his legs has asked her to this dance."

Jess hugged Thomas. "I don't care what they say. I think she's just tired of those macho guys. They're all fakes. I'm happy for you."

Thomas hugged her back. "See? Someone who actually understands." He flipped the other two off behind her back.

"That being said," Jess continued. "The look on people's faces when you two walk in...it is going to be *awesome*."

I already saw it in my head. Sam is tall, lean, and muscular. She has light brown hair and a tan to match. And like most rich girls, she wears skyscraper heels and dresses that probably cost more than my entire wardrobe. And she dresses like that on a daily basis. Not to mention her handbags and accessories.

And then I pictured Thomas walking in, black jeans and boots, a blazer with the arms ripped off, and his perfectly sculpted blonde mohawk. Followed by the most feminine strut as he showed off his prize. It really would be awesome.

I'm not gonna lie, but I think we all believed there was something more going on. It just didn't seem to fit.

Like, why didn't Thomas tell us earlier? And why has no one actually seen the two of them together? We all had questions, but none of us chose to ask them. Me, I didn't want to ruin Thomas' moment.

Thomas' date reveal was by far the most interesting thing that happened that night. We hung out for a few more hours, then Thomas drove me home. Most nights ended that way because Thomas lived closer to me than anyone else.

Before he pulled away from the curb, he leaned over the passenger seat and asked, "You believe me, right?"

"I do," I said, "but it would have been a little more convincing had you told us right after it happened. Not a week after the fact."

He smiled. "Yeah, well, believe it or not, she actually wanted it to be a surprise to everyone on the night of the dance. I'm not sure why. But, you know, she's actually a sweet girl."

I believed him, but I still didn't quite understand. "And how did you find that out?"

"Well...she asked me to the dance, not the other way around. I may have left out that detail earlier." He started to pull forward.

I kept up with the car. "That sure changes things."

"I was shocked, too," he yelled out the window.

"Either way, she's a lucky girl," I called as he drove away.

He honked in acknowledgment.

My night ended as I watched his yellow jeep drive two blocks down the road and make a right turn.

Chapter 14

September 2, 2013

I am not naïve enough to think for a second that my life is on the up and up for good. I've been through way too much in eighteen years to develop such a positive outlook. And I've said it before: I'm a natural-born pessimist.

I think of my sister Kim's first stint in rehab. I can remember her coming home when I was a child and just how utterly happy she looked. And I remember her telling me that things were going to be different this time. That she would never go back to that dark place. But after my father had his way with her for about a month, her smile faded…and what little hope I had as a child faded with it.

I use this story, as I sadly imagine that what happened to me today may be the beginning of the same fadeout.

I am supposed to be with my friends. Right now, I should be studying for my chem test. Hannah and Reuben should be awkwardly making out in front of me. Ana should be getting ready to leave for the night. Thomas should be working. Jess should be telling me "I'm over this science crap!" over and over again.

But none of that is the case. I'm home on a Saturday night. Because something terrible happened.

Or let me correct myself. *Nearly* happened. Or kind of happened. I don't know. Whatever. I don't know why I feel the need to have such long introductions sometimes. I suck at them.

I stopped by the house after school for what I thought would be a short pit stop. It was the usual plan. Grab something to eat and then head off to the Coffee Shop to spend countless hours working on homework—well, an hour or so working on homework—and the rest of the time in mindless conversation and worthless activity. So I went into the kitchen and discovered that Ariel had so graciously left some brownies on the counter for me. Actually, I doubt they were solely for my enjoyment, but that didn't hinder me from taking a few.

Rarely do I ever see anyone home at this time in the afternoon, so after grabbing my snack, I started for the front door. But as soon as I came to the bottom of the stairs, Ally jumped out and wrapped her five-year old arms around my right leg.

"You're home!"

"And so are you," I said. It was unusual for her to be home from school so early. "But why are you home?"

Ally looked up at me with a big smile that showed all her teeth. "Mommy picked me up from aftercare early today because her job let her come home early."

I kneeled down so we were face to face. "Is that so? So what's on your agenda—"

"Wilbur and I want to play hide-and-go-seek! Please!"

I looked at the door, then back to my pleading niece. "Ally, I can't, I have to—"

"Please, please, please! Just for a little while?"

She gave me her bottom lip, and, as usual, I found it impossible to say no. "Okay," I replied. "But just for a little while." By a little while, I meant, like, five minutes.

Ally hugged me again, then started up the stairs. "You count first," she yelled.

"Tell Wilbur he owes me one," I called back as I dropped my stuff beside the left staircase.

I only counted to twenty, as Ally was quite decisive on her hiding spots, even if it was just one of the same three spots every time—Butler Charles' room, Brandon's study, or the fancy spare bedroom beside her parents' room.

I climbed the stairs, making as much noise as I could. Ally likes knowing that I'm coming after her. Remember the whole "jumping out" thing.

When I reached the top of the stairs, I only had to decide which one of her three spots she'd chosen. I decided to look at the spare bedroom first, as it was the furthest away.

If only I'd gone to one of the other rooms first. If only I'd listened a little harder to Ally's footsteps. If only…then maybe what happened wouldn't have. Maybe it would never have been possible. And then my day wouldn't have turned out like it did. Maybe I wouldn't be questioning my future right now.

Well, I started toward that freakin' spare bedroom.

I know, you're probably just thinking *stop talking and get on with it.*

So here it goes.

As I opened the door to the spare room, I noticed Brandon and Jen's door was cracked a little, which was unusual. I stopped and looked in.

And that's when I saw her.

Jen was standing across the bedroom and looking into a full length mirror. There was nothing necessarily out of place about that. Except for the fact that she was wearing nothing but a black bra and panties.

My first thought was to quickly move on, but unfortunately, I was stuck in place. Her body is beautiful, and I'm an eighteen-year-old, testosterone-filled teenager.

So what do you expect?

As my brother's wife stood there, almost naked, combing her hair, I studied every detail of her body. Yes, that's what I just said. If only to show you how absolutely shameful it sounds—and, well, how shameful it was.

I noted the scars all over her body. Some large ones, including the one that ran down her right side until it met her underwear, and continued on below, all the way down to her knee. I couldn't imagine what could have caused such a scar. Or how painful that had to have been. I remembered her telling me about her scars the day I met her and she took me shopping. That was the day I stripped in a department store. Some of her scars came from her abusive father. Some she gave herself.

And that's when I realized that I wasn't the first person that Brandon had tried to save. Clearly, he had to get past the dark parts of Jen to marry her. And look how that turned out! Maybe Brandon actually knew what he was doing.

I hadn't quite finished that thought when Jen turned around. My mind told me to move, but my body wasn't fast enough. Her eyes met mine, quite briefly, before I slammed myself against the wall between the two bedroom doors.

My mind was screaming every curse word I could think of.

I wanted to run, but I knew it didn't matter. I'd been caught drooling over my brother's half-naked wife. Every negative consequence possible started flashing in my mind, from sheer embarrassment to being kicked out of the house.

Then I heard some unidentifiable noises, then footsteps coming toward the door. And in that split second I decided to be proactive. I'd been caught. There was no need to cower. I spun around just as Jen was opening the door. She had put on a white robe.

"I'm sorr—"

She grabbed the front of my shirt and pulled me toward her. As she planted her lips on mine, she pulled me through the doorway, then pushed me up against the wall just inside.

And what she gave me was no small peck. Her tongue was squarely in my mouth.

I can't describe what I felt at that moment, but I can tell you that I put up little to no resistance. As a matter of fact, the momentary, stunned feeling went away. I kissed her back. Passionately. I wrapped both arms around her. At the same time, Jen reached over with one arm and pushed the door closed. But she didn't give it a hard enough push, so it closed slowly, and the hinges squeaked.

But she didn't stop kissing me. It was sloppy. The rapid breathing, the sighing. My heart beating loud enough to hear. It felt like that kiss lasted forever.

And then the door finally closed. The noise it made triggered something in me: I realized what was happening here. It was a sobering moment. And a struggle. Part of me wanted to continue, but another part kept telling me to stop.

Thankfully, I listened to the second part. To my better judgment. I pushed Jen away, maybe a little harder than I meant to. She looked desperate. Her face was sad but aggressive at the same time. I don't know if any of this makes a whole lot of sense. But I'm not sure how else to describe what happened.

"What's wrong?" she asked. She was breathing heavily.

I caught my breath. "What's wrong?" I repeated. "You just tried to seduce me."

"It didn't feel too hard," she fired back. "It felt like you wanted it."

I did. Well, my body did. But my mind wouldn't let me want it.

"We can't," I said.

"Why not?"

"We just can't."

"Come on." She leaned in and started kissing my neck.

And for another moment, I indulged in her passion. She kissed the left side of my neck before moving up to behind my ear. It felt absolutely wonderful.

But I just couldn't do it. As she moved toward my lips again, I turned my head. I sidestepped, putting a couple feet between us.

"We have to stop," I told her again.

She stepped toward me. "We do? Are you sure that's what you want?"

I couldn't answer her the way I wanted to because I wasn't sure I really wanted to stop. "Yes, I seriously think we need to stop."

She frowned. "So I'm pretty enough to stand there and gawk at, but not pretty enough to sleep with?"

What could I say to that? I was absolutely stunned that the Jen I thought I knew would say something so inappropriate. And stunned at the amount of raw emotion, or desire, or whatever it was that was running through me. I saw the bed behind her and knew how easy it would be for me to take her and do whatever my body wanted.

But, again, my better judgment won out.

"Do you hear yourself?" I asked. "You're married to my brother. This is *wrong.*" I'm not the most moral person in the world, but even I knew how terribly wicked this was.

"He doesn't have to know. He's never around. And he's not here now. He's probably off with one of his secretaries, anyway. Who knows what he does when he's gone. I've had my suspicions."

I didn't care about any of that. It was wrong, no matter what, no excuses. "He'll find out," I said.

"No, he won't."

"Yes, he will."

"How will he find out?" she asked. "Do you see him? He's not home."

"But Ally is."

At the mention of her daughter, Jen's face immediately softened. The sexual charge disappeared. The heat in her eyes had dissipated. "I...uh..." She started crying. For a second, I thought she was going to faint as she looked around her room. She looked disoriented.

I stepped toward her just as she broke down. "I'm so sorry," she repeated over and over again. "I'm so sorry."

I had nothing to say. I just stood there and let her cry on me, just like I'd let Ally cry a week ago.

I think this was by far the longest part. She continued to cry and apologize, while I repeatedly looked at the door. I wanted to get out of there. But every time I thought she was done, she started again. Finally, after what had to be at least ten minutes, she stopped sobbing. And when she pulled away and looked at me, I saw the gentle face of the Jen I knew before this. It was as if there were two different people inside her.

She bit her lower lip, and I knew she had no idea what to say. Neither did I. I just wanted to get out of there. I started toward the door.

She tried to grab my arm, but she couldn't get hold of it. "I'm sorry," she said again.

But I was out in the hall now, and she barely had the sentence out when I slammed the door behind me. I didn't wait for her to come out and try to apologize again. I started walking—jogging—toward my room.

I was just about to the first staircase when Ally poked her head around Butler Charles' door.

"What took you so long?" she asked, crinkling her nose. She surprised me. In the heat of the moment, I'd forgotten our game.

I knelt down to her level. "I was trying to find Wilbur." I put my hand on her shoulder. "But we're going to have to play another time. I can't play right now."

"But we just start—"

I interrupted her. "I just can't. I'm sorry."

She didn't respond. She put her hand on my shoulder, mimicking my gesture. "Grown-up stuff?"

As bad as the situation was, I couldn't help but smile. At that moment, Ally was the only light in a very dark situation.

"Yes. Grown-up stuff."

Ally looked back into Charles' room. "Okay Wilbur, it's time to go." She turned back toward me. "You couldn't find him because he was with me the whole time." She started toward the staircase and called back to me. "Okay, go do whatever you have to do." She sounded just like a grown-up.

I ran straight to my bedroom.

And I've been in here ever since. Well, in between the times I've thrown up in my bathroom. Dry heave after dry heave. My stomach won't settle down.

I hope Jen hears it all.

In between the vomiting, I've been sitting in front of this computer. But as I type all this, it's still hard for me to believe that it actually happened. It just pisses me off so much that Jen has ruined everything. How am I going to face Brandon the next time we have dinner, with her sitting across from me, acting like nothing is wrong?

Worse, how am I going to face Jen at breakfast every morning? I guess I'm going to starve for the rest of my life.

I'm so angry right now! But not just at Jen. Brandon should get some of the blame, too. He's never home, and apparently he's not sleeping with his wife very much. Either that, or he just sucks at it. Part of this has to be his fault. So much for him saving anybody.

And now I'm worried about everything. Will what Jen and I did stay secret? Did Butler Charles or Ariel see or hear anything? For all I know, Ariel could have been in her room, just two doors down, listening to it all.

Or maybe Ally saw it. Or heard it. There are so many terrible possibilities.

It doesn't matter. These things have a way of being found out. And when it does come out, everything good that has happened this past month could be gone. Just like that.

I can't help but look at the bottle of sleeping pills Brandon gave me. How easy it would be to put myself out for a very long time.

Chapter 15

September 7, 2013

Nothing seems more familiar to me than New York City at night. It's the thugs in the alley behind the thrift store. It's the two Cadillacs parked on the corner, some teenage boys spotting for them halfway down the block. It's the girl wearing the trench coat and strolling slowly near the curb, her pimp casually walking a few feet behind her. It's the exchange of bills and powder in front of the old drug store. It's the young boy with the bulge of a gun showing through the back of his shirt. The familiar things are everywhere. And the temptations are never ending. The highs, the money, the fame—they all pull me toward them.

But this is all outside my cozy neighborhood. It's a lot harder to get away with this crap in a place where the residents own security systems and the streets are routinely patrolled by the police. Not to mention, rich people usually buy their drugs and women in the poorer areas of the city, away from where they lay their heads at night. I know I sound matter-of-fact, but I've had plenty of experience to back up what I'm writing here.

I guess my point is that all the crap I just told you about is where I fit in. My native habitat, so to speak. Not some mansion. Not some high school. Not a coffee shop.

I try to remind myself of this every day, either in hopes of waking myself up from too pleasant a dream or, if I'm not dreaming, to prepare myself for the worst.

Luckily, Ana has a way of dispelling such thoughts. When she looks at me with those emerald eyes and tells me I'm wrong about something, I feel very hard-pressed to disbelieve her. The conviction behind her words leave me no choice. Everything she believes in, she believes with such conviction—childlike conviction. Stupid conviction. But that doesn't matter. The more she tries to convince me that she's right, the more I fall for her. I have never felt such an attraction to anyone. Maybe it's because I can't have her. Or maybe it's because she's beautiful. And real. And genuine.

Best of all, when I'm with Analeigh, I almost forget the fact that less than a week ago, my sister-in-law's tongue was in my mouth.

"She had a lapse of judgment. And she's just desperate," Ana told me.

"Well, gee, thanks for giving me some credit," I responded.

She laughed. "Don't get me wrong," she said. "It would be hard to have a prime-A piece of meat in your house and not eat it—I mean, not take advantage of it."

"Thanks."

***

But the war in my head goes on. For one thing, how can a "Christian" family be so screwed up? My brother is forever absent. He was absent during my childhood, and he's still absent now. In my depraved mind, I feel he should expect his wife to stray. *Hypocrite.* That's the go-to word.

Which brings this question to mind, the one I asked Ana. "Why do all of you go to church and play the part when you clearly don't live by what the church says?"

I've asked a lot of questions like that this week. I guess my encounter with Jen has forced them out of me.

We were sitting in the Coffee Shop. Ana leaned back in her chair. "Because the church is our family," she said. "Plain and simple. If we ever needed anything, they would be there for us."

"Could that be because your father is the lead pastor?"

"No. It's because Christianity is about love and servanthood."

Of course that brought on many more questions. But we had plenty of time. As awful as last week was, this week hasn't been too bad. The rest of the clan left for their senior trip on Tuesday. Ana's a sophomore, and I guess my special enrollment didn't allow me to go on senior trips, not even with my brother's connections. So that meant a whole week of just the two of us, together, no distractions.

Well, no distractions except for Levi, who constantly cuts into my time. He's on the senior trip, too, but his phone calls seem constant. I know I shouldn't expect less than that, but when she talks to him, I find myself imagining ways to kill him.

But tonight was different. I couldn't help but think how few days we had left together, just the two of us. It's not that I don't want to see the rest of my friends, but being alone with her has been amazing.

Though it hasn't been without its moments, too.

I invited Ana over to the mansion yesterday so she could suffer with me through one of the rare family dinners. But dinner didn't happen last night, so we dodged that bullet. That left us with extra time. I showed her around the mansion, and we eventually found our way to the piano. I sat down and played a song from my newest book.

"*Well Tempered Clavier* by Bach," Ana said as soon as I finished.

"You actually know that?" I asked. "When Ally played it for me, I didn't have clue. I got a lecture."

Ana walked around the piano and sat down beside me. She touched a few of the keys with her index fingers. "How long have you been playing?"

"About a month."

She pulled the book off of the stand and looked at the cover, then showed it to me. "This primer is for serious players. It's all classical pieces. You're telling me you've learned how to do this in a month?" Disbelief was written all over her face.

She had a point. Even I was surprised by how fast I'd picked it up. It had taken Ally much longer to get to this point, and she still hasn't perfected the primer I was playing from. But I can't really compare myself to her, as her five-year-old fingers are about half as long as mine, and her mind clearly isn't as sharply developed at her age.

"Yes," I said. "Only a month. Jen says I have talent." But the minute I spoke her name, I became angry.

Ana must have noticed. "You're gonna have to get over it."

"Easy for you to say."

"True," Ana said, smiling. She put the music back on the stand.

"It just pisses me off," I said. "And it's hard for me to say no to my anger. Always has been."

Ana put her elbow on the piano, and rested her head on her hand. She gave me her inquisitive look. I like this look. Her green eyes get even more beautiful than they already are.

"It's not easy for you to say no to other things, either?" she said. "Is it?"

I didn't know what she was talking about. I started to speak, but stopped myself. I tried to figure out what she meant.

When I didn't answer, she smiled again. "Come on," she said. "You know what I'm talking about."

"I do?" It felt like an awkward moment was coming. It felt a lot like Jess's dance invitation. I wondered if Ana knew how much I really liked her. Was she going to call me out on it? I didn't think I'd ever made it obvious in any way.

"Yes, you do."

At that moment, silence was my friend.

"Oh, come on," Ana said. She sat up straight. "You know how much Jess is all over you all of the time, and the things she says."

I immediately felt relieved. This had nothing to do with Ana and me. Which was great, because I wasn't ready to tackle anything like that.

"What about it?" I asked as smoothly as I could.

Ana's inquisitive look came back. "You know that's just what she does. It's not because she is, like, in love with you or anything."

"I never thought she was."

"Come on! You haven't done much to stop it. I just don't want you to lead her on." Ana's voice was stern and motherly, her tone made even more pointed by her English accent.

"Just when I thought I wasn't going to get another lecture at the piano," I replied sarcastically. "I'm not trying to lead her on at all. I don't like her like that."

And I never thought this would be an issue. I just thought that was how Jess is. But, clearly, I was wrong. Or right, depending on how you look at it. If everyone knows this is just the way she is, then why is this even a problem?

Ana wasn't finished. "It's just, like, I feel if you continue to not have any boundaries, she's going to actually fall for you, which I guess wouldn't be a bad thing." Ana's voice was a little less stern now. "I guess I'm just trying to not make things awkward. We all like you, and I don't want a silly relationship getting in the way, especially if someone gets hurt in the end."

Ana's words were very sincere, even if I didn't need to hear them. I wanted to defend myself, but I'd not heard

Ana ever speak so seriously, nor so directly, about Jess or our "friendship." Which meant she really was worried. Which meant maybe there were ulterior motives behind this conversation. Wishful thinking, right?

"I promise I will try to do better," I said.

Ana smiled. "Okay, I trust you. And I didn't think you were that type of guy. You—"

"*Trust me*," I interrupted. "If I liked someone, they'd know it." I followed that by putting my hand on her arm. I don't know why I did it. It was completely stupid and, well…just stupid.

Ana looked at my hand. Then she looked into my eyes.

An awkward silence followed as we sat there and looked at each other.

And from that point, I imagine it like a movie. Our faces slowly came close to each other…

Like super slowly—

But then I saw the confusion on her face. It was a look I've imagined I've had many times. That look, like, when your emotions and thoughts are at war with each other.

I tried to ignore it, but the tension was strong.

"I have to go," Ana said. She stood up.

It was at that moment that I realized what an idiot I had been. I had just turned a simple night into some kind of romanticized fairytale where I thought there would be some sort of happy ending.

"I'm sorry. I—"

"It's okay." But she was not okay. "Thanks for hanging out." And with that, she left.

I was too embarrassed to do anything. I couldn't believe I'd turned a conversation about Jess into, what? A catastrophe.

I buried my head in my hands when I heard the front door close.

Then I sat there at the piano for who knows how long until Ariel walked in and asked me what I was doing.

"Shouldn't you be doing something?" I said in a cold voice.

Ariel frowned. "You should do something, too." Then she walked away.

***

Thankfully, Ana didn't seem to hold onto yesterday's debacle at all. As a matter of fact, I'd been with her since school let out, and not a single word about it. At first, I think I made it a little weird because I really didn't know how to go about being with Ana as if nothing had happened. But Ana acted so normal that it forced me to just be myself. And I'm glad I did, because tonight was a great night—no, dare I say, the *best* night. Sure, we studied for a little while, but then Ana asked me to come over to her house. I said yes. Of course.

And I couldn't have been more elated. I just hope it didn't show too much. Sometimes, I'm afraid my dark outer shell is not doing very well at concealing my childish self. And I think my hardened criminal being is slowly giving way to my average-teenager-doing-average-things being. If that makes any sense at all.

Ana's house was much smaller than I expected. Her father was the lead pastor of a church of thousands of people, so I never imagined his family lived in a small, tan, two-story home at the end of the cul-de-sac, a house that matched all of the other houses around it.

As soon as I stepped out of Ana's car—she drives a newer Ford Focus—I know, real hard-core, right?—I saw her father sitting on the porch. He was reading a book, which I assumed was the Bible. Makes sense. He was wearing gray sweat pants and a T-shirt. It was a different look from the flashy suit and tie I was used to seeing on Sundays. Not to mention, his salt-and-pepper hair wasn't slicked back, but was a disheveled mess. He looked normal. He stood up as we reached the porch.

"Hey, Daddy," Ana said, wrapping her arms around him.

"Hey, Baby," He returned the hug.

I never pictured Ana being one to show a whole lot of affection to her adoptive family, but, as you've surely noticed, being wrong about people is kind of my theme lately.

"How was your day?" he asked her.

"Fine."

That's when I noticed the book in his hand wasn't the Bible. It looked like some type of novel or biography.

The two of them seemed worlds apart, and it was hard for me to reconcile that they lived under the same roof. Her father looked like your average American working man. She looked like she just returned from a death metal concert. Or maybe even a satanic ritual.

"And Alex," he said. He let go of Ana and reached out with his right hand. "Ana has told me a lot about you."

"Daddy!"

I shook his hand. "Hi, sir." I smiled at Ana. She looked a little embarrassed.

"Please don't call me sir," her father said. "Am I that old looking? Call me Jim. Or Pastor Greene, if you must." His grip was firm.

I didn't know what to say.

And then it got a little awkward. Ana looked at me as her father took his time shaking my hand while seemingly studying me over.

"Okay," she said. "Time to go inside."

Her father, or Jim, let go of my hand. "Yes. Certainly. Don't let me hold you up. Make yourself at home, Alex. I'll just go back to reading." He lifted his book up and showed me the cover. "Nothing like a little sci-fi to enjoy this fine evening."

I nodded, then followed Ana into the house.

I met Ana's mother next. Her name is Sarah, and she was busy making dinner. Like her husband, she seemed quite down-to-earth and very friendly. "I'd like to talk to you more over dinner," she said. "You are staying for dinner, right?"

I couldn't say no.

Ana's house was quaint, but very well organized. It was a minimalist dream, in fact, very clean and uncluttered, kind of an odd setup, like a painting with Ana in the foreground. Her dark character was enhanced by the very white, very plain interior. It looked nothing like the mansion. This house actually looked like it belonged in this century.

As soon as her bedroom door was closed, Ana let out a huge sigh and leaned against the door. "I know. My family is weird."

"I like them."

"You do, huh?" She raised her eyebrow.

"No, really," I said. "It's nice to meet a normal family." We all know mine isn't.

Ana's room was simple and clean. As a matter of fact, there was very little in it. It didn't make the same statement that her every day appearance did. I walked around, inspecting it, because I didn't know what else to do. I'm not often in girls' bedrooms. Unless I'm pulled in by a family member.

"Well, they may have their charm," Ana said as she stepped away from the door. "Hands off my stuff."

I immediately put the picture I'd picked up back down on her dresser. "Who are the little ones?" I asked. There were two little, curly blonds posing on either side of

Ana. They looked younger than Ally, but the picture seemed to be a few years old, as Ana wasn't wearing black in it and she had long hair.

She straightened the black frame. "Those are my stepsisters. Adopted like me. They're twins, if you couldn't tell. They're probably in the playroom in the basement."

I'd always thought of Ana as the only child in the family. I don't know why. Maybe because she seemed like she would be hard enough to handle on her own. "How come you never talk about them?"

"You've never asked."

Then she grabbed my arm and pulled me toward a door opposite the one we came in. "Come on, I want to show you my favorite part of the house."

I went with her. She was touching me, and that was a win already. Hanging around Jess had forced me to get over my "don't touch me" attitude.

"I come out here all the time," Ana said as she opened the door.

And we walked out onto a small balcony that sat just above the front porch. I'd noticed the railing when we pulled up to the house, but hadn't given it any thought. The balcony wasn't very large, just enough room for a lawn swing—those swings with the floral cushions on them— and a small table with a potted cactus on it.

"Come on! You'll be the first boy I've ever brought out here. Jess and Hannah hang out here sometimes, but never Thomas. I don't know why."

"I feel honored," I said sarcastically. Although, deep inside, I really did.

The view was amazing. Her house sat on one of the higher elevations in the neighborhood, so there was a vast amount of landscape to see. This was one of the few parts of New York one could call hilly. It's just north of Manhattan. It was also one of the nicer neighborhoods in the vicinity of the Bronx. Several other neighborhoods were visible, and the contrast of houses with lights on and off made an arresting image. It also helped to have the New York skyline as a backdrop. If I had this balcony and this view where I lived, I'd probably be outside all the time.

But nothing was as beautiful as Ana. Even in the dark, her eyes sparkled. Her pale skin seemed to glow in the moonlight. And all of those other comparisons that novelists use to describe their gorgeous leading ladies held true.

We didn't say anything for a while. We just sat there on the swing and enjoyed that comfortable, quiet summer night. Ana initially sat away from me on the swing, but then she moved over until she was up against me.

"So tell me, Alex, who are you, really?"

And for the next, oh, I'd say fifteen minutes, I told her nearly everything about myself. I told her about my parents, the abuse, the poverty. I told her about running away and living on my own. I told her about my sister Kim and her suicide. And of course, I told her about Brandon and his absenteeism—not that I haven't already mentioned that to her a thousand times already. I even told her about juvenile detention, and what a wonderful time I had there.

She seemed to accept my narrative, for a time, but then she started to get that inquisitive look again.

After I finished telling her how I started writing while I was in juvie, and that I'm still writing, which is weird, because I'm writing right now, she nodded. "Okay, you've told me enough about the things that have happened in your life. But I want to know about *you*. I want to know who you actually are inside. Who are you are as a person?"

I wasn't sure what she meant. "Like, you want to know the bad things I've done? Because I'm sure you can look it up on the Internet."

"No, I could care less about that," she said. "But, like, what do you feel? What do you want to do with your life? And, besides, everyone knows what you've done."

If only that were the case! Then I wouldn't have so many guilty feelings deep inside me all the time. People only knew what I was charged with. But I've done much worse things than what is laid out in my petty drug charges.

"That's a tough question," I finally said. But I gave it my best shot. "I'd be lying to you if I told you I'm a good person. As a matter of fact, if Brandon hadn't taken me in, I don't know if I would have been able to stay away from the things I used to do. I promised myself I wouldn't, but sometimes I think the allure and the ease of that life would have pulled me back in. But who really knows? Right?"

"God knows," she said. "At least, the rest of my family thinks so." She smiled. "Okay, go on."

I sighed, hoping to fill the gaps in my thinking. "I don't know. I just feel like this is all a dream sometimes. A dream that I don't belong in."

"And why do you feel that way?" she asked. She sounded like a psychiatrist. Side note: I hate psychiatrists.

"Because I've been an adult for so long. I'm not sure how to do all of this? That's all."

"All of what?" She wasn't giving up.

"This right here. Being a teenager."

"You seem to be doing well," she replied. "I mean, you've infiltrated our group in next to no time. "

"Yeah, well you're all freaks like me," I said.

She laughed. "I can't argue with that. But we freaks are teenagers, too. So see? You've got it."

"That's what I'm afraid of. This past month has been wonderful, but what if my life goes back to that hell I came from?" That is always my underlying worry. Could all of this, even this moment with Ana, go on?

Her smile faded. She leaned back in the swing and stared at me. "I knew some day we'd crack you open. Jess said she'd be the one to do it. She's going to be pissed when she finds out I did it without her."

I immediately felt embarrassed by the whole conversation.

"But no more questions from me," she said. "I'll be easy on you now." She leaned back up against me. Let's just enjoy this—"

"No, it's your turn." This was the perfect time to turn the tables and learn a little more about this girl I'd fallen for.

She shook her head. "No, no, no. I'm a closed freaking book."

"Are you serious? I just went off into never-never land, telling you all that crap. And you're a closed book? Come on."

Ana laughed again. Then she went quiet.

"So…?" I wasn't going to give up that easy. It was my turn to play psychiatrist.

Ana rolled her eyes "Okay. What do you want to know?"

"I want to know why you're with that worthless jerk, Levi." I didn't really mean to be so blunt. Normally, I would have thought better than to ask such a direct question, especially to someone I cared for so much.

Ana's eyes grew large. She let go of my arm. "That's my boyfriend you're talking about."

But I'd already started down that path, so I didn't let up. "You know…all he wants is your body. He doesn't want you." It sounded way harsher coming out of my mouth than it did in my head.

Ana frowned. "Who are you to judge my relationship? And what makes you think I don't just want his body, too?"

I had no real proof regarding Ana's motives, but it didn't make me believe what I said any less. "You know, people think that about you," I said, "but I don't. I think it's just a wall you hide behind so people don't see the real you."

"And *you* can see past it?" Ana asked, clearly upset now. It wasn't my intention to make her mad, but it was too late.

"I don't know," I said, "but I just think you're better than that."

Ana laughed. An angry laugh. "You really don't know me that well, then. If you've heard about me, then you know I'm the girl that has slept with practically every cool guy in the school. That's who I am!"

"No. I beg to differ. That's *what you do*."

"Oh, wise one," she said, her voice dripping with sarcasm. "You know, this is part of being a teenager. It's learning that people don't give a crap about us. You know, we freaks come in all colors. Some of us are criminals and some of us get used. I happen to—"

"That's a cop out."

"Whatever." She rolled her eyes again. "Every man I've been with wants one thing. And you know—"

"I wouldn't. I want you for *you*."

Ana's face immediately softened. I was becoming pretty good at awkwardly expressing my interest. I'd just done it the second time. I'd turned a conversation about something else into a conversation about Ana and me. And I felt stupid again.

She gave me the same confused look she did at the piano last night. But this time she didn't stand up. She just looked at me.

"I'm sorry." I didn't know what else to say.

She sort of smiled. "For some reason, I believe you."

"Well, I really am sorry."

"No," she responded. "I believe that you really care for me, not because you want to sleep with me. But just because you care." The anger in her voice had completely vanished.

I let out a huge sigh. "You do?"

"I don't know why, but when you say things like that, you are just terribly convincing." She continued to stare at me with that intense look in her eyes. "And it's not just me. I think you'd do anything for Jess and Thomas, too. But when you look at me, it's different."

She was a lot more aware than I gave her credit for.

Like yesterday, I wanted to kiss her that very moment. But I tried to be a little less obvious this time. "I don't know why, either," I said. "I've never really been wired that way, but for some reason, I do care a lot about all of you. But especially you, Ana."

"I know." She turned away, breaking the staring contest.

For a few moments, we sat there, silent.

And it killed me. This was definitely better than the night before. Ana wasn't walking out the door. (Which would have been weird since it was her house. But you get the point.)

She finally leaned against me again. And as she did, I felt like I was a thousand feet tall and invincible.

"So what now?" I asked.

She laid her head on my shoulder. "Let's not make more of this than we already have."

I had no idea what that meant. And since I'd already laid everything out there so plainly, why not ask? Right? "And how would we make more of it?"

Ana didn't look at me. She exhaled deeply. "Well, for one, I'm not going to throw myself on you right now. Trust me, though. I'd like to."

I didn't respond, but I'm sure she felt my heart beat ramp up a hundred times faster. It felt like my entire body was moving with each thump. I wanted the same thing, even though I was content to just sit there and dream about it. I just hoped it wasn't a dream.

Man, wouldn't Levi just love to see this!

It wasn't much longer before Ana's father walked out into the front yard and looked up at us. "It's dinner time, you two."

I hadn't even thought about her father sitting just below us. Ana knew what I was thinking, though, and assured me that he couldn't have heard anything. "From down there," she whispered, "we were just mumbles and vague noises. Besides, when he's engrossed in reading, he doesn't pay much attention to anything else. Ask my mom."

Dinner was much rowdier than what I was accustomed to. The "bundles of joy"—that's what Ana's mother sarcastically called them—were devious kids. And loud too.

Cara and Abby were their names, although they preferred to be called C and A. I didn't find the nicknames all that strange, considering that Ally has an imaginary friend that she talks to. I don't remember being that weird and imaginative when I was a kid.

Cara and Abby made Ally look like an angel. The constant badgering, the complaining, and the blunt—and very inappropriate—questions made for a very interesting thirty to forty minutes though. One of them—I don't know which one, because they look exactly alike—introduced herself by asking me how many times I'd kissed her sister. Let that be an indicator of their behavior. Their father was very lenient to start. But after about ten minutes of being nice, he finally threatened the girls with a "severe whooping." I was initially taken aback by the word choice, but then I remembered that these religious people don't "spare the rod."

Other than the devil twins, the dinner was good. The food was delicious, the conversation, pleasant. I expected to be force-fed some religious garbage along with the delicious pot roast, but not once did the conversation turn into an attempt at indoctrination. There were the occasional references to God, but overall it was just small talk.

And again, Ana just didn't seem to fit in. The family was the picture of your average American family, except for this dark, short-haired outcast that seemed to be superimposed on the center of it. Yet somehow it just seemed right.

After dinner, Ana rushed me away to save me from more "domestic torture." I tried to tell her I was fine, but I think she was ready to get out of there, too. After meeting her sisters, of course I understood.

The drive home was quiet. The moments we'd shared on the balcony didn't seem to match the night, and I didn't really know how to broach the subject again without sounding stupid or desperate. I assumed Ana felt the same way, or maybe she was just trying to make it disappear, like she had after our conversation at the piano.

When she pulled up to my house, she didn't even put the car into park. That was my cue that she didn't want to have another long conversation.

When I started to open the door, though, she grabbed my other hand. "So…about tonight?" She bit her bottom lip like Jess does when she's nervous.

I let go of the door handle. "What about it?"

"Remember what I said about Jess yesterday?"

I did remember, every detail, in fact. "About not screwing up our friendship?"

"Yes. I just don't want us to—"

"—yeah, I know, screw it up. Got it."

"Yes," she said. But she didn't seem convinced.

But if this was going to be the extent of anything beyond a friendship, then I figured it was going to be my only opportunity. I decided to take a chance

"I just think we need to—" Without finishing the sentence, I leaned over and kissed her. She didn't struggle. She kissed back. But only briefly.

Then she took her foot off of the brake and the car moved forward a little. She slammed her foot down. The car jerked hard. It was enough of a jerk to separate us. And I know, yes, it's becoming a theme, but for a few moments after that, we just stared at each other. Then Ana started to laugh. I did, too.

"I thought we weren't going to screw it up," she whispered.

"Well," I answered. "I just thought if this was it, then I better get it in. I've been thinking about it too much not to do it while I had the chance."

Ana laughed even harder.

I opened the door. "Good night."

It took a moment, but she stopped laughing. "Night."

I started to put my feet out of the door when Ana grabbed my hand again. As I turned toward her, she leaned over and kissed me again. Not nearly as long, but very firmly. I barely had time to respond before she backed off. But she still held on to my hand.

"And what was that one for?" I asked, my heart beating, my mind racing.

She grinned. "Well, I like your philosophy. So that was my turn to get it in."

I was content to leave it at that.

***

I'm not going to lie. After tonight, I don't care anymore about what happened with Jen. And I don't care about Brandon's inadequate job as a big brother. I don't even care about all of that "fitting in" crap that I told Ana earlier.

I've been up writing this for about three hours. All I can think about is the taste of her lips. And the warmth of her body. And that look in her eyes. And did I mention the taste of her lips?

And you know what? I don't care about that whole screwing up our friendship thing. Whatever it takes, I'm going to kiss that girl again. I promise.

Chapter 16

September 21, 2013

I think in everyone's life, there are those moments that define us, that forever change who we are and who we want to be. And when we look back on them, good or bad, we can see how those moments affected us for better or for worse. But we probably wouldn't want to change the fact that they happened. That's because without the good, we wouldn't recognize the bad. Without good moments, we wouldn't know what it means to be happy or feel success. And without the bad moments, we would never have climbed out of the ashes as stronger people.

For me, my parents dying, my going to juvenile detention, and my kissing Ana twice could be defined as "those moments." I'll never forget them. I'll never be the same because of them.

But other memories haunt me, too. They haunt me every day. I've refrained from writing about them, but the more my life becomes normalized, the more these memories burn in my mind. I've done some terrible things. Things I try to forget. Things I don't want to talk about.

***

Well, enough philosophy. I can say without a doubt that going to the homecoming dance will not be one of those defining moments for me. As I struggled to put on my suit, I remembered dressing formally only one other time in my life. That was at least three years ago, after one of my friends—or partners in crime—was gunned down in an alleyway only a few miles from my current residence. I stole a suit just for his funeral.

This suit cost a little more than my stolen one. But that's not a big deal when you live with a rich family.

That's a great segue into my family life. It took several silent and very excruciating mornings before Jen and I were able to start talking to each other again. Actually, it was Ally who sort of forced it to happen as she began to notice the tension between us. Neither she nor Wilbur liked it at all. In her little five-year-old mind, though, she didn't know how to say what she meant. She just made strange faces at the both of us, faces we couldn't ignore.

And, finally, Jen broke the silence by leaning over and whispering, "I'm sorry," while Ally was putting away her dishes. "I've just been so angry lately, and I wanted to spite Brandon. Please forgive me."

After two weeks of agony, I couldn't hold onto my anger anymore. "Okay."

"That's not me," she continued. "I promise, that's not—"

"Let's just forget about it," I whispered back.

And from that point on, Jen and I started talking again.

And as I struggled to put my tie on for the dance, Jen was there to help me. The tie came out too short twice and too long the third time. After four tries, Jen stepped away, and I looked at myself in the mirror and laughed even harder.

"I look ridiculous!"

Ally sat up on her bed—yes, we were in her room and I was looking into a full-length princess mirror—and laughed too. "You do look funny," she said.

"Oh, stop it Ally." Jen straightened my tie. "Alex, you look dashing."

"Almost as dashing as his big brother."

I turned just as Brandon took my picture from the doorway. The flash nearly blinded me.

"What the he—" I remembered Ally was beside me. "—heck?"

"Hey," Brandon said as he came in and patted me on the shoulder, "this is a big step for you. From criminal to homecoming date."

"Take another picture," I said in a pretend-threatening voice, "and I may be back to criminal again."

Then we all laughed together, kind of like a normal family, I suppose. If only Brandon knew what had happened.

Meeting Jess's parents was, let's just say, different. They were both very short people—short in stature, I mean—and very quiet. Their daughter didn't look like either of them. But they were very nice, nonetheless. Her father offered me a glass of whiskey as I waited at the bottom of the staircase, which I declined, reminding him that I was underage. He didn't seem the least worried, so I was forced to awkwardly explain that it wasn't because I didn't want to drink it, but rather because I couldn't drink it. By the time I was done, he practically knew my entire criminal history.

Thank God, Jess didn't keep me waiting for long. I was looking away when she came down the stairs, but the gasps from her parents caught my attention. I looked up to see Jess looking more beautiful than ever. I did a double take at first. I barely recognized her. Her normally straight, blond hair was curled, and her bangs covered one eye.

But her dress was what amazed me the most. It wasn't at all her normally provocative style, but was very long, a shade of red, and sparkly. It went all the way down to her ankles, and believe it or not, even though it was strapless, it was not at all revealing, definitely not as revealing as her norm.

I took her hand. "You look beautiful," I told her.

"And you clean up well, too," she responded with a wink.

Her parents drove us to the dance—yeah, not exactly how I thought it would go—and I couldn't help but think about how crazy this was. It was barely a month ago that I had met Jess. And here I was, holding her hand and going to a dance.

And then, to my shame, I thought again about kissing Ana, a girl I'd known for an even shorter time. My mind seems to go back to that night often. Like, all the time.

And while I'm on the subject, let me tell you, I practically lost my breath when I saw Ana walk into the school gymnasium. If Jess was beautiful that night, then Ana was some type of goddess. She wore a white dress with a red belt, like something from the fifties. It was a stunning look, as her tattooed arms and back set off of the outfit like a steampunk cover girl.

"You like it?" Ana asked.

"You look beautiful," I told her, repeating the words I'd said to Jess earlier.

Ana and Jess hugged each other, and I was left standing there next to Levi. We just stared at each other. Thankfully, Hannah and Reuben joined us a few seconds later. Hannah was the picture taker for the night. Reuben just seemed antsy most of the time. I learned later that Reuben's night was mainly filled with selling prescription drugs, and he was a little nervous about the public arena. He seemed to be growing his business.

The homecoming dance wasn't really that enjoyable. As much as we all tried to fit in, it just wasn't our scene. Ana was the only one who even halfway fit in as Levi dragged her around most of the evening with his group of witless morons. But the food was good, and I danced with Jess a couple of times, which seemed to pass the time.

The big shocker of the night was watching Thomas walk in, hand in hand—like he'd promised—with last year's homecoming queen, Sam Reams. I kid you not, there wasn't a jaw in the room that didn't drop. Yeah, Thomas and Sam got the reaction they were looking for. Sam was stunning, but Thomas was the real surprise. The mohawk was gone. Now he sported a clean-shaven head along with a very sharp tuxedo and a dark blue bow tie that matched Sam's dress.

"You just stole the show," I told Thomas as he grabbed my outstretched hand and pulled me in for a hug.

"I know."

"Hi, everyone." Sam was very soft-spoken and clearly nervous to find herself in our group of misfits.

Jess and Hannah did everything they could to help her relax. It didn't matter, though, because as soon as Sam seemed to be getting comfortable around us, she was made Homecoming Queen for the second year in a row. As she gave her speech, the rest of the class suddenly found time to congratulate Thomas for his unbelievable catch. Although I suspect many of them probably thought Thomas was her gay friend, not a real date. But I wasn't going to spoil it for him.

Thomas would have been my choice for Homecoming King, and I think I speak for the rest of our group when I say that. Much to my dismay, however, I heard Levi's name called. I cringed as he kissed Ana before walking up on the stage and making a fool of himself with his half-arrogant, half-stupid declaration of how wonderful he was.

Ana looked at me, half frowning and half smiling, during most her boyfriend's tirade.

It was the after party that made the night. Hannah had done wonders with the warehouse, and at least half the school was there. I'd not seen the place even half that full. But that was no surprise. It seemed like half of New York's drugs and alcohol were there.

The furniture was all pushed up against the walls, making an enormous dance floor. And for hours upon hours, several hundred students danced, drank, and danced some more, some of them until they couldn't stand anymore and were forced out by their intoxication.

I mostly stood in the darkest corner and watched. I wasn't drinking. I had an unsatisfying bottle of water. I laughed as my friends and people I didn't even know made fools of themselves. As more cans of beer hit the floor, the louder the party got. I wanted to join them. I wanted to get drunk. I wanted to smoke. But somehow my conscience won out. It was no easy fight, though.

Like my first time at the warehouse, I eventually found myself sitting in the back of Thomas' jeep, staring up at the stars. Jess wasn't far behind me, so I made room for her and helped her as she struggled to climb up.

"Clearly," she said, "I'm not used to wearing this much crap."

"So it couldn't be the booze?"

She laughed. "Maybe."

The view here wasn't quite as beautiful as the view from Ana's balcony, but the skyline was still breathtaking from this side of the city. It wasn't as quiet, either, as the dance music mixed with the sounds of industrial buildings still in production.

But it was enough to keep both of our minds preoccupied for a time. I was happy in the moment, as I knew Jess wouldn't stay quiet for long.

"I see you're sticking to your guns," she finally said, nodding at the empty water bottle in my hand.

I threw the bottle over my head and into Thomas' front seat. He liked his jeep to be clean, so I knew it would drive him crazy. I was probably the only one not drinking tonight, so he'd figure out whose bottle it was soon enough.

"Trust me," I said, "it's not easy."

"It would be a lot easier if you just gave in and joined us for a little fun once in a while," she said. "It's not that bad to have a little drink here and there. Even our good old pastor man would say that."

I laughed at her odd way of referring to Pastor Greene.

"Seriously, though," she added, "just do what you want."

"I am."

"Seriously?"

"Dead serious," I answered very matter-of-factly.

Jess smiled, then leaned back against the seat. "You know, we all thought we were freaks until we met you. You take the cake."

I lay back beside her. "Thank you."

She turned on her side, then scooted over against me. Just because it felt like the right thing to do, I pulled her closer. At the same time, though, I again heard Ana's warning in my head.

"I know your life has changed a lot in the past month," Jess whispered, "but do you ever wonder what it will be like when we no longer have any of this? I mean, what happens when we all go off to college in different places? And we find careers that could take us to different parts of the country?"

I hadn't really thought of anything like that. For one, after a month in high school, college was the last thing on my mind. And two, I didn't want to think about change. I didn't want to think about my life without Ana in it. I know, it's only been a month, but I can't even imagine my life without Jess or Thomas, either.

Jess looked up at me. "I'm taking your silence as a sign that you haven't?"

"No," I replied. "Not really. Or at least not to the depth that you have. I'm still trying to figure out how one morning I woke up in lockdown, then I went to sleep the same night in a mansion. Or how I went from no friends to taking such an amazing, very hardcore, girl like yourself to the homecoming dance."

"You left out the part about how beautiful she is."

"Yeah. Both inside and out."

She didn't say anything. She just nudged her head against my chest.

I was doing exactly what Ana had told me not to do. But it was just how Jess and I were. I didn't know how to change it.

After a few minutes of silence, Jess looked up at me. "Can I ask you a serious question?"

It's phrases like that that still make me nervous. But for some reason, I knew that no matter where the conversation went, my relationship with Jess would be officially defined tonight. Because for some reason, with that simple question, I decided that it needed to be. She needed to know how I felt. And who I really had feelings for.

"Sure." I waited for the inevitable awkward moment.

She sat up. "Okay." She paused for a second. "Uhhmm…you don't have to tell me…but…" It was a lot like the night she asked me to go to homecoming with her. Only this time, Thomas wasn't here to help her out. She took a breath. "…uhhmm…can you tell me what you did before juvie?"

I was preparing myself for a totally different question, so I wasn't ready to answer that one. It was my turn to stammer through a response. I started to laugh.

"What?" she asked.

"I just…I thought…I thought you were going in a totally different direction." It was hard to talk through the laughter.

She looked confused. "And what direction was that?"

"Well, about *this*. About *us*."

Her eyes grew wide. She shook her head, and then she looked like she just knew something important. "Wait—what the heck? *Us?*" She climbed off the jeep.

I sat up, intending to follow her.

"What do you think this is, Alex?" She sounded hostile. Needless to say, I wasn't laughing anymore. And I didn't know how to answer that question, either.

Then she flashed into anger. "*What?* You think because I joke around with you…oh, and we hold hands sometimes…you think there's something going on between us? Was the back of Thomas' jeep the place where you were going to make your move?"

"I…I, uh—"

"I'm not done! You're probably just like everyone else. You think I'm that slut who's ready to give it away after a few drinks. Ready to fall into your arms—"

"I don't—"

"Shut up! Alex, I'm not the dark, edgy whore everyone thinks I am. As a matter of fact, *I've never slept with anyone*. There you go. Now you know. Jessica Lynn, the virgin. And now you can go tell the whole world."

I couldn't speak. I didn't have any words. I couldn't tell if this was the alcohol talking or if I had really pissed her off that much.

Jess turned and pointed her finger at me. "Alex Lane, just when I thought—"

I reached out and grabbed her by the shoulders. I didn't know what else to do. I didn't know what I was going to say, but I had to stop her ranting.

"I'm in love with Ana." It came out of my mouth before I even knew I was going to say it.

Jess stopped immediately. Her jaw dropped. And then she smiled, before wrapping her arms around me.

To say I was confused is an understatement.

"I knew it, I knew it, I knew it!" She stepped back. "You know, I almost slapped you across the face."

"What? I don't even...I mean..."

"I'm sorry. But I thought you were going to ruin everything by trying to get in my dress tonight."

She has such a way with words.

"Why?" It was all I could say. And it seemed like an appropriate question, since her wild rant had come out of nowhere.

"Because...because, you know how I am. I flirt, and well, you know..."

I did know. "But why?" Yeah, I was a total mess by that time.

"Ana has never been like me," she said. "We're kind of the opposites. I, well, now you know, I don't really do those types of things, but I'm the biggest flirt in town. Ana, on the other hand, sleeps with every guy that will have her, but she won't listen to her heart." Her rant was turning into some strange kind of rambling, like a preteen girl talking about her crush on some famous singer or actor. "Ana won't step up and take what she wants. I've been trying to tell her to take charge. To talk you away from me, and to start putting herself—"

I grabbed Jess's shoulders again. "What are you talking about?"

"She's wants you, Alex. Ever since she met you, she's wanted you. And not for sex. Not for status. She just wants you *for you.*"

Now it all made sense. It was like the puzzle pieces just fell together in my mind. Those things Ana had said about Jess and me had come from Jess in the first place.

"Did you know about—"

"About your little late-night trysts on the balcony, and in the car? Oh, yeah, she told me. I also know about your impatience at the piano. Ana wasn't ready for that crap. That's how all of the other guys are. And that's what I thought you were going to do just now. I thought my friend Alex was being a player."

"But I'm not those other guys," I objected.

"I know," Jess said, almost gleefully. "I really do know that now. But you have to show *her*. And it's going to take a lot. Because she doesn't do this whole relationship for love thing, as you know."

"I..." What could I say? Just hearing that Ana had feelings for me—especially hearing it from her closest friend—made this whole night go from amazing to...well, to whatever word you can think of that is better than amazing.

This was far from me sealing the deal, but at least I had a chance. I was a least on the right path to being able to kiss Ana's lips again. Hope was all I needed.

Jess grabbed my hands. "You know, from the very get-go, we all knew you liked her. There was just something about the way you looked at her. Spoke to her. She didn't see it, but Thomas and I sure did. I guess our senior trip was enough time for you guys to get the steam going."

We both laughed.

"But now," Jess said, "now to answer my question...."

"What?"

"My question! Before I delivered my virgin monologue."

I stopped laughing. I remembered. "Why I was in juvie?"

"Yes."

It took a lot for my mind to go from all of that new information I had absorbed back to where we'd started. I tried my best. I told you when I started writing tonight that there were memories that haunt me. Well, Jess was that first person to hear them. And you know what? It's amazing how easy it was to tell her...when my thoughts were so engaged in the knowledge of Ana's feelings.

Sorry, but I'm not writing down what I told her. I'm not ready for it to be out there in the open yet. Another day, another time.

When I finished my answer, Jess hugged me again. This time, I hugged her back. I even picked her up off of the ground and swung her around. When I set her back down, she didn't let go.

"Alex," she said, "we've only been friends for a short time, but I love you. I really do."

I would be lying if I told you that, at that moment, I had to fight hard to keep tears from forming in my eyes. I don't know if it was the excitement of Jess's revelation regarding Ana or the relief of sharing my past.

"I love you, too, Jess. And for the record, I never thought you were a slut."

She pushed away. Then she slapped me on the arm. "Way to ruin the moment! I take all that back. You're a jerk."

I laughed.

"And for *that*," Jess yelled, "you're going to come inside and dance with me."

There was no saying no.

Part 2

The Light in the Darkness

Chapter 17

October 8, 2013

This was my chance. It was just me and the girl of my dreams sitting on the bottom step, our feet stretched out on the sidewalk. We faced each other. Ironically, it was the same exact spot where I sat with Jess the day after Levi knocked me out.

"I don't know what to say," Ana replied.

I grabbed her hand. "Why do you need to say anything? We both know how we feel. Why keep hiding it?"

Ana looked pained, as if she were fighting something with all her might. She bit her lower lip. "Do you really know what I feel?"

The longer it dragged on, the more let down I felt. "I know you don't want that dumb—"

"He's my boyfriend, Alex!"

"No, he's not. He's a loser that uses you for sex. There is so much more to you than that. You know there is."

Ana pulled her hand away. "You say that like you truly know me. We've only known each for like a month. How can you be so pretentious to think you know who I am, or what I want?"

This was not where I wanted this conversation to go. In the million times this moment played over in my head, I've never seen it go quite like this.

"See?" she said. "You don't know."

I guess my silence made her come to that conclusion.

"I just know that's not who you are. That's it," I said.

Ana shook her head, and gave me one of those disbelieving smiles. "But how can you? You sound so freaking confident, like you're some kind of—"

"Because I love you, Ana! From the day I first met you, I've loved you. I can't explain it, but I do."

Her face looked blank, which did not often happen with Ana.

I really thought those words would come out at a time when we both were ready to hear them, not just blurted out as Ana chastised me. But then again, it's taken two weeks for me just to get up the nerve to talk to her about it. And that's why I've been too embarrassed to write anything down during that time. I've been so afraid to do this.

"No one," she finally said, "outside my family, and Jess, of course, has ever said that to me." Ana's lips settled into what could only be described as another disbelieving smile. Her face turned a little red. And then she grabbed my hand, and looking me squarely in the eyes, she asked, "Do you really mean that? Because I'm not ready for it if you don't."

"I've never said anything as true as what I just said to you." Bring on the Oscars for that line, right?

Ana bit her lip again, then showed her teeth with an ear-to-ear grin. "Well, I have to tell you, all I've wanted to do was kiss you again. Since that first time, I've found it hard to think of anything else. I still remember the taste of your lips."

Talk about my heart pounding! "Whatever you just said is exactly how I've felt, too," I managed to say.

"Then kiss me again."

I wasn't about to pass this up. I leaned in to do the thing that I've wanted to do more than anything in the world.

She closed her eyes and waited.

And right then—perfect timing—just as we were about to connect, Brandon's Maserati pulled up to the curb.

Ana heard it, too. She opened her eyes.

But I wasn't going to let my brother steal this moment. She turned her head, and I fell into one of those embarrassing misses. Rejected at the last second.

"I'm sorry," Ana said. "I better go."

"No! Wait!" I kept her hand in mine as she stood up.

She semi-pulled at me, but didn't put up much of a struggle.

"Just...uhhmm..." and I let out a string of curses.

"Don't worry, Alex. Because I love you, too." She gave me that huge smile again.

I was able to let go of her hand, probably because I was too weak to hold on. At that moment, I knew what "feeling the butterflies" meant. It was somewhere between complete shock and the need to throw up.

"I..." Words were not coming to me.

Ana leaned down and kissed the top of my head. "I'll see you soon."

By now, Brandon was out of his car. He nodded and said, "Good evening," as he passed her on the sidewalk. Then he started up the steps. "I'm sorry about that," he said as he passed me.

"About what?" I said. I'm sure I sounded stupid. I probably looked stupid, too, as I watched Ana get into her car.

Brandon started laughing. "I was your age once, little brother. I know what just happened. You know, people are going to start talking about this once it's out. My criminal brother with the pastor's rebellious daughter." He laughed again. "You really know how to make a story."

"Yeah, well…" My mind was elsewhere. Believe it or not, I didn't even have a sarcastic or mean comment right then.

Brandon shook his head, still laughing. "I've seen it all." He started up the stairs. "And by the way," he called down to me, "good job tonight."

"Thanks."

He walked into the mansion, leaving me to my stupor.

You're probably thinking about what he meant by "good job." For just a second, I'll leave you with the image of me sitting on the steps in shock so I can tell you how I got to that point—the point of almost kissing Ana again and hearing the word "love" come out of her mouth.

Let's just call this the short version.

With Brandon's help—yes, I've just confessed to getting help from my brother—I had secured a three song performance at one of his charity gala things. Well, *performance* is a strong word. I played the piano while a bunch of rich people were dining, then spent a long time introducing myself and explaining, well attempting to explain, how I learned how to play the piano so quickly.

As this was my first time playing in front of anyone, my friends were not going to miss it. Just imagine a bunch of punk kids in a crowd of old people in tuxedos and evening gowns. I think Brandon spent most of his time explaining why he'd allowed these freaks into the hotel's fine dining room. But it was Brandon's event, so who could question him?

I played some music, mingled, then got out of there.

To my surprise, I found Ana waiting for me outside the hotel. Honestly, that was the plan the entire time, so it really wasn't a surprise at all. Jess and Thomas have been trying their best to make this happen ever since homecoming. But Ana's been very hard to get alone.

Impossible, actually. And of course, there's always Levi in the way. So Thomas and Jess made up some story about why they had to leave early. I think Ana knew something was up, but she didn't seem let on too much. I could tell she was suspicious, though.

My excuse for leaving was that I needed a ride home and didn't want to wait for Brandon to get done mingling with his wealthy friends. Truly, I didn't. So it wasn't really a lie.

Like the last few weeks, Ana's been acting like nothing ever happened between us on that balcony or in her car, so the ride home was filled with small talk and a lot of silence. I was waiting for some way to broach the subject of what happened between us. But nothing she said made for a natural transition.

"I'll freaking kill you if it doesn't happen tomorrow," Jess had told me the night before. So I couldn't let this opportunity pass, or I'd never hear the end of it in chemistry class tomorrow.

We were just about to pull up to the mansion when Ana said something about Thomas and Sam. In case you were wondering, our metro friend and the homecoming queen weren't technically dating, even though they were pretty inseparable at school. Ana went into a long speech about how they were perfect for each other. I didn't hear any of it, though. I just know that I took it as my opportunity and interrupted her monologue.

"I agree, Thomas and Sam will be great together. But what about us?"

Ana put the car in park and just sat there for a moment, looking straight ahead.

I didn't say anything, either. I was too busy holding my breath and wondering what would happen.

Then she turned the car off and looked at me. "I guess it's time we talk."

And the rest, like they say, is history.

***

After Brandon went inside, I sat on the steps for a while. During that time, Thomas texted me once, and Jess texted me countless times. I finally responded when Jess sent me the hundredth variation of her "I'm going to kill you" line.

I sent both of my anxious friends the phrase "mission accomplished." I didn't pay any attention to any other texts from them. They could wait until tomorrow to hear the rest of the story.

I was so nervous that my stomach never returned to normal that night. What would it be like tomorrow? I mean, she does still have a boyfriend. Would it be awkward now that everything was out in the open? I'm ashamed to admit this, but I've slept with more women than I can count. But as far as real relationships go, I'm as novice as they come.

I haven't gotten over the sick feeling yet. I haven't been able to fall asleep tonight. But if I could, I'd dream about Ana's smile. That's because about fifteen minutes ago, Ana texted me a picture of her smiling. The caption read *How I feel tonight.*

I didn't know what to say back to her, so I just told her I felt the same way. It was kind of a lie, because at that moment, what I really felt like was running into the bathroom and puking my guts out.

As a matter of fact, I still might do that.

I can honestly say that when I first started writing in juvie over two years ago, I never thought that I'd be writing about a girl who is the love of my life. Seriously, if you picked up any one of the many notebooks I now have stored under my bed, you'd be amazed at how desperate and dark I was. I've read a couple of them. Even I can't believe some of the things I've put on paper. But I hope this is a testament to where my life is going now. To see the contrast between then and now is amazing. Or maybe it's miracle. My Bible-wielding family would probably say that.

I hope Ana never has to see the person I used to be. I will have to tell her someday, like I told Jess in the back of the jeep. How that will go, only time will tell.

Like I've said before, I fear no man. But now that this has happened, there is one thing I fear more than anything else. I'm afraid of losing her.

I keep saying that my life can't keep going this well. I thought my rendezvous with Jen was the start, but even a horrible thing like that faded away. All the same, I can't help but think that something bad is bound to happen.

And with that, I think I'm going to find my way to the bathroom now and see about losing my dinner.

Chapter 18

October 9, 2013

Ifinally fell asleep, but the morning came way too fast. I could have thrown my alarm clock out the freakin' window if I'd had the energy to actually roll over and grab it. Instead, I listened to the blaring for fifteen minutes or so, before willing myself to get up.

What got me up was another text from Ana. It was the same picture of her smiling with the words *and this is how I feel this morning* under it. I sat on the edge of my bed for at least another ten minutes, wondering how to respond. I didn't want to sound stupid, or too forward, so I chose the easy route and sent back the simple response, *me too. see you later*.

I tried to act normal that morning, but Jen immediately noticed something was different about me. Maybe it was my unnatural urge to smile, or the fact that I barely said two words after I joined her and Ally in the kitchen.

She looked at me inquisitively from across the table. "What's wrong with you?"

"It's just a good day," I responded.

I could tell she wasn't buying it, but she graciously let it go.

Then Ally put her hand on mine. "Did you take your happy pills this morning?" There was a deep sincerity in her voice.

Jen and I both laughed until I dropped my fork on the floor.

"Where did you hear that?" Jen was finally able to ask.

Ally looked at her mom as seriously as she had at me. "Well, I see Ariel taking her medicine some nights. She told me they were her happy pills."

"And to think," I said, "she's still crazy, even with drugs."

"We don't know what she's taking," Jen said. "But maybe it's the drugs that make her that way."

I think Jen had tears in her eyes as she said that.

Ally just seemed confused. Finally, she stood up and said, "Come on, Wilbur. It's time for school."

Brandon's driver, Andy, usually took me to school, but this morning I decided to take a cab. Andy is a fantastic driver, and riding with him usually makes for great conversations, but he drives way too slow. I couldn't wait to get to school. I wanted to speed through the day, get classes done, and see Ana again. That's the curse of being two years older than her. We had no classes together, so I wouldn't be able to see her till lunch.

And I had no idea what that moment would be like. Levi and Ana never sat together, and quite honestly, they never really talked to each other at school. But something in me knew it would be different today. I had this gut feeling that it wouldn't take long for a confrontation to begin. And I knew Ana well enough to know that Levi wouldn't be kept in the dark for long. It was just a matter of *how long*.

I couldn't have been more right.

As soon as Jess sat down beside me in chemistry, I could tell something was wrong. She wasn't excited enough. I had expected a flood of questions, followed by squeals and more questions. But that wasn't what I got. What I saw on her face was a façade. She didn't look nearly happy enough.

I could only play along for a while. Jess was not good at hiding things, and it was painful to watch her trying.

"Okay, Jess," I finally hissed at her, "what's—"

"Quiet, class," Mr. Gregg said. He was staring straight at me.

I nodded and waited until he started talking again. Then I leaned over and whispered into Jess's ear. "What's wrong with you?" It's ironic that I asked her the same question Jen had asked me only an hour earlier.

"Nothing," Jess responded. But she said it with so little conviction that she had to know it wouldn't convince me.

I pushed at her. "Come on," but all she did was flip her chemistry notebook open. Then she then turned toward me. "I'll tell you after class."

I saw the concern in her eyes. Everything in me wanted to drag her out of the classroom and force the truth out of her.

It had to be Levi. I just felt it. Only he could ruin such a wonderful day.

As soon as class was over, I grabbed Jess's leg and held it down as she tried to stand up and leave with everyone else. She sighed and looked at me.

"You know," I said, "you don't hide your feelings very well."

"It's a curse." She gave me her fake smile.

"Will you just tell me what's wrong?"

Jess reached under the table, took my hand off her thigh, and threw it back at me. "I've been trying this whole period to make up some story," she muttered, "but, either way, you're gonna find out soon enough."

I knew it. Levi. "What did he do?"

Jess bit her lip and scrunched up her face like a little kid does when they don't want to say something. "You knew this was going to happen."

"What. Did. He. Do?"

"Okay, just hold on. This morning, when she told him, he pushed her and called her—wait, just—"

She tried to grab me, but I was already on my feet. I didn't even bother to pick up my backpack.

Jess ran out behind me, carrying both of our stuff. "Alex, don't do anything you're gonna regret!"

But my mind was made up. And, besides, I wasn't going to *regret* anything I was about to do. That's what I told Jess.

It wasn't hard to find Levi in the cafeteria. He and his letter-jacket thugs always huddled around a large table squarely in the middle of the room.

Our eyes met as soon as I stepped through the door. He knew this was going to happen. For all I knew, they may have been planning for my arrival.

As I walked past other kids, with Jess still grabbing at my arms, Levi stood up and grinned.

"How low can you get?" he shouted across the room. "Now you're taking my garbage? That's okay. She's damaged goods, anyways." He stood up.

I kept walking. I noticed Ana and Thomas standing across the room. They started walking toward me, but I was already near the middle of the cafeteria, so they wouldn't be able to stop me.

Levi's friends were also coming at me. I wasn't worried. I was going to make a fool out him first, and then I'd do the same to them. This time, I wouldn't be waking up in the nurse's room.

Levi smiled as I passed the last table before I got to him. "You're a real sucker for the dramatics," he said. "Now everyone gets to watch me bash your face in again."

"Hey, everybody!" I yelled. I didn't need to. Everyone was watching by now.

"Alex, please don't do anyth—"

I pushed Jess away. "It's okay," I assured her. She didn't look convinced.

Then I turned to the rest of the kids in the cafeteria. "This fool in front of me put his hands on my girlfriend this morning," I said. I hoped Ana was okay with me calling her my girlfriend.

Levi and I were about a foot apart now.

"She was my—" he started.

"Shut your mouth!" I yelled and I pushed my index finger hard into his chest.

He shut up. His face was turning red. Yeah, he was pissed.

"So," I said to the crowd, but I was really talking to him, "here's what I'm going to do. I'm going to hurt him. A lot. And then I'm going to hurt every one of his friends if they choose to be stupid enough to try me."

The letter jackets started laughing. "We heard that last time," Levi said. "Right before I laid you out."

I laughed, too. "Yes. But this time I'm going to punch you in the throat. And then I'm going to crush your balls with my foot. How does that sound?"

Levi wasn't smiling anymore, but everyone else was still laughing. His face was redder now.

I could tell he was about to lash out at me, so I kept going. "And then, all of you back there," I looked straight at James. "I might just do the same to you. It depends on—"

"Okay," said Levi. "I'm sick of this." He pushed me hard with both hands. I stumbled back a few feet and ended up sitting on the table behind me.

I saw Thomas and Ana with Jess. They didn't move. They didn't try to stop me. I saw one of the teachers running out of the cafeteria, probably to get Principal Covington.

Levi took a step forward. "It's time to shut you up for good," he shouted.

I sat there on the table as he came at me. As I expected, he went for another haymaker. It was easy to dodge.

As his whole body caromed past me, I grabbed his hair and slammed his head on the table. Then I pulled him up and punched him in the side of the throat. When I let go, he stumbled backward. He was too busy gasping for air to do anything else. But I had a promise to keep. I kicked him hard between the legs.

He collapsed and curled up in pain.

Everyone was silent. Then James made a decision. He walked up to me and tried the same move as Levi. The punch missed. I pulled him through and kicked him in the back of his right knee. He stumbled and turned, and then I walked up behind him and kicked him between the legs, too. He fell over right beside his friend.

The cafeteria was still silent.

I turned to face the rest of the jocks. "Who's next?" I stood there calmly, waiting for one of them to be stupid enough to come at me. But nobody did.

As fast as it had started, it was over.

When I felt someone grab my arm, I thought it was Jess again. But when I turned around, I saw it was Ana. She had tears in her eyes.

"Come on," she said. "One of the teachers went to go get Mr. Covington. Let's just go sit down at our table before he gets here."

She was probably right. What else could I do but wait for my punishment. The whole school saw it happen. The principal was coming in. Brandon was going to kill me.

I grabbed Ana's hand. "Okay."

Jess grabbed my other arm, as if to make sure I didn't turn around and do more damage.

"Until next time," I spat down at Levi. He was on his hands and knees now, but still crying in pain and not moving. He flipped me off, but he didn't say anything.

Thomas was walking backwards in front of me. "Earth to Alex," he called. "You realize you probably just got yourself suspended again."

I had realized that.

Thomas slapped me on the cheek. "But I think it was worth every day of it."

Jess and Ana laughed nervously.

By the time I reached the table and began to sit down, I heard Principal Covington "Alex Lane, get to my office now!"

***

"You told me it was a good day? Really looks like it."

That was about all Jen said on the ride home.

I was grateful. I didn't feel like explaining myself again. I'd just had a long phone conversation with Brandon.

"Come on, Alex," he'd said. "One more suspension and you're done. Done," he repeated. "I had to promise to give an *anonymous* donation to the school to keep you from getting kicked out for good. I really don't like getting blackmailed into charity. That principal of yours is a real piece of work. I don't want to have to talk to him again. You hear me?"

"Yes," I'd said. "Loud and clear. I'm sorry." I hadn't tried to defend myself. Brandon hadn't sounded as angry as I'd expected. In fact, he sounded disappointed, which honestly made me feel worse. I now understand what people mean when they say that disappointment is more of a punishment than anger.

"Just, stop it," he said. "Okay?" Then, before I could begin to answer, he hung up.

When I gave Jen back the phone, I told her, "He said he was proud of me and that I deserved the best meal you and Ariel can whip up!"

Jen just laughed. "Not gonna happen."

After we got home, I sat on the front steps for about an hour until I saw my friends coming around the corner.

"Well," Thomas shouted, "if it isn't Rambo himself!"

I stood up. "I don't feel like it," I shouted back.

When they got closer, Jess took a look at me. "Are you okay?" She looked worried.

"I'm fine."

"Yeah, well, you didn't look so fine beating the crap out of those idiots. I don't like that side of you." She looked me over like she needed to see if it was the real me.

"Boy," said Thomas, "you became my hero today. I knew you were bad, but come on! You would have hurt them all, wouldn't you?"

"Probably."

"Whatever." Jess punched me in the arm. "It was just plain stupid. But I'm glad Levi won't be able to have children." She punched my other arm. "You did the whole world a favor." And then she smiled.

Ana stepped up to me. "You are stupid, you know?"

"Yeah."

She grinned, then leaned in and kissed me.

Thomas shook his head. "Wow…this just got freakin' weird. Would you look at the clock?" I wasn't looking at him, but I knew he was looking at the watch on his wrist that didn't exist. "I think it's about time for me to go to work."

"I'm right behind you," Jess said, following him as he walked away.

Ana and I were still kissing when they walked back to us. Thomas pointed and whispered. "I forgot. We parked that way."

Ana and I both started to laugh.

"Carry on," Thomas said.

"So what do we do next?" Ana asked, looking up at me with a huge smile that matched the selfies she'd sent me.

"Coffee sounds about right."

She laughed again. "No. *With us*."

"I know what you meant," I gave her a little peck on the cheek just to keep in practice, "but some things are better off said over free coffee."

She shook her head. "Stupid and sarcastic. What a winning combination." She gave me a short kiss. "We better catch up to them. They drove me here."

I looked up. Thomas and Jess had already rounded the corner. I glanced back at Ana. "They'll wait. If not, I guess we'll have a long walk ahead of us."

Ana smiled. "I wouldn't mind that at all."

Chapter 19

October 15, 2013

I often feel like the most miraculous thing has happened to me. Or, according to my so-called church family—very loosely stated—a miracle has occurred. I mean, I have changed significantly. Not that there aren't times that I feel like my old self. After all, I did just beat the crap out of Levi and his friend. But I could have done much worse to them. The temptation was there.

That was always my problem. No one has ever felt sorry for me or ever cared how I felt. So I grew up with no remorse and no idea what caring for others meant. My love for Kim was probably the closest thing to caring about anyone else, but that was mostly out of duty, because I always felt like her childhood was stolen from her. And she was my sister, so what else was I supposed to do?

That's what makes these feelings I have now so hard to understand. No, I do not feel remorse for what I did to Levi and James...but for some reason, I feel ashamed that my friends saw me that way. So angry. And that Brandon was disappointed in me. I know what you're thinking: *Alex actually cares what Brandon feels?* Yes, for some reason, I do. And that's proof enough that a miracle has occurred.

"What are you thinking about?" Ana asked me.

I wasn't thinking at all, unless staring blankly into space counts for using one's brain. "Huh? I don't know."

She smiled again. She just couldn't quit smiling at me. "Well, you know what? I've waited awhile for this."

"For what?" I asked.

"For us to finally be alone. We finally have the chance."

I hugged her and kissed her on the forehead, but I had nothing to say.

"Do you think Thomas and Jess will survive a night without us?" she asked.

"Happily. I don't think they quite know what to do with us yet. Especially Jess."

"It has been awkward," she said dryly.

"It will get better." I wasn't completely sure of that, as I had no prior experience, but it sounded like the right thing to say at that moment.

***

These last few days have been strange. Thomas is still courting the homecoming queen, so his mind has been somewhat preoccupied. But Jess? I don't think she's quite sure how to handle this revelation. I wouldn't go as far as to say it's been awkward, like Ana said, but it has been different.

Of course, tonight that didn't matter. I was on Ana's balcony, just me, her, and the New York skyline. And I wasn't about to spend our time talking about our friends.

"I think we should try to get to know each other better."

"What do you mean?"

"I mean, we know each other, but not really all that well. I don't even know if you have, like, a hobby or something you like to do. Or maybe you see dead people, or something?"

She chuckled. "That sounds like a Jess question."

"Well, maybe she's rubbed off on me."

"I do satanic rituals and make voodoo dolls. Everyone in school knows that."

I laughed. "You and Jess both, huh?" Then I got serious. "No, really, I mean it, what do you like to do?"

She just shook her head. "You're weird, you know that? Most guys would be unbuttoning my shirt by now. Not asking about my hobbies."

"I'm not most guys. Come on. Anything?"

She leaned back, looking up into the night sky. "Hmmm...I can't really say I've ever been good at anything, really. I'm not like you. I can't become a professional piano player in two months."

I ignored that last part. "Nothing at all?"

She shook her head. "No. I just do what's expected of me and that's really it. I mean, well, I like to read, I guess."

I laughed. I wasn't buying it. "Analeigh, I know you have so many layers to you, but all you like to do is read?"

"What's wrong with that?" She tried to sound offended. "And you know nothing about my layers, whatever that even means."

"I just can't believe you don't have just one thing, besides reading, that you like to do. Or something besides riding an old train car for fun."

That's when she gave me a more serious look. "Yeah, well my life hasn't been all fun and games and fairy tales. Have you ever wondered how I got here? How I came to be the preacher's daughter?"

I stopped laughing. I had wondered that. Many times. But I'd never had the opportunity to ask her about it. "So tell me."

She sighed. "Do you really want to know?"

I nodded. "Yes. I want to get to know you better, however that's possible."

"Well," she took a breath, "I'll try to keep it short, but—"

"Don't," I interjected. "We have all the time in the world."

"You are by far the biggest freak I have ever known. But whatever." She sighed again. "Okay, so I've never actually had real parents. Or at least I've never known them. I grew up in an orphanage just outside of London."

It seemed strange that this girl I loved had come from so far away. I was only ever reminded of that fact by her slight accent.

"Do you know who they were?"

"Great question. No, not a clue. Can I continue?"

I nodded again.

"I don't remember a whole lot, except that kids came in and kids left. But I never did. Don't get me wrong, the orphanage was a nice place, but it was an orphanage, and I learned pretty quickly that it wasn't normal. That my life wasn't normal. And that's just how things were for me. I'd wake up, go to school, come home, and sleep. That was life as I knew it. The only thing that kept my mind off of how mundane my life was, was reading. It's a great way to escape, you know."

It sounded like reading for her was what writing was for me.

"And that was it. Until I was twelve." She paused.

"What happened then?"

She took another deep breath. "Well, I met a boy who was seventeen at the time. I knew nothing about real life, so he was like a dream to me. He lived across the street from the orphanage." Ana looked up at me. "Are you sure you really want to listen to this?"

"Yeah, I'm sure." I wanted nothing more than to listen to her.

"Okay. I snuck out most nights to be with him. And we had sex. A lot of sex. That's really all we did. We had sex until I realized that's all he wanted from me."

Her present lifestyle was starting to make sense.

"Well, once I figured that out, I didn't want to do it anymore. He wasn't very happy, as you can guess. But we stopped for some time, and then—"

"He forced you, didn't he?"

"Who's telling the story here?"

"Sorry, but that's what happened, right?" I knew enough men, including myself, to see where her story was going.

"Yes. That's what happened. He forced me, but I became more unwilling every time he came on to me. It wasn't like I really fought him, but I made it clear that I didn't want it."

I was beginning to feel angry at this unknown man. The way she told the story, it was as if she'd been an adult at the time. But she was only twelve! She'd been taken advantage of. That's one way we're alike. We've both had to become adults too early.

"So one day," she said, "I told him no. That I was done. And of course, he got mad and started cursing and throwing things. Et cetera. So guess what I did?"

"Was that my cue to say something?"

She raised one eyebrow.

"Okay," I said obediently, "what did you do?"

She nudged me with her elbow. "Come on. Just guess. You'll be proud of me."

I didn't have a clue, but I guessed anyway. "You yelled rape," I said sarcastically.

She laughed. "No. I grabbed a metre rule, what you call a yardstick here in the States, that his mom used—she sewed clothes—and I hit him in the face with it. To this day, I don't know why I did it. I could have just walked away.

The story was starting to go in a good direction now. "So what did he do?"

Her face turned serious again. "He hit me. And he hit me again. He actually hit me so hard that it left bruises on my arms and chest. Along with busted lip and a black eye."

Hearing that made me pissed off again.

Ana smiled. "But you know what? I'm glad he hit me. Because, two days later, it was those bruises and my busted-up face that made my father notice me. He was speaking at a church in London. When he and mom stopped at the orphanage at a friend's request, they saw me. They wouldn't leave without me. And that's my story."

Like my story, something seemingly bad worked out for her good. I made a mental note to walk through my parents' car crash and relate her experience to mine...but at another time. I had another question.

"What happened to the boy?" I had to have some resolution.

"Oh, his mother came in and beat the crap out of him. I've never seen a seventeen-year-old boy cry so hard."

"And then when you came here? To New York?"

"I was thirteen," she said. "I had no clue what it was like to be an American teen. It was a rough first year. But then I met Jess. She changed everything. And Thomas, too, but mostly Jess. She really is stronger than we give her credit for. She's a great person."

"I know."

"But," Ana continued. "I also let myself go. I started cutting, and then when that didn't work, I went back to what I knew best. Until I met you. Levi knew something was up, because I didn't give him any for, like, three weeks. You would have thought I was torturing him."

"So I'm the knight in shining armor?"

"You're something, but I haven't quite decided what yet." She smiled. "So there you have it, that's been my screwed up life. And now you get to be a part of it.

You're dating the pastor's rebel daughter, a sex-addicted, church-attending freak of nature."

"*My* sex-addicted, church attending freak of nature."

"You say that, but does it make you feel any less of me?"

If only she knew the things that I had done, she wouldn't have asked me that question.

"Not at all," I said.

"And that's what makes you a freak!"

"It's because I love you."

She shook her head. "And I don't know *why* you do."

I didn't have an answer. I just did. From the day I met her.

She leaned in and started to kiss me then. It was very passionate. I kissed her back fully. Once her tongue entered my mouth, and she crawled onto my lap, it was over. She had me totally in her control.

I carried her into her bedroom and practically dropped her on her bed, then fell on her. We started kissing again. I'd been waiting so long for this.

But her parents were only one floor below us, and at one point, we saw a shadow pass under her door, so there was a quick break. It didn't last long. We laughed nervously and started kissing again.

She took off my shirt. She was unprepared for the tattoos that cover most of my chest, stomach, and back. For a moment, she traced the swastika on my chest with her finger. Then she pulled me down across her lap to read the excerpts from *Mein Kampf* on my back. She felt the scars my tattoos covered.

When she stopped touching me, I sat up.

"This isn't who you are anymore, is it?" she said in a quiet voice.

"No. No way."

She smiled. "Good!"

I figured this was as good a time as any to tell her where I came from. "Maybe it's time for you to hear my story."

She put her finger on my lips. "Another time."

We fell back on the bed.

And this is where you can see how I've changed. As soon as I felt her unzipping her pants, I stopped kissing her.

"What's wrong?" She asked, breathing heavily.

I leaned up on one arm. "I'm not that guy...remember?" Okay, I used to be. But not now. I could tell she was confused, so I caressed her cheek. "I'm not going to sleep with you. Trust me, I want to. But then I'd be no different than any of those other guys."

"But you *are* different. You—"

"It's not gonna happen," I repeated. "It's not right."

She collapsed back against the pillow. I thought she was going to cry, but she suddenly started laughing. "I can't believe you! How many times do I have to tell you how strange you are?"

"Well, at least three times tonight," I answered.

"And why isn't this right?"

I had several reasons. "Well, first off, you're the pastor's daughter. And you go to church. And according to our church, this is wrong."

"*Our* church?" She gave me a funny look. "We only go there because we're forced to."

"That's not true. If I remember correctly, you told me once that it was your *family*. That in the church, you had people you could trust."

She sighed. "Okay, I give you that one. And?"

"It's illegal. I'm eighteen and you're sixteen."

"That's a really strong point," she said sarcastically. "And I can tell you have more reasons. So what else."

"Well, you're worth more than this. You deserve better than illegal and morally questionable sex."

She didn't respond.

I backed off the bed and stood up. "I'll take that as point taken."

"Holy crap!" she almost shouted. She sat up. "Can you really have once been that person?" She pointed at the swastika on my chest again. "Ever since I've known you, you've done nothing but defend our group of misfits. You've never gotten high. You've not had one drink. You've done whatever your absent brother has told you to do. You turned down your hot sister-in-law's advances. And now you won't even have sex with me? Even though you've said it yourself, you love me. What would it take for you to go back to being that old person?"

"Losing you."

She opened her mouth, but no words came out. She shook her head. Then she smiled.

"What?" I asked.

"You're so freaking perfect, I'm annoyed."

I started to put my shirt back on. "I'm sorry."

"No. It's fine. Everything you said is right. I hate losing an argument, but I just can't argue against anything you've said."

I sat down beside her and took her in my arms. "Then don't." I brushed my lips against her hair.

She started to say something, but was interrupted by a knock on her door. I immediately stood up, as to not get caught on her bed.

"It's time for dinner," Ana's mom said.

"Okay, Mom, we're coming right down." She turned to me. "Are you staying for dinner?"

I grabbed her hands and pulled her up off the bed. "Of course I am. I need to show your parent's I'm a respectable young man, even if I've been suspended from school twice in, like, two months."

Ana kissed me. "Well, I know I've said it, like, four times tonight, but you are such a freak."

"I'm fine with that." It didn't matter what I was. As long as I was with her, I didn't care.

Chapter 20

October 19, 2013

I t was 2 a.m. The odds of someone being awake were next to none, but I wasn't taking any chances. I could just see Ariel stalking down the stairs, Bible in hand, ready to pounce on any intruder. That was not quite how I envisioned my night ending.

I tiptoed slowly up the stairs, but my steps seemed to be making more noise than usual. After about five steps, it became obvious to me that walking slowly and softly wasn't any quieter than running up the steps. So I ran.

I nearly made it all the way up in the dark, but the last step decided not to play nice. It tripped me. I fell forward, but when I reached out for something to grab, I came up short and landed on my hands and knees, dropping some of my books and my house keys. It made a lot of noise.

"Way to go, genius," I whispered to myself. "That's what I get for not turning on a freaking light."

I stayed still for a few seconds, waiting for a door to open, hopefully any door but Ariel's. I didn't want a scene at 2 a.m., and Ariel had a knack for being loud. Luckily, no doors opened. When I thought it was safe, I made a beeline for my room.

"Alex, is that you?"

I was almost in my room. Hearing the voice, I looked down the hall. There was Brandon, silhouetted in the doorway of his study.

"No," I joked, "I'm an intruder."

"Very funny. We need to talk," Brandon said before he stepped back into his study.

I guess it was too late for humor. I left my stuff just inside my room and walked down the hall. When I knocked on the open study door, I could see him sitting in the dark at his desk. I couldn't help but notice how much he looked like he had the day he'd picked me up at Hillbrook. His beard was fully grown out again and he was wearing that same suit—the one I thought of as his secret agent mafia suit.

"Come in." He didn't even look up from his desk.

What did I do? I thought.

I took a few steps inside, then stopped and leaned against a bookshelf a few feet from his desk. Brandon's office was built in the same style as the library downstairs, with a lot of bookshelves, some furniture, and copious amounts of detailed woodwork. There was even a skylight. It was very nice, although not quite as breathtaking as the room on the first floor it was styled after.

"Someone's up late tonight," I said in another attempt at humor.

"What have you been up to?" he asked.

"Just hanging with friends. You know."

"With Ana, you mean?" He still didn't look up.

"Yeah. With Ana."

I ran my hands across the spines of some of the old books on the shelf next to me. When Brandon didn't say anything, I decided to try my first comment again. "You know, it's pretty late for you to be up."

"I know you kissed my wife." He looked directly at me.

I nearly fell down.

Brandon pointed at the chair in front of his desk. "Sit."

First, I made sure there wasn't a gun or some other weapon sitting on his desk. Then I vainly tried to find something to say. But no words seemed appropriate.

"You kissed her," he said again. "Right?"

I'd never planned for that question. After a few weeks, I thought the incident with Jen and I had disappeared forever, so I hadn't rehearsed what I would say if we were found out. Being hit with a Bible by Ariel didn't seem all that bad at that moment. I had no options. I had to be honest. "Yes, I did. But—"

"Just shut up." Brandon leaned far back in his chair and sighed.

Every time things seem to be going well, something bad has to happen. That seems to be my lot in life.

"Brandon, I…"

"I said shut up!" He leaned forward and whispered. "We're not going to end this in a yelling match, little brother. No one needs to know we talked about this." His face was as tense as I've ever seen it.

This was it. I was sure I was going to be kicked out of the house. I could just feel it.

"When did you find out?" I asked the question before he could interrupt me again.

Brandon rubbed his eyes and sighed. "The night after it happened."

"Wait. You knew and you didn't say anything?"

"I didn't know what to say." He just stared at me for a minute. "What do you say to something like this? I would rather have just killed you that night, but that wouldn't have been right, either, now, would it? You don't know how hard it has been, playing the nice guy these past few weeks. Killing you would have been a lot easier."

"I would have deserved it," I responded. "I'm sorry, Brandon. I really am."

He stood up and walked around his desk, then sat on the edge, just inches from me.

"What are you doing?" I asked.

"I want you to see my face when I tell you this," he answered.

I leaned back, away from him. "Are you going to kill me now?"

At this, he actually smiled. "No. I'm not going to kill you."

"Then…what?" I'm sure I sounded ridiculous. I'm also sure I looked nervous and dumb at the same time.

"I'm going to forgive you," he said. "And I'm going to thank you."

I was dumbstruck. "Wait…is this some sort of—"

"No, it's not a joke." He reached out and put his hand on my shoulder. "I forgive you, Alex. And thank you for showing me that I can change."

I wanted to just say "Forget about it," and get out of the surreal dream our conversation was turning into. But I was at a loss for words. Again.

That's when Brandon started to laugh. "Let me explain."

"Please do."

"Jen told me everything. She told me how you stopped it. How you were the bigger person. That's the only reason I didn't kill you."

"Well, gee," I said sarcastically. "That's a relief."

"Do you think this was easy for me?" His voice was sharper now. "Acting like nothing had happened?" He waited for me to answer.

"No."

"No," he repeated. "No, it wasn't. I was angry at Jen. I was angry at you. But most of all, I was angry at myself. I've not been around much these past few years. I've been practically non-existent, except for one lousy movie night a week. I've ignored the things that are important for what? Money? Power? Popularity? What else could Jen have thought? I know she's had suspicions that

I've been unfaithful. Why shouldn't she feel that way? You know, I didn't even ask her before I picked you up. I pretty much just told her I was going to do it, and then I did it. I didn't bother to get her opinion. I left her help behind." He paused. "I've even taken the very thing that's made me who I am and left it behind, too. Guess how many times I've been to church since you've been here?"

I didn't know, so I guessed. "Twice?"

"Once." He let that sink in for a minute. "The very thing that changed my life has become nothing to me. And, therefore, my life has turned into what it was before I married Jen, before I found my career, before I found God." He stood up and started pacing behind me. "This is not who I want to be, Alex. It took you kissing my wife to make me realize that."

I had to correct him. "She kissed me."

He stopped. "Yeah...right. Shut up and don't remind me again."

I still didn't know what was going on here. Was I going to be punished? "So...I'm not getting kicked out of the house?"

Brandon laughed again. "No. You're welcome here for as long as you need to be here. This is your house, Alex."

And then, out of nowhere, my brother threw his arms around me. This wasn't like the awkward hug in front of the juvenile detention center. This was a real hug. He wasn't letting go.

And in my twisted mind, I imagined that a hug would be a great time for him to insert a knife into my back.

He held on for a few minutes, and just when I thought he was going to let go, he whispered in my ear. "But if you even *think* about touching my wife again, it won't end so nicely."

"Understood."

As he loosened his grip, I felt his hand drop something in the pocket of my hoodie. I pulled away. "What are you doing?"

"Just read it when you get the chance," he said.

"Read what?" I felt around in the pocket and pulled out a small book.

"It's my first Bible," he said. "It's what changed me. I've been reading it a lot these past few weeks. That's the only way I've been able to be kind to you. Believe me, the *only* way."

I had a sudden flash of being hit in the head by Ariel's large-print Bible. It made me laugh.

"What's so funny?"

"Oh, nothing." He wouldn't have understood.

"Just read it, okay?"

I thought I saw tears in Brandon's eyes, but it could have been the dimness of the room. "You know," I said, "I'm not really into religion and stuff."

"Just read it."

"Okay. I will." I had no intention of reading the Bible, but my brother had just forgiven me and thanked me for kissing his wife, so I thought I needed to at least be polite.

Brandon smiled. That was probably the biggest smile I've ever seen on his face. "Okay," he said, "are we good?"

"Sure," I answered. I stood up and started walking toward the door. As much of a relief as this was, though, it was still awkward. "Good night," I said.

"Good night. No. Wait!"

I stopped and turned around. "Yes?" I imagine I gave him a pained look, realizing that this surreal conversation was not yet over.

Brandon was back behind his desk. He looked at me. "I'm sorry."

What did he have to be sorry for? "Okay...."

"I'm sorry for everything I didn't do while you were growing up. I'm sorry for leaving you and Kim alone. I'm sorry for not being a brother for eighteen years. Can you forgive me for all of that?"

For the second time that night, I almost fell down. I never thought I'd hear that word—*sorry*—come out of my brother's mouth. I didn't know what to say.

He didn't give me a chance to say anything. "I was young and stupid, and I was running as fast as I could away from that situation at home. I left you and Kim to fend for yourselves. I was a terrible person. And for that, I owe you my life. But I need to know if you can forgive me."

Now I felt tears welling up in my eyes, but I was determined not to break down and cry. I didn't want to say anything, either, because I knew my voice would break. My heart was racing.

"Can you?" Brandon asked again. "Can you forgive me?"

When I thought I could control my voice, I said, "I think I already have." But I didn't need to say it. As soon as the apology came out of his mouth, I was more than willing to forgive him.

I walked out the door and ran to my room. When I was inside, I closed the door and slid down it till I was sitting on the floor. For some reason, just hearing my brother's apology was enough. I wasn't mad at him anymore. I couldn't be. Even if I wanted to be, my heart—my soul—wouldn't allow it.

I had forgiven him.

And for the first time in as long as I can really remember, I broke down. I cried uncontrollably. I cried until I fell asleep right there on the floor.

Chapter 21

October 21, 2013

"So now you're best friends?" Thomas asked. We were fishing, and he cast his line without looking at me.

"Yeah. Sure." I had just told him about my late-night conversation with Brandon. He listened carefully, but after weeks of hearing me complain about my brother, he couldn't help but be skeptical. "So," he said, "what's next for the misunderstood and wickedly in love Alex Lane? Wedding bells?"

I struggled to put a worm on my hook. "Haha. What about you and the homecoming queen?"

Thomas looked up at the sunny sky. He was the picture of a contradiction in his black sweater, black jeans, and tall army boots. Along with the tattoos and the freshly trimmed mohawk, he was the last person anyone would think was a fisherman.

"Uhhmmm...," he said after a minute. "I don't think that's gonna happen."

That was news to me. "Why not?"

He tugged at his line and pulled his hook out of the water. There was nothing on it. "Another one freaking gone. What the heck? Hand me the worms."

I handed him the dirt-filled Tupperware bowl he kept his live bait in.

I was content to let the conversation drift away, but as Thomas effortlessly put another worm on his hook, like, the thousandth worm that day, he explained.

"Let's just say, Samantha pictures a two-story house with a picket fence and three kids playing in the back yard. I think she'd let me put a ring on her finger if I wanted to."

"So what do you want?"

He laughed. "A good time!"

I was about to respond to that when Reuben stumbled out of the woods, cursing wildly and wiping his hands on his jeans. "Go into the woods to relieve myself," he said, "and I'm gonna end up with poison everything."

Thomas laughed. "At least now you'll have an excuse when you scratch your crotch in public."

Reuben flipped him off, then climbed into the front seat of the jeep. "It's okay," he said. "Nothing a little jane won't fix." He pulled a joint out of his pocket and lit up.

Thomas reached back and knocked the joint out of Reuben's mouth. "What are you doing? I told you, nothing illegal on my grandparents' property."

"Oh, come on!" Reuben yelled, scrambling to pick up the joint. "That stuff isn't cheap."

"No! Don't do it!" Thomas yelled again.

Reuben banged his head on the dash. "Whatever," he mumbled. "When are you guys gonna be done with this torture?"

"We've got all day," I said.

He banged his head again. "No, no, no."

"I'll tell you what," Thomas said, giving me a private smile. "We'll leave when we catch our next fish."

This made Reuben perk up. "Great! When did you catch the last one?"

"Well, my grandpa said he caught one about two years ago."

Thomas and I laughed as Reuben jumped out of the jeep. "Real freakin' funny! Good thing I brought extra." He pulled another joint out of his pocket and waved it at us before disappearing into the woods again.

"If you get my grandparents arrested," Thomas yelled after him, "I'll kill you!" And right that minute, he jerked back on his line, and I saw a small fish rise out of the water and struggle to get away.

"Holy crap! You caught one?"

"Holy crap, you're right."

It took him about five seconds to pull the little fish in. It was a tiny little thing, no bigger than a few inches long.

I grabbed at the fish, but its texture and sliminess were too much. As you can obviously guess, this was the first time I'd ever been fishing. It was bad enough sticking a hook through the worms, but the way that fish felt was just gross.

Thomas laughed again. "If the girls weren't out shopping, or doing whatever the heck girls do, I'd let Jess show you how it's done. She's not afraid of any fish or worm."

I wiped my hands on my jeans. "Yeah, well, good for her."

Thomas pulled the fish off the hook and threw it back in, laughing the whole time.

"Speaking of the girls, though," I said, "what time do you think they'll be done?"

There was no cell phone reception on his grandparents' farm, which I thought was strange because I could see the city past the other side of the pond we were fishing in. It wasn't like we were out in the middle of nowhere. So I had no clue if I had received any calls or texts from Ana. Thomas said that was the best thing about the place—it was free from distractions.

"Are you serious?" he asked, looking at me like I was stupid. "It's girls' day out. It'll be dark before they get done. You have a lot to learn, my friend."

"I guess I do. So…are we going to tell Reuben you caught one?"

"Caught what?" Reuben called from somewhere in the woods.

Thomas shook his head. "Nothing," he yelled. "I just got snagged on a rock or something."

Reuben shot a string of curses at us.

"And when you're done throwing a hissy fit like a little girl," Thomas continued, "and doing illegal things on my family's property, you can come out here and be a man and fish."

"Yeah," Reuben called back. "Like I'll do that when you stop pretending you're not gay."

Thomas didn't reply. Instead, he put his finger over his mouth and said "Shhh." Then he pointed at the front of the jeep and leaned over and whispered in my ear, "Pull your line in. Let's see what Reuben does when the jeep fires up and we leave him here in the middle of nowhere."

Trying not to make any noise, I did what he said. It was really hard not to laugh, though.

As soon as Thomas had the engine started, I heard Reuben yelling. Thomas put the jeep into gear.

The funniest thing was watching Reuben come running out of the woods, cursing and yelling and giving us the finger as we drove away. In reply, Thomas flapped his hand out the window, trying to make as feminine a gesture as possible. I just waved and smiled.

Reuben didn't think it was funny. Apparently, his sense of humor didn't match ours right then. We let him sit out there for fifteen minutes before we came back.

Chapter 22

October 30, 2013

I don't often have nightmares. Perhaps the life I've led leaves little to the imagination. Or maybe it's possible that I'm immune to the debilitating fears that dreams can produce. I'm not really sure, but I'd trade a million nightmares to go back three days and change what happened.

My life was turning into everything I'd ever wanted. It was becoming the opposite of a nightmare. It was turning into a beautiful, unforgettable dream.

And now it all just feels like it's over. Done. Gone.

Today is the funeral, and I'm not there. I can't be there. They won't let me leave. And I can't blame them. My bloodied knuckles and the bruises on my back are enough proof that I'm a danger to society.

Prison, I know. A state-run mental health facility is a new experience altogether. Physical confinement is easy, but a forced cocktail of sedative drugs is torture. I used to pay for this crap on the streets. Now I'd do anything to get off of it.

How did I get here? I've asked myself that question a million times since I woke up between these white walls. Not because I have no idea what happened, but because the few pictures I've pieced together in my mind are so hard to believe. What little I've pulled from my nurses also confirms the unbelievable reality that I've come to know is true.

You probably have more questions than I have time to answer, so I'll just start from the beginning. You can assemble the pieces of the story, just like I had to.

***

When I woke up to a knock on my door, I figured it was the morning. Why else would Ariel be trying to wake me up? As usual, I ignored it. Ariel knew me well enough by now to know that I heard every one of her obnoxious morning raps on the door, so thankfully she never knocked more than once.

So when the second knock came, I knew something was different. I thought it was probably Jen or Ally. As far as I knew, no one else in the house had even been near my room. I looked at my alarm clock. It read 11:45 p.m. I'd only been asleep for thirty minutes.

By the third knock, I was getting pissed. "What do you want?"

"It's just me," I heard Jen say.

I immediately got out of bed. I pulled a blanket around myself, and opened the door. "What's up?"

She looked noticeably worn out and yawned before she could say anything. She had a blue robe on, and her hair was a mess. "Some guy is at the door for you," she said. "I told him you were asleep, but he said it was urgent."

Some guy? Was that really all she could tell me?

"Hey," she said, "don't ask me. Just take care of it." She started to walk away.

"Did he give you his name?" I asked.

She stopped and thought a minute. "Oh, yeah…he said he was Reuben." She didn't even turn around.

"Well thanks, sunshine! You've been such a help, and so forthcoming with information."

"Whatever." She was already back in her bedroom. She closed the door behind her.

I did feel a little sorry for her, as it seemed my friends liked to wake her up at awful times.

I had not the slightest idea why Reuben would be at my doorstep so close to midnight. I checked my phone.

There were no calls or texts from anyone, so I doubted it was an emergency, or anything of importance that couldn't wait until the morning. That said, I had every intention of making sure Reuben knew how annoyed I was.

As I stumbled down the stairs, I started wondering if this was some kind of joke he and Thomas had thought up. If it was, they were probably going to get the reaction they were looking for.

I opened the front door. Reuben was pacing back and forth. "Alex—"

"What are you doing here this late? You better have…" Then I saw Reuben's face. It was ashen, covered with sweat. Or maybe tears. I'd never seen Reuben look so distraught.

"What's wrong?" I asked, stepping out the door and into a frigid wind.

Reuben grabbed my arms. "You've got to help me."

"Of course I will," I said immediately. "Is something wrong with Hannah?"

"No, no." He let go of my arms and leaned against the fence. "It's nothing like that."

"Well, it's definitely something. You look like you're burning up." There were sweat beads all over his head, which was strange because he only had a T-shirt on and it was freezing outside.

"It's this deal."

I waited for him to continue, but I could tell he didn't want to tell me what was going on. I finally said, "What deal?"

"A drug deal." He refused to look at me.

I immediately regretted telling him I would help. He knew I didn't live that life anymore. Part of me wanted to punch him in the face just for asking, but I could see the fear in his eyes. It felt like I was his last option.

"You know I can't help you," I said.

He looked like he was about ready to cry. "Dude, you know I wouldn't be asking if I didn't really need your help. I don't have anywhere else to turn. I—"

"No! That part of my life is over. I'm happy. I'm in love. I have a family. I'm not going to lose all of this for some stupid, little deal. Why would you even need me?"

"It's a lot bigger than that," he burst out. "This is bigger than any other deal I've ever done."

"What? Why?" I'm not sure why I asked. I wanted nothing more than to go back inside, but curiosity got the best of me.

Reuben started pacing the sidewalk again. "It's heroin, man. And it's some gang or something."

That's when I knew he was in way over his head. "Are you freaking kidding me?" I asked him. "What are you doing? This is way out of your league!" I pushed him hard. "You're freaking peddling this stuff and you come to me? Why would you even think about doing this? This is the big league, and I'm sorry, but you're not the big league. Not even close."

I'd seen the big sellers in person. I mean, I was one of them. We were willing to risk it all and pay with our lives. I knew Reuben was not.

Reuben began to tear up. "I know, I know. I shouldn't have, but I saw dollar signs all over it. It was stupid. But I've heard stories about you, how you used to do all of this stuff. How you were some type of bad a—"

"*Used to be*, Reuben. Used to be. I'm not anymore. I chose not to go back to that life." Reuben wasn't my family, or Ana, or even Thomas or Jess, for that matter. It might have been a different story if it was one of them standing there in front of me.

Reuben grabbed my arm. "But you have to. You have to help me."

I pulled away. "No, I don't. I don't have to help you. Go home. Quit thinking about the money and start thinking about an honest life. Come on, do something legal for once. Hannah doesn't deserve this."

There was a time when someone said those words to me and I didn't listen. I never thought I'd be on the giving end of that speech.

"I'm going to bed." I started to walk away.

Reuben fell to his knees. "They'll kill me."

I stopped immediately. I'd heard friends say that before. Most of them aren't alive today.

"These guys are serious, Alex. If I don't deliver, they'll kill me. I promise. They know who I am."

I turned around and pulled him to his feet, then pushed him against the rail. Hard. "Reuben, are you an idiot? You told them your name?"

"I know it was stupid."

Now, he was really pissing me off. "If they know your name," I said as calmly as I could, "then they can find out who your family is. Who your friends are. I should just kill you myself!"

"I'm sorry. I'm so sorry!" Tears were streaming down his face.

I was so angry, and I really wanted to kill him myself. The old me wanted to throw him on the street and run him over with Brandon's car. But the new me could see the panic and desperation in his eyes. He was my friend, even if he was the least of them.

He just kept apologizing, over and over, his eyes squinting, waiting for my fists to meet his face.

I was holding his shirt so tightly my hands hurt. My heart was beating fast and I felt hot. "I can't help you," I said again. I let go of his shirt. "I have Ana now. And you know I have a family, too. I have a life, Reuben. A life!

Come on. Don't try to take that away from me. If I get caught, it's all over."

"But you know I wouldn't ask if I didn't need your help. You know that."

I honestly didn't feel like I knew Reuben well enough to trust him. What I did know was that he was an arrogant individual. Seeing him groveling at my feet meant he really had nowhere else to go. He wasn't lying about that.

Maybe it was the cold October air. Or maybe it was some miniscule part of my soul that needed to be released. But at that moment, it was like a switch went off inside me. I could help him. But with that knowledge came a hard edge that I hadn't felt since I'd dispatched Levi a few weeks ago. It was the criminal side of me that I'd learned to suppress. He was forcing his way back into me.

"Okay," I said, "how well do you know these people?"

Reuben sighed. "I don't." He flinched, as if he thought his answerless answer deserved punishment.

"Well, then who connected you to them?" I asked.

"A friend."

"How good of a friend?"

Reuben slid back along the rail. "Okay," he said when he thought he was out of reach. "More of a friend of a friend."

This time, I threw my hands in the air. "Reuben, you have got to be the dumbest person I know. Seriously. That means this person doesn't care whether you live or die."

"But you can help me?"

I punched him the face. He fell hard against the rail, then rolled down to the sidewalk. When he grabbed his face, I saw the blood from his nose running through his fingers. He started crying hysterically.

I crouched down beside him. "I can help you. But, so help me, if you ever sell anything else in your life, a bloody nose will be the least of your problems. You understand me?"

He barely moved his head.

I slapped the side of his face. "I said, do you understand me?"

"Yes," he cried out. "I understand."

"Okay. Do you have a gun?"

Reuben reached into the back of his waistband with his bloody hand and pulled out a .22 pistol.

I grabbed it from him and wiped the blood off with my shirt. "Where'd you get this?"

He tried to wipe the blood and the tears off his face. "I stole it from my dad's case. It's actually my brother's. He and Dad like guns."

"Well," I said, looking it over, "you're too stupid to use it, so I'm going to keep it, okay?"

"Okay."

As I looked at the gun in my hand, memories—bad memories—flooded into my mind. But it felt so natural between my fingers, as if my hand was made for it. Once I felt that cold metal, there was no going back.

We got into his car and drove several miles through New York City. Reuben kept whining and saying he wished the trip was longer. I couldn't have thought more the opposite. I anticipated the sell—the sweaty palms, the fear, the chance of dying. These were the feelings I'd vowed when I was in juvie to never feel again. How I ever managed to give them up, I don't know. I felt so powerful, so in control.

This was my element.

Now that I think about it, after I told Reuben I'd help him, not once do I remember thinking about my family, about Ally, about my friends, about Ana. Not once.

That world was immediately gone, replaced by the narrow mindset of a criminal.

And you know what? It just confirms that the monster inside of me will never leave. It may have been dormant for two years, but it's never been completely gone. It just needed a chance to come back out.

Where we were going wasn't very far from our warehouse, maybe a block or two. I had Reuben park his car on the back side of the building where the deal was supposed to go down. That way, if something went wrong, we had a better opportunity to get away without anyone seeing what we drove away in. Reuben's stupidity was even more evident by his choice to drive his mother's white SUV, instead of his own car, a black Honda Civic. But there was no real benefit in telling him that.

The building was just another abandoned manufacturing facility, one of many on the street. I'd been there several years prior, as it was a hotspot for anything and everything illegal.

I casually started to walk down the sidewalk when Reuben grabbed my arm. "What do I do?" he asked, a fresh set of tears running down his cheeks.

I pulled away. "First off, stop crying like a baby. Own up to what you got yourself into."

He shook his head and wiped the tears away with his sleeve.

"Second," I said, "just hand over the drugs. Don't say a word unless you're spoken to. I'm Reuben tonight. You're just my mule. You hand over the drugs. That's it."

"Okay." he said.

Rounding the corner, I saw two men standing by the front door. One was black, short, and stocky, and he was wearing a New York Knicks hoodie. The other guy, who was taller, was also wearing a black hoodie, but the hood was up, concealing his face.

"Yo," the stocky fellow said. "You Reuben?"

"Maybe," I said. "What's it to you?" I noticed that his right hand was behind his back. "Stop playing with yourself and tell me where we need to go."

The tall guy in the hoodie laughed.

"Smart mouth you got there, fool," the short guy said. He pulled his hand around and showed me his gun.

I could feel Reuben's fear. He was standing behind me, so I couldn't see him, but I could hear his rapid, shallow breathing. He sounded like he'd just sprinted a mile. I slowly lifted my shirt to show the thugs my own gun.

"Mine's bigger than yours."

The tall guy laughed again.

"I wouldn't be laughing, tough guy," I said in a level voice. "Mine's probably bigger than yours, too."

He didn't laugh at the joke.

The guy in the Knicks hoodie nodded his head at the warehouse door. "They're waiting on you," he said. "And trust me, they ain't looking for no pissing contest in there."

"That's too bad." I stepped through the doorway.

It was dark inside, dark and musty and quiet. There was one long hallway with doors on both sides, little empty rooms that had once been the offices of a booming manufacturing facility. But for years, the building had housed the scum of the earth, people like myself.

At the end of the hall was a large door that opened up into an open workshop. I knew the place by memory. From the front door, it was probably a good several hundred feet to the large work area, but the long hallway was mostly just dark, plus cobwebs and smoke.

I grabbed Reuben's arm. "Stop breathing so hard," I told him. "You sound like you're dying."

"I am."

I squeezed his arm hard. "No you're not. But if you walk into that room up ahead acting like this, you will be. Now take a deep breath and give me your best poker face."

He tried, but it wasn't very convincing.

I felt confident walking down the hall. Like I said, I was made for this. I felt like whatever or whoever was going to meet us on the other side of that big door at the end of the hall, I was ready for it. I can't say I felt much confidence in Reuben though. Part of me thought it would be better just to tell him to hide in one of the offices, where I could retrieve him after everything was over. At least he'd have a chance of getting away if things didn't go as planned. Unfortunately, the guys on the outside had already seen his face, and if they knew his "friend of a friend" very well, they knew how to get to him.

As we neared the door to the workshop, I let go of Reuben's arm. "Poker face!"

He nodded, although his swollen eyes betrayed him.

"Okay, let's go."

I walked through the doorway first, and when the light hit me, it made it hard for my eyes to adjust. The hallway had been so dark, the lights in the large room seemed amplified.

I saw a lot of figures standing around an open area, behind them were rows and rows of industrial shelving where large metal parts lay dusty and unneeded.

My eyes were still adjusting, but the group looked the part of low-life hustlers and thugs.

No one said anything at first, so I took it upon myself to get the deal rolling. "Well, if I must say, I was expecting more."

"What is this?" said someone with a gruff, scratchy voice.

It was a very familiar voice. As soon as I heard it, my heart sank and I felt sick. All my confidence disappeared. Not out of fear, but because that voice could mean only one thing.

Reuben and I were not walking out of this building alive.

"I said, what is this?" Stefan asked again. He walked out of the crowd of low-lifes, his gray beard and short stature setting him apart. "I was told that some peddler named Reuben was coming to sell me some drugs," he said very casually, "and instead I get the reformed convict, Alex Lane."

"Wait, Stefan," I said. "I can explain."

Guns all raised and pointed at me as I took a step toward him.

"Explain what?" he asked. "I know you've been fraternizing with your rich family, Alex. I know you have yet to do any business around here since you got out. So what are you doing here now? Is this some sort of set-up?"

"It's not a set-up." I was resolved not to show an ounce of fear.

Reuben was sobbing behind me again.

Several of the men started laughing as Stefan came closer and clapped his hands like he was applauding a performance.

"So this must be Reuben," he said scornfully. "The low-life scum I was waiting for."

"Only you can honestly claim that title," I said as he circled around my friend, mocking him.

Stefan stopped. "I see your little stint in lock-up hasn't tamed your mouth."

"And I see you're still wallowing in your filth."

He laughed again. Now he was inches behind me, leaning in between me and my sobbing friend. He brought his mouth up to my right ear. "You picked the wrong time to come back, my friend. I've been in a foul mood for a long time."

I didn't turn to face him. "Couldn't replace me, could you?" I whispered back. I saw a lot of faces staring at me. Stefan wasn't an easy man to work for.

I had never actually worked for him, but I did a lot of business with him. And I made him a lot of money. But he wasn't the type of guy that held onto loyalty. I'd seen him shoot guys over a few dollars.

And I'd seen him kill small-time punks like Reuben. The man would do anything for a cheap purchase, but he had little patience to strike up long-term business deals.

Stefan started back toward his posse. "No, no, Alex, I couldn't replace you. And for a little while I thought your getting out would mean you'd be back. But then I found out you were pissing around with your wrought-iron fences and family values."

"Do you need a definition of values?" I asked. "Or maybe spelling it would be a better place to start." While I was doing my best to get under Stefan's skin, I was also trying to signal Reuben to shut up with my left hand. Unfortunately, Reuben was too busy crying to notice. He was beyond help.

Stefan reached out with one hand and was given a small pistol. "This, Alex," he held it up so I could see it, "this is my value." He held the gun above his head.

"So you're just going to kill us because you can?" I asked him.

"Why shouldn't I? I haven't seen any drugs yet."

"We have drugs," Reuben whimpered.

"Shut up, Reuben!"

The whole room, except me, started laughing at Reuben.

Stefan applauded again. "So he can talk." He took a few steps forward.

I watched the gun dangle from his fingers.

"Reuben," he said, "come over here. What do you have for us?"

For the first time, I felt my heart beating fast as I watched Reuben shuffle toward Stefan. Every ounce of me wanted to pull my gun out and shoot Stefan right there, before he had a chance to do anything to Reuben. But shooting him would mean the death of both of us, so I quickly scratched that option.

Stefan reached out and gently wiped a tear from Reuben's eye. "Son, show me the merchandise."

Reuben fumbled through his coat pocket, trying vainly to bite back his sobs. Everyone but me was still laughing at him.

Just give him the drugs, Reuben. Give him the drugs and get back over here.

There was no way I could protect him where he was standing. Not that I could protect him, anyway, even if he was standing behind me. But at least there was some ounce of possibility that we'd get away if we were both closer to the door.

As Reuben clumsily handed over the drugs, I scanned the room. My eyes were adjusted to the light now, but that didn't help. I could plainly see all of the rows of shelving behind the thugs. The only thing near me was a short row of metal filing cabinets that looked out of place. Besides that? Open concrete floors and a room filled with guns.

Stefan took the bag out of Reuben's hand. Reuben winced as their hands touched. Stefan ran his gun through Reuben's hair. "It's okay, son. If your drugs are good, you have nothing to worry about."

That was a lie.

"Okay?" he asked.

"Okay," Reuben repeated. That just got more laughter.

Stefan threw the bag to one of his grunts. "Test it." He turned back to Reuben. "Do you know who you're hanging out with? Do you know what your friend Alex did before he was locked up?"

Reuben hesitated. "Some."

"And how do you know?"

"Me...and my friends...googled his name," Reuben answered.

Just shut up I thought.

"You googled his name?" Stefan repeated. "How enlightening! Well, let me tell you about your friend Alex over there. When I first met him, I—"

"Really, Stefan?" I cut in. "Don't you think this is a little juvenile?"

Stefan pointed his gun at me. "I wasn't talking to you." He turned back to Reuben. "Alex was a cocky little kid. As I'm sure you know by now, he hasn't changed much."

"Stefan, can we just go now?" I was trying to irritate him. Anything to keep his thoughts off Reuben's obvious weakness.

Stefan walked toward me and touched my forehead with his gun. "I said I wasn't talking to you, Alex." He let out a string of curses, then asked if I was done talking.

"Sure." I smiled. "Go on with your story."

Stefan, visibly annoyed, pulled the gun away. "Now where was I... Oh, yes, your friend Alex here, he was—"

"Stefan," the tester said, coming forward.

Stefan waved the gun over his head. "Can't a man just tell a simple story without being interrupted?"

"Tell me about it," I muttered.

Some of the guys started to laugh, then stopped. They knew Stefan wouldn't be pleased if they acknowledged my stubborn humor.

"Okay," Stefan said to his tester. "How is it?"

This was the moment of truth. The grunt would have placed some of the merchandise in some foil and used a match to light it to see if it was good. The one thing I never asked Reuben was whether or not his stuff was a fine product. He had a knack for lying. I couldn't be sure it was good stuff.

And my fears were confirmed. The tester just shook his head and dumped the bag out on the floor.

It was time to act.

As soon as I saw the drugs leave the man's hand, I reached for my gun. But I was too late. Stefan—he didn't even look at Reuben—raised his gun and fired.

Blood splattered out of the back of Reuben's skull as he fell on his face.

I no sooner had my gun out when I saw a whole circle of guns pointed at me. I dove to my left and slid down behind the row of filing cabinets just as a barrage of gunfire erupted.

There was no fear in me. No sadness, either. Reuben had gotten what he deserved. He was an idiot, and in this arena, idiots die. But he meant something to my friends— and to Hannah. And that brought on a rage that I can't even describe.

As the first round ended, there was only one thought in my head. I was going to kill Stefan. No matter what, he would pay, death for death.

And here's my last memory of that night.

I stood up and started firing.

***

They said that when they found me, there were two other guys dead, plus Reuben. All were single shots to the head. And I was kneeling on top of Stefan pounding his face with my fists.

I hadn't shot him. Though his face was broken beyond recognition, he was still alive. At least he was alive when they dragged me off his motionless body. They also said that as I was pounding him, I kept repeating, "You idiot." I was like a deranged animal. It took four Tasers to take me down.

But I don't remember any of that.

My state of mind is what landed me in this empty room in this freak house. All I've had since I woke up was a pen and paper—by request—and food and water. I've had no interactions except with the nurses and some quack-job doctor.

My favorite nurse, Ashley, is my only link to the outside world. That's how I knew Reuben's funeral was today. I'm sure my friends and family are there right now, paying their respects.

The last time I was locked up, I felt nothing. This time, I feel lost—lost and alone. I miss the ones that I love. I miss Ana. I miss Ally. I even miss my brother. But I'm afraid this was the screw-up that ended any chance I'll ever have for a normal life. This screw-up belongs to me alone. I can't blame anyone else.

Just one decision, and my life went away. I could have said no to Reuben. I could have let him go and die alone, the coward that he was. Or I could have tried to protect him. Maybe there was something I could have done with the power of my name. Then Hannah would not be alone now, and Rueben's twin would not be watching his brother get lowered into a hole.

But ashamedly, I don't think I would have changed a thing. Once the adrenaline rush came back, once I said yes to Reuben, I felt more than alive. *I was made for crime.* I don't know how I can run from that. I only survived crime-free for three months. And what did I get out of it? I learned how to play the piano. I had a glimpse of true love—but just a glimpse.

I remember Ana's father preaching one Sunday about the spirit-against-the-flesh battle. I have no idea what he actually meant, but it's the closest thing I can think of to describe how I feel right now.

Part of me knows what I was made to be. I was made to be a name that criminals like Stefan know. I was made to put fear in others' eyes.

But the other part of me wants to break down and cry. That part of me wants just one more time to feel the warmth of Ana's embrace. I'd do anything to feel that again. Anything.

Chapter 23

November 7, 2013

I woke up, completely alert. But instead of the hospital white I was used to, my home strangely greeted me. Then I heard the faint sound of Ally's voice as she came running down the hall, undoubtedly playing hide and go seek with one of the staff. I knew somewhere in my mind that I shouldn't be here in my room with the sun shining through my bay window.

But I didn't care.

Suddenly, I heard the refreshing sound of Ariel's usual knock. "Come in!" I nearly shouted. I welcomed even the smallest semblance of normalcy in the housekeeper's routine.

But Ariel didn't come in. Instead, I heard another knock, fainter this time, followed by Ally's voice again, but slightly muffled.

The door started to open. I saw long, slender fingers wrapping around the edge of the door. The fingernails were painted black. I immediately knew whose hands they were.

"Ana!" I shouted, jumping out of my bed.

The door immediately slammed shut. It sounded much louder than it should have been, which caused a buzzing in my ears.

I ran to the door and grabbed the knob, but the stainless steel was so hot it started melting the skin on my hand. Gasping in pain, I fell backward. "Ana, help!" I called

Nothing. Not a sound.

I looked at my hands. They were both burned…but I'd only grabbed the door knob with my right hand. What was going on? I looked again. The skin was hanging off my hands, showing the pale muscle and the red of blood. The pain was unbearable. I felt the room starting to move around me.

Before I knew it, I fell over, and lying flat on my back looked up at the ceiling. It was swirling in some kind of unnatural pattern. Then the room grew darker.

I turned my head. I should have been startled, but the face looking back at me only brought despair. It was Reuben lying there, only a few feet away, his eyes open, the rest of his face hidden by smears of blood. It was as if he were reaching out with his eyes, and asking for help. Any kind of help.

The pain was suddenly gone, and now all I felt was an overwhelming sorrow. Not for Reuben. It was because Ana wouldn't open the door. I needed her now, more than ever.

And then it all went black...but only briefly.

That's when I woke up.

***

Now it's 2 a.m., and I can't go back to sleep. My chest hurts. My heart hurts.

And my pen is running out of ink.

Chapter 24

November 10, 2013

Over a week went by, and I was still in the mental hospital. Though the initial impact of my crime had passed, the agony of my loneliness had not. I hadn't seen Ana in more than two weeks. But it wasn't the length of time that hurt so badly. It was the fact that she had every opportunity to visit, but she chose not to.

When her father came in to check on my spiritual well-being, he told me that something had changed in his daughter. Something good. But apparently that *something* did not involve me. I was changing for the worse, she for the better.

The words *heartache*, or even *heartbreak*, do not even begin to touch what I feel deep down inside of me now. There are no words to adequately describe how I feel.

Pastor Greene left me with the following words: "Don't worry about her. You need to worry about yourself. Worry about your own soul."

Maybe he had a point, but I can't help but think about Ana all the time. She's the first true love I'd ever had, and without her I couldn't care less about my soul.

Brandon came with some fair news the next day. I think the connection we were building before this is probably gone forever, though, because he seemed cold and calloused. Well, I can't blame him. It had taken months for us to figure each other out, so to lose that is very disheartening.

"The bad news," he said as soon as he stepped into room, "is that our lawyer is pretty much convinced that the evidence is overwhelming. All we have is the argument that it was self-defense. It *was* self-defense? Right?"

"If that's what you call it," I answered. "I'd call it murder. Or attempted murder in Stefan's case."

"No!" Brandon said. "It was self-defense. Right?" It sounded almost like a threat.

"Sure thing."

"Good. But even if it's proven to be self-defense, the drug charges will probably put you away for a long time. There's no stopping that, Alex. This is well beyond your third strike. From the looks of your criminal record, it's like, strike twenty."

"And the good news?" I asked.

Brandon sat down on the end of my bed before he spoke. "The good news is you've been determined competent, so you'll be getting transferred to jail in a few days. And at that point, I can pay your bail so you can come home while we wait for the trial."

That was very good news. But it was also hard to believe. "What judge in their right mind would let me out on bail?"

"A judge who believes that you were just helping a friend and got caught in a fight. A judge who believes you were just defending yourself."

"You mean a judge that's a friend of yours," I said in a flat voice. Rich people seem to have so many rich friends.

"No," Brandon responded. "A judge that's seen some of the evidence. A judge that believes what I believe. Alex, I know Reuben came to you. And I know you did everything you could not to go. Ariel overheard most of your conversation. You wouldn't have gone if the buyers hadn't already known Reuben's name. I know you did it because you were afraid for Ana's safety. For *our* safety."

"You say that," I countered. "But you don't really *know* that. You don't know how right it all felt. You don't know—"

"No, Alex. I do know. I know that you are not the person you once were. I believe you've changed, even if it's just a little."

I conceded the fact that I didn't need to convince him otherwise. I was the one locked up in a mental hospital. My actions had spoken louder than my words. "Well, either way," I told him, "I don't think you should waste your money on me. I don't deserve to wait for my trial in the lap of luxury."

Brandon stood up. "You're right," he said. "You don't deserve anything I've given you these last few months. You don't deserve a family. You don't deserve friends. You don't deserve anything."

I wasn't sure where he was going with this. But he wasn't helping me feel better.

Brandon wasn't finished. "But you know what, Alex? I don't deserve any of that either. You know the boy I once was. You know what I allowed you and Kim to go through. But now, by the grace of God, I have what I have."

For a second, I thought the conversation was going to be all about my brother's guilt. Again. I wasn't in the mood. "So," I said, "this is all about *you*? You're going to bail me out again just because you owe me? Because I don't want that. I don't want—"

"No, it's not about you or me at all," he said. "It's about Jesus, Alex. It's always been about Jesus." Brandon came closer and leaned down in front of me so we were face to face. "Can't you see that? Every change I've made, the changes you've made, they were never because of *us*. They were because of the mercy of God. Nothing else."

And here we go again, I thought. Pastor Greene had had his shot, so now it was Brandon's turn. "So let me guess," I said, "even your change from workaholic to family man was because of this Jesus, too? It couldn't have been that your wife threw herself on me."

I saw a flash of anger in his eyes, but it quickly faded. "That's exactly what I'm saying, Alex. Everything in this life, the now, the future, even the next life; it's all about Jesus, plain and simple."

Inside, I was laughing. But outside, I didn't let on. I'd heard this kind of thing every Sunday for three months. And it meant nothing to me. It didn't make any sense.

"I'm sorry, Brandon," I said, "but I just don't see it."

He exhaled. "I know you can't. But I believe that you will." He reached into his coat pocket and pulled out the same little Bible he'd given me in his study two weeks ago.

I didn't have the slightest idea where I'd left it. "Where'd you find that?"

"It was next to the grandfather clock in your room. Doesn't look like you ever opened it, though. Did you?"

I could have lied, but it wouldn't have been very convincing. "No, I didn't. I didn't even know where it was."

Brandon put the book into my hand. He held my arm with his other hand, then folded my fingers over the Bible so I was holding it tight. "Well," he said as he let go, "you have plenty of time to read now, don't you?"

I didn't want to read it, but what else did I have to fill my time with? I could only write so much before even that turned into pure boredom. He was right.

"Okay," I said, "I'll take a few glances."

"That's all I can ask for," Brandon replied. "From what I can gather, you have less than a week in here. Then you'll be transferred to jail, where I can bail you out. Until then, little brother, please stay out of trouble."

I thought he was joking and laughed, but he didn't even crack a smile. "As if there's a whole lot of trouble I can get into here," I said. "Maybe I can refuse my meds or something. Maybe I'll get a straight-jacket for that."

Brandon smiled for the first time. "Or maybe you'll do what's right."

"Maybe," I muttered, as my nurse, Ashley, walked in.

"How are you doing today, Alex?" She always had this cheerful voice.

"I'm doing fine."

Brandon nodded and walked out the door. No sooner was he gone then Ashley had my sleeve up and was poking me with a needle.

"You really know how to get to a man's heart," I told her.

"Straight through the veins, huh?" she asked with a smirk.

I laughed for real this time. "Back in the day, that's exactly how it was. Straight through the veins."

***

It was nice to see Jess and Thomas yesterday. But in the end, it only reminded me that Ana hadn't come. I tried to ask them what she was doing, why she hadn't visited me, questions like that, but all they said was a vague "Ana's changed," the same nonsense Pastor Greene had spouted off at me. Apparently, whatever Ana was telling them wasn't much. Maybe she didn't even know what the change was.

"She is better for it, though," Thomas admitted, but that made no sense to me. "Let's just say, she's been at church a lot more lately," he added.

I didn't press the matter because I knew I'd probably hear more about this Jesus fellow, and that was the last thing I wanted.

Other than that, they filled me in on what had happened in my absence. They told me about Reuben's funeral and how hundreds of students were there. He was a very popular kid. Jess told me how Hannah rarely left her house anymore. They'd seen her a few times at school, but she never went to the warehouse anymore.

"She must hate me," I said.

"I don't think so," Thomas answered. "She knew Reuben was a rebel. And everyone thinks you were just trying to help him. He was a screw-up, so he came to you, a hardened veteran. At least that's the story I've been hearing."

"But that's enough about that," Jess said like she did every time the direction of the conversation went negative. "Can I just say we miss you so, so much?" She wrapped her arms around me.

"I've missed you, too."

"A lot has changed since you came around, my friend," Thomas said. "But I wouldn't change a bit of it. These last few months have been awesome. And I know this isn't the end of it."

"Always so positive." I made sure not to say anything negative so Jess wouldn't change the subject again. "Anything else new?"

They exchanged glances, but neither of them said a word. There was a long minute of awkward smiles and silence.

"What is it?" I finally asked.

Thomas looked at Jess, who gave a tiny nod. "Well, this may come as a shocker," he said, "but I'm over the homecoming queen. I've found an awesome girl who is just, well…awesome."

By the look on Jess's face, I knew who he was talking about. "You're kidding me!"

"Nope." He put one arm around Jess' shoulder. "Two weeks now."

I was not expecting that at all. It was awkward, but I can't say I wasn't happy for them. "Well, congrats. I guess. It's kind of weird, though."

Jess laughed. "Well, I have you to thank for this…you know?"

"You do?"

"Yep. You remember that night after the homecoming dance? When we were sitting in the back of Thomas' jeep, just looking at the skyline and talking?"

"Yeah." Of course I remembered. "You were drunk off your—"

"Okay!" She slapped me on the arm. "Besides that."

But that was all I really remembered. "To be honest Jess, I really don't remember anything I said that night. Well, maybe I wrote it down somewhere."

"You and your notebooks," she said with a grin. "But no need to try to remember. You actually didn't say anything particularly enlightening. But you weren't afraid to tell me that you were in love with Ana. And that gave me the confidence to tell Thomas how I think I've always felt."

Thomas nodded and grinned. "The day after Reuben's funeral, she just walked up to me and told me she loved me." He squeezed Jess with one arm and reached down to pat me on the leg with his other arm. "And that's it."

"So you're really not gay?"

"Oh, stop it!" Thomas said as falsetto as he could get, waving his hand in an exaggerated manner.

Everything was changing. I was silent for so long that Jess finally asked me if something was wrong.

"Nothing." I was lying, of course.

"Your eyes are telling me differently."

"I hate that you can see that. I just wish I could have been with you guys these past few weeks. I just wish things didn't have to end like this."

"What do you mean by end?" Thomas asked. "You're gonna get out of here and we're gonna be waiting."

"But will Ana?" I asked pointedly. "Will she be waiting?"

That made Jess stop smiling. "Ana's changed...but I can't imagine she wouldn't be there for you."

"I can't imagine it, either," I said after a minute. "Actually, I don't want to imagine it."

"Then don't," Thomas said.

"I'll do my best."

"And you'll forget the rest," Jess said.

Chapter 25

November 12, 2013

It's 3 a.m. I've barely slept at all. What little sleep I've managed to get has been filled with the same nightmares, over and over again. Different places, different stories, but always the same ending—Reuben's lifeless eyes staring back at me. And no way to reach Ana.

But tonight, I can't keep the tears from streaming down my cheeks. There's no way I can control them, and I have no desire to. I can't shake the depression I'm in. I can't shake it without her. All I want is to see her face, hear her beautiful accent. To touch her.

She's changed.

What does that even mean? No one will tell me. No one can explain it. I guess I never really asked, but I think that's because I'm not altogether sure I want to hear the answer. I can't help but believe the change doesn't include me. Or else she'd have visited me by now. The downward spiral's started. The life I'd come to know these last three months is over. And I get that. I accept it. Except for the idea of living without her. We'd only dated a few weeks, but now it feels like we had a whole lifetime of bliss.

What am I saying? I don't even know if any of this is true. When Brandon bails me out in a few days, maybe she'll be waiting for me, arms open wide. Maybe she just needed space to figure some things out. Maybe this whole mess gave her that opportunity.

Or maybe not.

She probably hates the monster I really am. How could I blame her? If she knew the terrible things I'd done before…well, there would be no way to win her back. I honestly don't think there's a way now.

But I give up on trying to figure this out. I might as well hang myself with my sheets. Or worse, I could start reading that little Bible.

Chapter 26

November 21, 2013

Being immersed in a God-fearing family, I have found that the term "born again" seems to find its way into many conversations. Whether it's during a prayer or during the Sunday service at church, those two words wedge their way in, even if the current topic is anything but religious in nature. It's another one of those annoying things, among a whole list of other uncommon phrases that only Christians say.

I have to imagine that walking out of lock-up for the second time is as close to being "born again" as my life will ever be. Pastor Greene has talked several times about the first and second births, in both a physical and spiritual sense. And after reading through the Bible that Brandon gave me at least ten times, I can see where he found the idea. Maybe I was the one lucky guy who had a third shot at life. I've been born again twice. I know I'm totally out of context, and I think the religious folks would call that blasphemy, but walking out of a lock-up facility and into the frigid, open air can only be described as a new birth.

And this time, I knew where I was going—*home*. That monstrosity of a place neatly squeezed between two other brick buildings, that palace with its massive foyer and double staircases straight out of a Victorian castle, with its library with painted glass ceilings, my room with the ivory-inlaid clock, my piano—that's my home.

And I had a family waiting for me, too. Dysfunctional at best, but no less desirable. I couldn't wait to play with Ally. Or find Butler Charles sleeping in some corner of the house. Or even to hear Ariel's annoying morning and evening knocks on my door.

Even more, I couldn't wait to see Ana. No sooner had I been handed my phone, then I sent multiple texts and left several voicemails. Hearing her voice on her voicemail message made me more eager to just talk to her. My thirty-minute ride home was filled with anxious waiting that had no positive end result.

"Just give her time," Brandon said. He could see how depressed I was getting when I should have been excited.

"She's had weeks," I said.

"And you've been convicted on drug charges and you killed two people. It could take months. Even years."

I didn't respond. The thought of years away from her choked me up.

The ride in Brandon's Maserati was all too familiar. Only there was no small talk or life story-telling. This time it was all business. Brandon talked about trials and lawyers and judges, and all kinds of other meaningless details. I stared out the window and wondered when my phone would ring. Just one ring was all I asked for. If there was a God, even a single text would do.

I would hold on to that petty, pathetic prayer all night.

But I found great joy in wrapping my arms around Ally.

"I missed you so much," she whimpered, and then she broke down into tears.

I picked her up and held her. "I missed you, too." I could barely choke back my own tears as she sobbed into my shoulder.

While I was holding Ally, Jen walked up and gave me a sideways hug, welcoming me home.

"Now," Brandon said, "I say we get some dinner and have a long overdue family night."

"Yes, please, Daddy," Ally got out between sobs.

And so we had a family night.

Ariel greeted me with an awkward hug that felt forced before she served us a grand meal—turkey with mashed potatoes, gravy, stuffing, and chocolate pie for dessert. Needless to say, I ate my fill.

"And," she said, "this just a trial run for Thanksgiving dinner next week."

"If this is just a trial," I said, "then next week is going to be heavenly." I was shoveling food down my mouth and gulping down sweet tea.

"The food wasn't good where you were?" Ally asked.

"Nope. It was awful."

She laughed. "Did you see my dress?" She was wearing a pink dress with sunflowers on it.

"Did I? You're looking gorgeous, young lady."

She blushed. "Mommy and I bought it just for you for coming home."

"Well, thanks." I smiled at Jen. "And thank you."

Jen nodded. "You're welcome. She's missed you a lot. We all did."

"And I've missed you all," I said. "Even you, Brandon. But not as much. No offense."

"None taken," Brandon replied as he helped himself to more mashed potatoes.

The door opened, and Butler Charles walked in and took a seat. "Sorry I'm a little late," he said. He noticed me. "Oh. You're back." And that was all he said.

Everyone laughed. Charles looked like he didn't have a care in the world besides eating his turkey.

We watched *Toy Story 3* that night. And we talked, and we laughed, and Butler Charles snored. But there was no more perfect way to spend my first night back home. Ally sat on my lap and wouldn't let me out of her sight until she fell sound asleep, her head nestled against my chest.

After the movie was over, Brandon gently picked her up and carried her to bed. "Goodnight," he said.

Then Jen stood up, stretched and gave a loud yawn. "Alex, we really are glad to have you back. You know that?"

"Not only do I know that, but I feel it," I answered. "You know, leaving the lock-up today was so different than the last time. Because I knew I had somewhere to go. I knew I was coming home."

Jen smiled. "Good. That's what we hoped for. Good night."

I grabbed her arm as she walked by. "Why?"

"Why what?"

"Why all of this?" I asked.

"I think Brandon's already told you that. It's all about—"

"Jesus. Right?"

"Right." The Jen that had kissed me all those weeks ago was no longer around. Like her husband, Jen seemed to have changed.

I let go of her arm. "I've lived here for three months," I said, "and you guys never shoved any of that stuff down my throat. Thanks for that. Thanks for everything."

"Yeah, well, as you've noticed, we all have our own issues to deal with. We have no right to hit you over the head with a Bible. That's not what it's all about. I'm just a white trash cutter/drug addict that was saved by God's grace. As you know."

"Brandon's good at that saving thing."

"No, not Brandon. God."

"Right," I replied. "God."

Jen laughed. "Good night."

"'Night."

I went to my room, leaving Butler Charles to snore all alone. But I didn't fall asleep. Instead, for maybe three or four hours, I sat on the bed I'd so sorely missed and read that little Bible that Brandon gave me. And when my eyes couldn't take any more reading, I just lay there and wondered how that little book made people like my brother and his wife, with pasts as dark as anyone's, change into what they were now. Not perfect, but far from the same.

There had been a few moments where I thought I could change, too. But then Reuben knocked on my door that night, and all those thoughts vanished with each blow I landed on Stefan's face.

After what seemed like hours of hopeless pondering, I started to fall asleep. The world slowly faded away and the colors melted together.

And then my phone went off.

Before I even grabbed it off my stand, I saw Ana's name flash on the screen. My stomach jumped as I opened the text.

It was one sentence. *I miss you Alex, but I just need some time.*

Though it wasn't exactly what I wanted to see, I immediately felt a wave of relief. I started to type a message back to her, but after a couple words I stopped.

She needed time, and a long response from me would not be giving her that. I deleted the original message, then sent back the simple response—*ok.*

If time was what she needed, then that's what I would give her. It hurt, but it was far better than the constant thought of her hating me. She said she missed me, which meant she still wanted me.

Maybe she still loved me. I thought about this until my weary eyes closed for the night.

One simple text. There is a God.

Chapter 27

November 25, 2013

I watched Ally play the piano for at least an hour. She never realized I was there, as I sat in the corner of the massive library, my back sharing space between a bookshelf and the adjoining wall. A few times, the soft music nearly put me to sleep, but each wrong note or time error jolted me back awake.

A few times I thought maybe I should reveal my presence, but each time I decided that ripping away the calm of the moment was just too depressing. She would never play well if she knew she was being observed. This isn't something I just made up, but something Ally had said in passing a few months ago when I first began to play.

I'd fallen asleep in that corner, who knows when. I had nearly read an entire collection of Tennyson, just one of about a million books in the room. That's probably a very poor estimate, but there are a lot of them.

It was actually the sound of the piano that woke me.

I had to have been asleep for a few hours, because I'd sat down not long after lunch, and the fact that Ally was home meant it was at least four o'clock. Either way, I'd wasted a lot of time.

But there was nothing to do. I was stuck in the house. I had been forbidden to leave by the judge until my court date, so there wasn't much left for me to do except play the piano and read. I don't have any other hobbies. Unless crime counts as a hobby.

But I'd already played the piano for a freaking long time today, and, like I said, I'd nearly finished a volume of poetry. There was no one there to abuse, kill, or steal from. Boredom was inescapable.

Then I heard Jen yelling from the kitchen, "Ally, let's do your homework."

Ally slammed several keys, making an awful noise. Then she picked up her schoolbooks and stalked away.

I didn't blame her. What five-year-old kid has homework? This private school of hers had to suck.

"She plays beautiful, doesn't she?" I heard Butler Charles say.

I was so startled I nearly threw a book at him. Then I hit my head on the shelf above me and yelled a string of curses.

Charles laughed.

"What are you?" I muttered. "Some kind of ninja? How long have you been there?"

"As long as you have." He peered over the arm of the burgundy sofa. "I saw you sleeping back there and decided it looked like a great idea. So I caught some shut-eye myself."

I had to laugh at myself, even though my head hurt. "Sorry for the language." I rubbed the sore spot.

Butler Charles stood up. "Young man, I was in the Navy a long time ago. And you know how sailors are with the cursing." He smiled and walked away.

A twinge of curiosity hit me, and I meant to ask him more about his past, but before I could spit out a question, he was already gone. I'd never seen him move that fast. Maybe he really was a ninja.

At that precise moment, Ariel walked in through the kitchen door, whistling some awful tune. She didn't see me. Now, normally that is a good thing. I rarely go out of my way to talk to the crazy woman.

But today was different. Like I said, I was bored out of my mind.

She nearly jumped out of her skin when I called her name.

"I'm sorry," I said, as I stood up and revealed myself. "Believe me, you're not the only one who's jumpy today."

With one hand on her chest and an exasperated look on her face, she sat down on an orange sofa. "Can I help you?" she finally said. She seemed as surprised as I was that we were conversing without being forced to.

"Not really," I answered, stepping beside her. "I was just saying hi."

"Oh, well…hi." She stood up again and gave me an awkward smile. "Well, I see you later." She scurried away as fast as she could.

That was a bust, I thought. I can't even have a conversation with the resident mental case.

I fell back across a chair adjacent to the sofa Ariel had sat on. I was content to endure another evening filled with doing nothing. I was starting to close my eyes when that flash of curiosity hit me again. I sat up and yelled Ariel's name. She was opening the foyer door, and my sudden call made her slam it shut and grab her chest again. She leaned against the wall.

"I am so sorry," I apologized again.

She waved her hand in acknowledgement and shook her head. "No need apologize. I scare easy."

I let her catch her breath.

Finally, she stepped away from the wall and looked at me. She had a very annoyed expression on her face, like I was hindering her from doing some dire task. "What you need from me?"

"I don't really need anything," I said. "I just have a question. Do you know anything about Butler Charles?"

She looked confused. "What do you mean?"

"Like his past, or what he did before he was here."

I expected her to ask more questions about my questions, as her language barrier hindered most normal conversation. Instead, a wide smile came across her face.

"You want me tell you about Mr. Charles?"

"Yes." Anything to make this day go by faster.

Ariel became her normally animated self and waved her hand. "Come, follow me. I show you."

I followed her out of the library and up to the second floor. She kept waving me on and repeating, "A lot to show you."

I was kind of freaked out by her sudden openness. Maybe, I began to think, this was just her chance to tie me up and exorcise my demons in the name of her God. That's why I was a little reluctant when she asked me to follow her into her bedroom. Maybe she was going to kill me and hide my body instead.

"It's okay," she said. "I think you will not mess up my room like you do all of the others."

That sounded like the housekeeper I knew. I had about ten smart things to say, but I held my tongue and walked in.

In my mind, I'd always expected Ariel's room would be like some oddly colored, hideous Mexican restaurant, filled with a gross amount of Catholic idols and incense. But much to my surprise, it was the emptiest room in the house. It was practically a replica of my own room, with just small differences in the color scheme. There was an antique armoire and an even larger, more ornate grandfather clock. But other than those things, the bed, and some other Victorian-like furniture, the room was empty.

Ariel pointed to a chair beside the lone window. "Please sit. I get photos."

I sat as she got down on the floor and started pulling things out from under the bed. After two boxes came out, I offered my assistance, but she waved me away with a "shut up and be quiet" gesture. It was a gesture I'd seen a lot in the past few months, usually after I said something either smart or rude. After a few awkward minutes of watching her in a very compromising position, I saw her pull out a small shoebox, which she slid over close to me.

"You can open that."

I picked up the box as Ariel pulled another chair closer. I started to hand the box to her, but she pushed it back. "You open it. Then tell me what you see."

Such a wide smile on Ariel's face seemed so strange.

I took the lid off the old shoebox. By the amount of dust, I could tell it hadn't been opened in a very long time.

Inside was a large stack of old photographs. I looked at Ariel and she nodded.

"Look at them."

The first few I picked up were of who I assumed was a younger version of Ariel. From maybe ten years ago, certainly not much longer than that. Several photos were her with other Hispanic individuals that I presumed were her family.

"That is my brother and sister," she said, pointing to the third picture I picked up.

"Are they in New York, too?" I asked.

"No, no, no," she answered, shaking her head. "They are dead."

"They—" I choked. I couldn't speak.

"It's okay," she said.

I put the picture back in the box. I saw other unfamiliar faces, but I was afraid to ask.

Ariel reached into the box and started moving photos around. "Somewhere in here," she mumbled, "is what you are looking for." After a few minutes, she pulled out a single picture and looked at it. "Yes. This is it." She handed it to me.

It was a picture of a gentlemen that looked very familiar. It was a younger version of Butler Charles.

"Why do you have a picture of Butler Charles in here?" I had to ask.

"That's not Butler Charles. That's Missionary Charles."

"Who?"

She laughed one of her crazy laughs. "It's Butler Charles twelve years ago. He was a missionary in Mexico. He was my savior."

I nearly laughed. "You're kidding me!"

"Kidding? What do you mean?"

That's how I knew she was serious. Navy? Missionary? Who was this old man?

"You look confused," she said.

I shook my head. "No. It's just hard to believe that the man snoring on the couch every night did anything but, well, do nothing. How did he end up here?"

"I'll tell you if you want to hear it."

I looked at the grandfather clock. The glare from the window rendered it unreadable, but I was just trying to be funny. "My schedule is a little crazy," I said, "but I think I have some time."

Ariel laughed. She took the photo out of my hand and looked at it. "I tell you about Charles, but only if you are willing to hear the whole story."

"Hey, like I said, I have plenty of time." If she only knew how bored I really was.

"Okay, here it goes." She took a breath and started. "I meet Missionary Charles twenty-two years ago when he passed by me in the main square of Malinalco, which is just over an hour outside of Mexico City. There is nothing special about him. He look like some other tourist that ventured through the city, except he smiled at me. Like a big smile, or very meaningful as you Americans would say."

"And that's how you met?" I asked.

"No. No, that was just the first time I see him. I remember smiling back at him, and then watching him stand up in middle of the square and talk about Jesus. Everyone laughed at him. Some mocked him and called him names, like lunatic or a disturbance of peace. Others shouted 'amen' and yelled for him to continue.

"I did nothing at all, except watch him go from tourist to riot starter in a few minutes. I didn't know at the time, but Missionary Charles was with a team of others who were handing out Bibles while he was speaking. One of the locals started set one on fire, and then some others did it, too. It was what you would call chaos.

"I was on the outside of the mob, so I was able to get away from anything dangerous. But by the time it was all over, the mob had set a fire in the middle of the square and they were throwing all of the Bibles into it. I watched as the men who handed out the Bibles shielded Missionary Charles and escorted him out of the square as people began throwing things at him and trying to hit him."

"Didn't the police come?" I asked.

"Yes," she answered. "But it was after the worst had happened. And I don't think they do anything anyways. I just remember sitting there and crying, I was so scared."

It sounded like a scene from a movie. Ariel looked distraught as she talked about the riot.

"So then what happened to Charles?" I asked her.

"Well, I tell you. Butler Charles made it out of the mess just fine. In...uhhmmm...the long run, like you say. But he did have a cut over his eye and some bruises. But I didn't find any of this out until much later. Actually, I didn't see him for a few years after the riot.

"But he made very big impact in my life. You see, I found one of his Bibles lying on the street, barely burned. I picked it up and took it home with me. I hid it for a while because I was afraid that my husband will find it. He wasn't very nice—"

"Wait," I interrupted. Something wasn't adding up. "You have a husband?"

Ariel laughed. "No, not *had* a husband, I still *have* a husband. And two children, too."

I let out a profanity, then a quick, "Oh, I'm sorry. But you're joking, right?"

"No, no, not joking at all."

"But where are they? Are they hiding under the bed? In the closet?"

I'd never seen Ariel laugh so hard. She'd never found me very funny before.

"No," she said, "my family is still in Mexico. They wait for me. But let me tell you the rest of the story."

I was too shocked and confused to not let her. "By all means, go ahead."

"Where was I? Oh, yes, I found the Bible. And then I hid it. But I read it every day while my husband was at the factory. He would hurt me if he found out about it. You see, he didn't let me do anything on my own. He was a mean man. And he hit our children. He would hit them or me over nothing. And the more he drink, the meaner he got."

Her face turned soft. "But I didn't know that he found the Bible the very first day I hid it. And he read it as much as I have. I didn't know that for a long time. But I did notice how much nicer he became. You see, my abusive husband find Jesus."

And then she went crazy. At least that's how I would have finished the story.

"And then my whole family found Jesus," she said, "all because of the Bible I found on the street. And my husband never hit me or the children again."

Now I really was confused. "So where does Butler Charles come into the picture again? And how did you get here? And where is your family?"

"I get to all of those questions now," she answered. She pulled another photo out of the box and handed it to me. "This is Charles and me six years ago at the airport."

It was amazing how much older Charles looked in this picture than the earlier one. This picture looked exactly like the Charles I knew. He had his arm wrapped around Ariel, and I saw the distinct figure of Jen standing in the background. A very pregnant Jen. But I didn't see Ariel's family in the picture.

"So, this still doesn't explain who Butler Charles is and where your family is now."

"I know."

I saw the glint of a tear in her eye. "I'm sorry." That was the first time I'd ever truly and sincerely apologized to Ariel.

"It's okay," she said. "You see, my husband was ridiculed by many of the men in our neighborhood, which means they also made fun of my kids and me. We lived like this for a few years before I saw Charles again. It was the same thing in the same square. But this time, I followed him and I told him my story. And that's when we started to work for the missionary organization with Charles. We did this for seven years until Charles retired. But during that time, we were able to build new home outside of Malinalco and open our house to others. And Charles lived with us for a while. We became like family with him."

I was still confused. Something bad had to have happened. "But then he retired and things didn't go so well?"

"Yes. Once Charles retired, things were never the same. The churches we planted closed down. And we lost our house and lived on the street for several years. But we never give up hope. And we never stopped talking about Jesus."

Of course not, I thought. With Jesus, all things are possible. And that's why she was stuck here as a housemaid. "Okay," I said aloud. "I get it. Jesus, Jesus, Jesus. But what happened?"

"You see, Butler Charles never forget about us. When we were at our very lowest, I wrote a letter to him. He was working here as a butler with your brother and his new wife. And he sent money, enough money to bring me here. And he got me my job here. And I'm here ever since."

"And your family?"

"They wait for me until I have enough money to bring them here, too. You see, Charles only had enough money for me. Being a missionary, he didn't have very much money."

I shook my head. The story didn't add up. "But couldn't Brandon give you money? Why haven't you asked him?"

"No, no, no…we cannot ask him. He doesn't even know. And you can't tell him."

"Why not?"

"Butler Charles and I don't want to take advantage. And we pray daily, but we let Jesus take care of us."

"You've got to be kidding me! I'll go tell him right now." I started to stand up.

Ariel grabbed my arm. "No! You can't tell him!"

I tried to pull away from her, but she held tight. "Why not?"

She looked panicked. "Because I promised Butler Charles before he got sick that I would not ask them. I promised." She started to cry.

I stopped pulling away and sat back down. "What do you mean by sick?"

It took her a moment to steady herself and stop crying. "Butler Charles does not remember any of this anymore. He barely even remembers who he is most of the time. He has this disease. I don't know what it is—"

"He has Alzheimer's?"

"Yes, that's it. He only remembers a few things. Like being in the army and that he works for your brother. And he remembers Jesus."

Now it began to make sense. The constant sleeping. The incoherence. His general demeanor. Not to mention my family's general allowance for his behavior, like letting him sleep instead of work.

Butler Charles was dying.

I leaned back in the chair. I'd wanted to learn about Butler Charles, but what I'd learned was way more than I ever expected. He had such a full life, but it was coming to an end.

"Brandon and Jen know, right?"

She nodded. "Yes, they know. This was more than you expected to hear."

I sighed. "Way more. I mean, I just thought he was lazy. I feel like a jerk." I looked up at Ariel again and noticed she still had tears in her eyes. "And you...you're separated from your family." I reached out and touched her arm. "I'm sorry."

"What are you sorry for?"

I had so much to be sorry for, I couldn't even begin to tell her all of it. "I didn't realize what you've had to go through," I finally said. "I've been a jerk to you. I've made fun of you. I've ridiculed you behind your back. I've—"

"Oh, stop it! You have a hard life, too."

"No, my own choices put me where I am. And I have my family. You don't."

She wiped the remaining tears from her eyes. "But I have Jesus. And I am afraid that you don't."

That left me speechless. How many times did that name keep coming up? And how strong were the people who used that name? They found joy in things that should have been joyless, peace in times of pain, love in a loveless world.

But I still didn't want to hear about this crazy man, Jesus. At that moment, though, I promised myself that I would never judge my friends or family for their faith.

Ariel didn't press me any further.

I told her I was sorry several more times as she showed me more pictures of her family and Butler Charles. She started crying again, and I felt tears welling up in my own eyes. I felt such great pity for this woman. And I felt the same for Butler Charles.

But neither one of them pitied their own situation. Why not? I guess Butler Charles didn't know about his condition, but I feel that even if he did, he would take it all in stride. The man Ariel was describing to me loved life but spent it sacrificing for others. He had no living biological relatives, but he lived his life in a way that everyone he met became part of his family. I only wished I would have known him before his illness.

It was over an hour later before I stepped out of Ariel's room. I was exhausted.

Just then, Jen stepped onto the landing. She stopped. "What's wrong with you?"

"Everything."

She looked confused. "Well, at least you're specific. I hope 'everything' isn't going to keep you from dinner?"

"Depends on what we're having." That was supposed to be a joke.

"It's a surprise." She went into her room.

"I see we're both real specific," I yelled through the door.

Either way, I was hungry.

And Ally was somewhere at the bottom of those stairs. I knew she was sure to cheer me up.

Chapter 28

November 26, 2013

Reuben's lifeless eyes stared through me, as I felt his warm blood flowing through my fingers.

"Wake up!" I screamed. "Reuben, wake up!"

The single warehouse lamp gave just enough light to outline his bullet-riddled body. His blood soaked my knees. It was the only warmth in the cold room.

I heard Stefan's laughter in the darkness. I tried to ignore it. But it got louder as I kept shaking Reuben's lifeless body.

"Just shut up!" I finally yelled. "Please, just shut up!" But he didn't stop laughing.

I continued to shake my friend until I noticed another stream of blood flowing into the light. It was not coming from Reuben's body.

I knew it was from the thugs I'd killed, but I felt no sorrow for them. I tried to move Reuben, so their filthy blood would not touch him. But we ran out of light and moving him would pull us both into the darkness. It was hopeless.

Then, slowly, the light began to expand as more bulbs lit up across the warehouse ceiling. I followed the dirty trail of blood, expecting to see the unfamiliar faces of the men that I had shot. I had no clue what they looked like. I didn't even remember killing them.

All I know is what I was told.

Stefan's laugh faded into the distance just as the light came to a foot. Then it illuminated the body the foot was attached to. It was very thin and not what I expected in a man.

Because it wasn't a man.

As I reached toward Ana's body, I fell over Reuben's. Ana's soul was gone. Only her dead, emerald eyes were left to show how beautiful she had been. The stream of blood started under her temple.

"No…"

I knew it couldn't be real. I knew it was a dream. This wasn't how the story went. But I still felt an immense sorrow.

Stefan's laugh grew even louder, but I didn't care anymore. I just stared back at Ana's green eyes with a longing I cannot describe.

And then I woke up.

My clothes, the sheets, and the pillow were all so soaked with sweat that I had to spend the rest of the night on the floor. I lay there on the hardwood planks, but I was never able to actually go to sleep.

The nightmares were getting closer together. But the problem was not the nightmares themselves, it was the immense sorrow that followed them, an overwhelming sorrow I knew was unfounded, yet could not shake. I felt that if I saw Ana's face, the nightmares might go away. But until then, there was nothing to do but deal with the dreams, and the emotions attached to them.

I kept trying to fall asleep. When it seemed to be out of the question, I found myself pouring through Ariel's box of old photographs. She'd left it in my room with a note that said, *Please return when done with.*

And for hours upon hours, I thought about Ariel and Butler Charles in a life that seemed to be so far from this one. Eventually I saw the first glimmer of light coming through my window.

Chapter 29

November 27, 2013

Considering what I knew about Butler Charles and Ariel now, it was strange to sit across the table from them. It was like they were new people, except nothing about them was different except for my perceptions of them. But it was like meeting the both of them for the first time now. My judgmental attitude was gone. My general disdain had vanished. And I couldn't find anything weird or abnormal about them to sarcastically comment on.

I was fine with that. If I hadn't considered them my family before, I did now.

As I dug into my potatoes, I couldn't help but hear Ally's constant humming. She was sitting two seats down and smiling and giggling and playing with her food. The humming was musical, but it wasn't the music that kept my attention.

It was definitely the smile. I'd seen that crooked grin before, and it always meant she was keeping a secret. It was her way of saying, "I know something you don't know. And I want to tell you, but I'm not supposed to."

Ally's smile, coupled with Brandon and Jen's general silence, turned me on to the fact that I was the only one there not in on some secret. I was too hungry to pursue it right then, but if nothing was said during the entire meal, it was going to be very awkward.

Once the small talk began, my suspicions were confirmed. For the past week, every family dinner we'd had was consumed with discussions of court dates, plea deals, and jail time. It was now to the point that Ally got upset more than once because the discussion made no sense to her. Tonight, Brandon told a long story about his day at work, then Jen commented on Ally's last piano lesson. Not that any of those things were inherently strange, but even before the present circumstances, small talk wasn't my family's strong point.

I listened for as long as it took for me to finish eating. After that, I decided to listen for a little while longer as I watched Ally's little angel face trying to hide whatever it was. Finally, I couldn't help but laugh.

"What's so funny?" Brandon asked.

"I don't know, you tell me."

Brandon shook his head and smiled. "We're not very good at hiding things are we?" He laid his hand on Jen's.

"Not at all," I said. "If there's one thing I've learned while living here, it's that we are a family that doesn't communicate extremely well. And by that, I mean the 'how was your day' and 'tell me about it' stuff isn't quite our forte."

"What's a four-tay...?" Alley asked.

Ignoring her question, Jen said, "You're right. We really do suck at it."

"Understatement of the century," Butler Charles commented.

While everyone laughed, except for Ariel and Ally, neither of whom knew what was going on, I leaned back in my chair and joined my hands behind my head. "Okay," I said, "let's hear it."

Brandon looked at Jen and she nodded. He looked back at me, but before he could say a word, Ally interrupted.

"All of your friends are coming over tomorrow!"

"Ally!" Brandon gave her a stern look.

I sat up straight. "Whoa, whoa, whoa. What's going on?"

Jen reached over and put her hand on mine. "What Ally is saying is that we thought it would be a fun idea to have your friends over for lunch tomorrow before we had our family Thanksgiving meal. Just make it an entire day of fun. What do you think?"

"What do I think?" I nearly shouted, giving Ariel another reason to nearly have a heart-attack. "Thank you!"

Jen patted my hand. "You're so welcome. We know how bored you've been these past few days. And I know your friends have been dying to see you."

I'd been dying to see them! Being locked in the house without seeing or hearing from them was terrible. Not to mention, I needed to learn more about Jess and Thomas' new relationship.

"When will they be coming?" I asked.

It was Brandon that answered. "Around noon," he said. "Thomas said they would have come earlier, but Hannah couldn't make it until then."

I instantly felt my stomach fall. "Hannah's coming?"

Jen squeezed my hand. "It was her idea. She called me two days ago."

I felt relieved and scared to death at the same time.

"Your friends love you, Alex. Hannah loves you, and she knows what happened was not your fault. She wants to show you that." Brandon reached across Jen and put his hand over both of ours. "Don't be afraid to let her back in."

I let out a sigh. "Okay, I'm happy she's coming. But I don't know what I'll say to her."

Ariel chimed in for the first time. "How about saying you're sorry?"

Jen nodded. "Agreed."

They were right. I had nothing else to say. But an apology just wasn't enough. It would never be enough.

"Are you okay, Alex?"

I looked at my brother. He was truly concerned. "I'm fine. I…just…thank you so much."

"No need to thank me for—"

"No," I interrupted. "Not just for this. *For everything*. Now I need to go shave and shower and try to look like I belong in the real world. May I be excused?"

"Certainly," Jen said, laughing at my strange politeness. "You don't want to look like your brother," she said, winking at his usual shaggy beard.

I stood up from the table. "Yeah. That would be a travesty."

Brandon didn't comment.

"Well, good night everyone."

A chorus of good nights came my way. I was nearly through the doorway and into the kitchen, when I felt a hand grab my arm. I looked down to see Ally peering up at me, her smile bigger than ever. I then looked back at the table. They were all smiling. There was more they were not telling me.

"What else?" I asked.

Ally tugged on my sleeve. I got down on one knee so we were eye to eye. She looked at her parents and smiled, then back to me.

"What is it? Spit it out, Ally."

She leaned in and whispered into my ear. "Make sure you clean up real good. You don't want Ana to see you like this."

I fell back against the doorframe. "You're kidding me?" The thought that Ana might come hadn't crossed my mind, because she hadn't been a part of the "my friends" group for some time.

Ally just laughed.

"She's not kidding," Brandon said.

"Ana was the first person we asked after we talked to Hannah," Jen explained. "She's had enough time. She wants to see you." She walked over to me and knelt down between Ally and me and put her hand on my shoulder. "So, Alex, are you ready to see her?"

"Yes." I'd been ready for weeks.

Ally started clapping. She didn't know what any of this really meant, except that Ana meant a great deal to me.

I was practically speechless. But I finally got the words out: "I don't know what to say."

"Don't say anything," Jen said. "Just be ready for tomorrow." She grabbed Ally's hand. "Come on, baby, let's finish dinner. And let's leave your uncle alone."

"Okay, Mommy."

I stood up. "Well…I guess, goodnight again."

I went straight to my room. I felt exhausted, but I knew there was no way I'd sleep well—if at all—that night. How could I sleep when tomorrow my life was coming back? What would I say to Hannah? What would I say to Ana? These were pointless questions.

So I was left with nothing else to do but write. I wrote for hours. And now I have nothing left to say.

Chapter 30

December 11, 2013

This is going to sound strange, but November 28—Thanksgiving Day—was actually five days for me. I know that makes absolutely no sense at all, so I can only give you the story and let you figure it out on your own.

***

I believe I left off writing the night before Thanksgiving, when I wrote into the early morning hours of Thanksgiving Day. It was not an easy night. Thinking about how seeing Ana would affect me, about my strong desire to see her, about where we stood—by "we" meaning us, as a couple, together—and my simple fear of talking to Hannah after everything that had happened…well, all this thinking gave me an anxious adrenaline rush that I cannot even begin put into words.

I sat on my bed with my back against the headboard for the longest time, just staring off into the distance. In my desperately tired state, I decided to do something that I'd wanted to do for as long as I'd lived in this mansion.

With my unique skill set, it only took me five minutes or so to pry the pearl inlays off that old grandfather clock. But when I held them in my hand, I did not feel the satisfaction I'd expected. It just never came. So I put them back in. And that took much longer than five minutes. Probably the better part of an hour.

And then it was back to the drawing board, which meant sitting on my bed for a few more hours, waiting for the sun to rise

It was worth the wait.

After I opened the curtains, my front-row seat was a pillow on the floor. I leaned back against my bed and had a perfect view of the New York skyline. As the sun rose above the horizon, I felt my chest ache with an understanding that I'd pushed away for so long.

I think it was Pastor Greene that said that all men know there is a God but choose to suppress what they know. As the sky turned blue, then orange, then yellow, I knew I was one of those men. Not that I felt like God's hand was raising the sun at that very moment, but how could I deny that something—or someone—much larger and more powerful than me had to have created such a beautiful thing? No random chance or act from nothingness could have painted the beautiful canvas outside of my window.

It was a relief to let that thought come into my head. As much as I disliked all forms of religion and the oppression I felt came with religion, the burden of lying to myself, of telling myself that I was and had always been my own god, was gone. It was like handing over the control and letting someone else, someone much larger than me take it. That's the only way I can describe it.

I felt no sense of revelation or spirituality. Just a moment of peace. But only a moment. Because then the realization that I'd been holding onto so many other burdens on my own hit me. My past and the terrible things I'd done—much worse than killing two thugs—weighed heavy on me. It weighed heavy because only two people shared the weight. Jess and I.

I needed other people to help me carry this burden. I needed to tell Brandon. I needed to tell Ana. I needed to get it all out.

And for some reason, I needed to read that little Bible that Brandon gave me again. So I did.

I was cleaned up and dressed by ten o'clock. I was so anxious that I did everything twice as fast as usual. After what felt like an eternal night, I got out of my room and found my way to the library, where I played the piano until the kitchen door opened an hour later.

Jen peered around the edge of the door. "You're playing like you're nervous."

I put my elbows on my knees. "Well, if feeling like I'm going to throw up means I'm nervous, then that would explain it."

"Euwww!" I heard Ally say from behind her mother. "That's gross." She stuck her neck around the door, just below her mother's elbow.

I patted the piano bench. "Well, come here and play a duet with me. Maybe that will help me get over my nerves."

She looked up at her mom for permission.

"Go ahead," Jen said. "One song. And then come back and finish your breakfast."

"Okay, Mommy." She ran into the room and jumped up on the bench and into my arms.

I hugged her tight, taking comfort in her excitement. "Thanks."

Ally leaned back. "You're welcome. What are we gonna play?"

I set her on the bench beside me, so she could see the piano books on the rack. When I moved the book I was playing from, we saw Ally's study primer. "How about the Well Tempered Clavier by Bach?" I asked.

Ally giggled. "That's the first song I ever showed you."

"I know," I responded. "And then you gave me a lecture like I was your first student. You inspired me to play, you know that? So I guess I *was* your first student."

She blushed.

"So, how about you take the bass and I'll take the treble?"

She nodded and I counted. "One. Two. Three. Four."

I think we played it without a single mistake.

Breakfast came and went quickly, and then I found myself sitting at the bottom of the staircase in the foyer, just staring at the front door. Brandon arrived home just before noon, briefcase in hand.

"Nervous?" he asked, taking off his pea coat.

I'm not going to lie, I'd forgotten he had some business that morning, so when the door opened, I was hoping to see my friends come in. "I'm fine," was all I said.

Ally ran down the middle hall and jumped into her father's arms, screaming, "Daddy!" several times.

"Hey, girlie," he said back, throwing her into the air.

Jen was not far behind. "Hey, hon. Just in time," she said with a noticeable hint of sarcasm. They must have had some pre-agreed time for him to be home, and he'd missed it.

"I don't see any guests," he responded smartly.

Jen kissed him anyway. "Well, Ariel's about done with the food, and Butler Charles kindly volunteered to help set the table since Ariel will be doing it tonight for our Thanksgiving meal."

"Butler Charles is actually awake?" I asked. I hadn't seen him yet.

"I guess so," Jen answered. "I think Ariel somehow baited him into doing it, if you ask me."

Brandon set Ally down. "Well, it's kind of him, either way."

Just then I felt my phone vibrate in my pocket. I pulled it out as fast as I could. It was a text from Jess.

Five minutes away.

I immediately felt sick again. "Well, here we go."

"Okay," Jen said. "Let's all get ready and leave Alex to greet his friends."

Ally wasn't very happy with that plan, but her father pulled her along as they went down the hall.

I found myself standing there, all alone, taking deep breaths as if I had just been on a run. Then I felt stupid. These were my friends. I shouldn't be feeling that way.

But I couldn't help it. I was beyond nervous.

I didn't have much time to think about it. I saw shadows come through the glass in the front door. Then the doorbell rang. I took one more deep breath and yelled, "I got it!" to make sure Ariel knew she didn't have to answer.

I opened the door.

The first face I saw was Jess's. She was smiling ear to ear. Thomas was standing next to her and they were holding hands. But only for a second, as Jess threw her arms—and legs—around me. Not expecting the weight of a girl jumping into my arms, I nearly fell over backwards.

"I've missed you so much!" she yelled in my ear.

Thomas walked in, as sly as ever. "I told her not to do that," he said.

I returned an 'it's ok' expression, before telling Jess I missed her too.

It was a long hug, but Jess finally let go and stood on her own feet. "Handsome as ever I see."

"It hasn't been that long," I told her as I peeled her off me.

"Yeah, but before you were in hospital clothes."

"Oh, stop it," Thomas said as he wrapped his arm around her. It was then that I noticed Hannah standing quietly in the doorway. I felt a tear slide down my cheek. Jess and Thomas stopped laughing.

"I'm sorry," I said to her.

Her eyes were wet, too, but she smiled at me. "I know." And then she threw her arms around me, too. "I know you were only trying to help."

Jess and Thomas joined in to create a group hugging session. But it was still a very somber moment, like I had imagined it would be.

That's when Jen came walking down the hall. "You're all here!" she said.

The group hug immediately loosened as Hannah wiped away her tears and Jess answered, "Of course."

Brandon and Ally were not far behind Jen.

The greetings were a little strange, as Jen and Brandon received hugs from Jess and Thomas while Hannah shook their hands. A minute later, Ariel presented herself and started taking their coats. At the same time, Jen went through the menu, playing up the deliciousness of cheeseburgers and fries.

"We wanted to do something different," she said. "That way, you all didn't get two traditional Thanksgiving turkey and mashed potato meals in one day."

I had to laugh. My friends were anything but traditional. Hannah—the stereotypical nerdy Asian—Jess and Thomas—heathen punks, clothed in black and covered with tattoos and piercings.

Once Jen was done with her recitation, Brandon asked the question I had wanted to ask but was too afraid to.

"Where's Ana at? Wasn't she supposed to be coming with you guys?"

I didn't want to hear the answer. My realistic side thought she'd probably flaked out on them. The scenario of her just staying away and trying to forget about me had already played through my head several times since they had arrived.

"She'll be here soon." Hannah answered.

I tried not to show the relief I felt.

"As a matter of fact," Jess said, looking at her phone, "very soon. She texted me, like, two minutes ago and said she was a minute away. Apparently she's not that good at time."

The sick feeling came back again. I knew I couldn't just sit on the bottom step and wait for Ana. But I wanted to see her so badly. I *needed* to see her.

"Excuse me," I said, and I went out the door and into the cold.

No one seemed to object to my leaving. I suppose they knew how big that moment was for me. But I can say with certainty that they had no idea that moment would be as terrible as it became.

Let me try to explain.

It couldn't have been more than a few minutes before a red car pulled up in front of the mansion, where Andy the Sunday driver usually parked. What was I thinking? I don't remember. I never thought it was her. Ana's car was black.

But then I saw her face. She was looking out through the passenger window. Just seeing her emerald eyes lifted a weight off of me.

I can only describe the feeling as sheer happiness.

Her door opened.

The driver's door opened, too.

I started to walk toward her. I don't know if I was walking or running. And I don't know why I remember this, but I distinctly recall the front door opening behind me. I could hear Jess's voice. "Oh, no," she said.

My memory gets really hazy here. I can only give you flashes of what I saw and felt...or at least what I think I saw and felt.

Ana gave me an awkward smile as she shut the car door behind her.

She looked so beautiful—black jeans and boots, a long gray coat and a black scarf. She looked gorgeous against the red sports car.

All she said to me was, "Don't be mad."

Which was very confusing, if only for a moment. Because the next thing I saw was Levi's head rising over the roof of the car. Now Jess's "oh, no" made perfect sense. Levi smirked. But this wasn't his normal "I'm better than you" smirk. That didn't matter. He had no reason to be with Ana. None. The monster inside of me instantly returned.

The rest of what I'm about to tell you is a mix of things I think I remember, plus fragments put together by the others who were there. If it doesn't make sense, I'm sorry. But I'll try my best to help you understand.

So here it goes.

My immediate feeling was rage. It was a rage that blocked out every other possible feeling. It blocked out *everything*. Why was he with Ana? The rage boiled over into adrenaline, the same rush that had allowed me to kill two people and nearly kill a third. It was like everything I'd been through was suddenly compounded into this—this unbelievable moment—a moment that felt like a slap in the face. More than just a slap. A fist.

But I didn't know that right away. I didn't know that until I found myself on top of Levi, looking down at his bloody face, pounding it bloodier, punching and punching. I was in the same exact position the police said I was in when I was beating the life out of Stefan.

I remember hearing screams. Then feeling hands all over me. But nothing could make me stop hitting him.

They told me I hit him in the face at least twenty times. They said he didn't even put up a fight. I kept punching, he just lay there. I broke several fingers. I can't even imagine what I did to his face.

Like I said, this is mostly lost to me. I know that eventually Brandon and Thomas were able to pull me off of him.

And what do I remember next? I was standing there in the middle of the street, looking at crying eyes and panicked faces. I had nowhere to go, nowhere to turn. Everyone that loved me was there. They were all terrified. They were all staring at me with expressions of sorrow and disgust.

And then, before I knew what I was doing, I opened the door to Levi's red Mustang and jumped in. The keys were still in the ignition.

I hadn't driven a car in years.

I started the engine. I could see Ana looking through the window. She looked sadder than I'd ever seen her before.

And that was it. The rest of that day is a blank.

***

When I woke up the first time, I thought maybe it was all just a dream. I couldn't see anything, but I could hear familiar voices. I thought the sounds I was hearing were just parts of a nightmare that just wouldn't end.

I couldn't feel anything. I definitely remember not smelling or tasting anything. Five senses. Check. That was fine because I was only awake for a few seconds.

***

I officially opened my eyes on December 2. The sun was very bright on the white walls of a room that I did not recognize. It took a few moments before I figured out that I was in a hospital bed. I couldn't move my body, but I didn't feel any pain. I knew there had to have been plenty of drugs involved.

All I could move were my head and eyes. I looked around for a few seconds.

And then I heard her voice.

"Alex?"

I couldn't see Ana's face until she was standing right next to the bed.

She smiled. My last glimpse of her had been through the window of Levi's car. She'd looked so sad I couldn't stand it. And now she smiled at me. Then I felt a sensation in my left hand and I knew she was holding it.

"What happened?" I asked.

"It doesn't matter."

She was right. It didn't matter. Seeing her face and feeling her hand was enough. But at the same time, I knew that what I had seen—what I had done—was not a dream.

I went back to sleep.

And the rest of the story will have to wait until tomorrow. My broken fingers can't type another word.

Chapter 31

December 12, 2013

"You wrapped the car around a light pole." Tears were streaming down Ana's cheeks as she told me what had happened. "Alex, you're lucky to be alive. You broke your arm and several bones in your face when you crashed. If you saw the car, you'd realize just how lucky you are. God spared you."

I cringed when I heard her say "God." God had decided to let me live. God had a sense of humor. And God must be very patient.

"There was blood everywhere," she continued. "I thought you were dead. I thought I'd lost you." She was lying on my numb body.

I would have reached up and wiped the tears away. I would have wrapped my arms around her and held her till she stopped crying. I would have done whatever it took to make her stop. But I couldn't do anything. I could barely move.

It took everything in me to ask her one simple question. "What did I do?"

You know from what I wrote yesterday that I eventually learned—and remembered—what happened on Thanksgiving Day. But it's taken ten more days to get to this point, and my recall is still hazy.

And it's still hard to take it all in.

Luckily for you, I shattered my left arm, so I can still write. But it's very painful with splinted fingers.

Ana has been by my side in the hospital from day one, when I could only utter a few sentences. Now I can sit up and talk. And write and eat. From the time school is out until early the next morning, she sits here with me. Day after day, I wake up to see her emerald eyes watching over me.

And to pass the time we talk. She tells me about her life in London. Orphanages. Adoption. Family. She talks about carving her body, about the demons she's held onto for so many years. She tells me about Jess and Thomas and Hannah, about school, about the life I would be living if I weren't lying in a hospital bed. She talks about God.

I love her attention. I can think of no better way to spend my time. I could listen to Ana talking for hours. Though I'd rather not be in a hospital bed.

I love her now more than ever. Even if she has changed, I still love her.

We laugh a lot and don't even think about the future that will soon take all of this away from us. Healing is my enemy now.

And Brandon is back to his calloused self. All he talks about are court and jail time and judges. I don't care about any of that.

"As soon as you are medically cleared," he told me the other day, "you have to turn yourself in." That was the second thing he said to me after I awoke for good. The first thing he said. "Hi."

This is my future: from the hospital to a jail cell.

I had broken the one rule the judge gave me. I'd left the house. Beating someone up and speeding down a busy street were among other laws I'd broken, but that one step out the door was enough to get my temporary freedom revoked.

It was a good thing I'd done enough damage to my body to keep me in the hospital for a while. But if Ana weren't here, I'd rather be dead.

And if I'd died in the crash? Then I wouldn't be able to run my fingers through her hair as she sleeps beside me. I wouldn't be able to read her to sleep with a Psalm or two from my little black Bible. I wouldn't be able to share this with you.

Maybe you—and the world—would be better off if I had died. Maybe my friends and family would be better off, too. I know I was better off after my parents were killed. I was happy they were gone. I needed them gone.

But this is so different. These people don't want me to die. They want me to be here with them. Even when Brandon is discussing the specifics of my crime and punishment, I see a profound concern in his eyes. Maybe it's disappointment. I think I've let him down in the worst way. I spent my whole life feeling let down by his absence. I'm sure he feels how I felt when I was kid and I watched him walk out the door every morning.

The fact is that I'm the center of their world. I'm the shameful subject of a shameful existence. Yet they still love me. My friends and my family love me. They love me without condition.

And the only reason they give for that unconditional love is their God. They can give me no other visible or logical reason. Only that this God saved them, and now they want him to save me. It's illogical, simplistic, and stupid.

But as I write this now, I find a hole in my heart—a heart that aches to know how any of these people can follow such ludicrous ideas to the point that they would be associated with a murderer like me. That they would do everything in their power to show me the love of this man, Jesus, if only to save my worthless soul. They can do nothing for my present life, nothing to change my sure sentence to a ten-by-ten prison cell, yet they will do everything in their power to ensure that my eventual death is not in vain.

At the same time, I can only welcome and embrace them. Ana and my family are patient. They're kind. They've suffered so much for me. How can I push them away when they've given me so much? How can I push Ana away when I know that as soon as she wakes up, she'll be careful not to speak about my past, my failures, what I did to Levi, or my impending imprisonment? She'll tell me stories, some that I may have already heard, just because I want her to—just because she loves me.

I've seen the change in her. I've heard the way she talks. And deep down inside, I secretly want that too. I've been broken too many times not to change my mind. On my own, I've done nothing good. But I don't deserve what she has. I'm clearly not worthy of it.

I'm not worthy. Maybe everyone would really be better off if I had died two weeks ago. I know they would disagree, but they can't argue with the facts.

I'm a murderer.

Chapter 32

December 14, 2013

Today brought a mixed bag of emotions. There was joy, there was disappointment, and there was the pain of realization.

The joy came when Jen set Ally on my lap. This was the first time my niece had visited since the "incident." That's because Jen and Brandon didn't want her to see me until my face was more recognizable. I don't blame them. Ana let me see the damage in a mirror, and it was disgusting. I don't think it was anything that Ally should have been subjected to.

Ally sobbed, just like she did when I returned from the mental hospital. I may have cried a little too, but I can't be sure since my face is still completely numb.

"I love you," she said.

It was music to my ears. "I love you, too."

They didn't stay for long. Ally had a piano recital that night. It was her first official performance.

"Knock 'em dead," I told her.

She looked at me with a wrinkled brow.

"Break a leg."

She looked even more confused.

I hugged her. "Okay, just play well."

She laughed and said, "I will. I promise! I'm playing our favorite piece, just for you."

"The Well Tempered Clavier?"

"Yes." She squeezed me one last time, then slid off the bed.

Jen was ready with her jacket. "We'll record it for you," she said.

"I'd appreciate it."

Brandon lingered behind after Jen and Ally left. When they were out of earshot, he came closer to my bed.

"What's the bad news?" I asked. I could see it on his face.

He gave a nervous laugh. "I didn't want Jen and Ally to hear anything negative. But I just got word that you only have a week left. Then you have to turn yourself in."

I looked at my arm. It wasn't even close to being out of the cast. Then my splinted fingers. I already knew my face was a mess. "How can I go to prison like this?"

Ana was still there, though she hadn't said anything while my family was in the room. "You can't be serious?" she said now.

Brandon looked out the door to make sure Jen and Ally were down the hall. "Because you can walk," he said. "If you had broken your legs, this wouldn't be an issue. I'm sorry. That's just how it is." He looked every bit apologetic as he said, "I have to go. We can talk later when Ally isn't here."

"I understand."

That was my disappointment. Only one more week, and I'd be living large in a correctional facility, broken and bruised, pain and all.

The joy returned briefly when Jess and Thomas came in. They apologized profusely for not coming earlier, but I forgave them. The stares they gave Ana, and her return glances, told me it was because of her that they hadn't come sooner. I don't think she wanted them to see me, the way I looked. Just like Jen and Brandon with Ally.

Jess jumped into my bed and practically smothered me. "You lunatic! What were you thinking?"

"Jess?!" Ana said sharply.

"It's okay," I told her. I couldn't feel very much. But I'm not sure if Ana was more taken aback by Jess's physical expression or the name calling.

Jess didn't care, either. She never left the bed the entire time they were there.

"Anything new?" I asked them.

"Are you kidding me?" Thomas replied. "You're the lucky one. School still sucks."

His statement prompted glares from both girls.

"Not that I would wish this on anyone," he backpedaled. "But…okay, that was a stupid thing to say. I get it."

"It's fine."

And so we talked for several hours about stupid things. Things that high-schoolers should talk about. Things that were nothing like the cold reality of my current situation. And then, somehow, the conversation came around to the future.

"We both got accepted to Syracuse!" Jess blurted out.

Ana and I congratulated them. "But how in the world did you both decide to go to the same school? And get accepted so early?"

"It was fate, dude! We were meant to be together."

Jess sat up and hugged Thomas. "Meant to be. That's right." They kissed.

Ana and I looked at each other. It was still weird. We were both uncomfortable.

"We actually sent in our letters at the same time," Thomas explained. "About two months ago. You remember when we had that career fair and we…" He told the whole story, but I don't think any of us cared for the detail he was giving.

Jess finally interrupted him. "Just get to the point."

Thomas frowned. "Well, the point is…. Okay, I don't have a point, but I was just telling them the story."

"And we appreciate it," Ana said.

"She's just being nice," I added.

We all laughed.

My friends left near dinner time. I hated to see them go, but I couldn't blame them. The hospital is not a fun place to be on a Saturday night.

It wasn't until they were gone that the realizations began to surface. "I can't believe it's only one more week," Ana said, choking back tears. She climbed up next to me where Jess had been and laid her head on my chest.

"I can't believe it, either," I said. "But it's harder to believe that our friends will be gone. Off to college. I'll be in prison. You'll still be in high school. But they'll be living life to the fullest. I'm happy for them." Inside, though, I felt extremely sad.

Ana started to cry. I held her close with my good arm.

Then she started to laugh.

"What is it?"

It took her a moment to respond, in between the giggling and tears. "It's just that I'm so sad, yet I wouldn't trade these last few months for anything. If I had the choice, I'd do it all over again."

"Because you love me?"

She smiled. "Yes, because I love you."

The planning started immediately after that. There was no way I was leaving this hospital and going straight to a jail cell. I had at least one more night at the warehouse. I had at least one more night in my home, with my family. I had one more night with Ana.

The question was how we could make it happen. Ana assured me there was a way. And I believed her.

Chapter 33

December 20, 2013

I f it had been the last memory of my life, the very pinnacle of my existence, I would have been content. I wrapped my arms around her, clasping her thin waist. The wind hit us hard, but it could very well have been blowing through us, the way she didn't allow it to move her. She stood firm. My presence wasn't needed.

Ana was a pro at flying.

"Just close your eyes," she said. "Dream."

But I could not close my eyes. They were glued to her, the most beautiful person I'd ever seen. She was the goddess of the wind. She owned the air. She defied gravity.

The railway car moved then stopped way too fast. I wanted to stand upon it forever, holding her until I could hold her no longer. I wanted to stay in that moment, with her hair blowing against my face, her frame barely touching mine, her smell blasting my senses.

Riding car after car for two hours was the next best thing. I watched her go alone four times. Then we flew together well over ten. But it never got old.

"You want to go alone?"

I shook my head. Of course not. If I was going to fly, it would be with her. I was awkward, tight, and clumsy on the rusty behemoth. She was weightless, free, the embodiment of grace.

"Then hold me again," Ana whispered, gently kissing my neck.

"Nothing would make me happier."

Only the sunset would stop us. I may be biased, but it was clearly the most beautiful sunset I'd ever seen. The sky was painted in oranges and pinks as the sun tried to play hide and go seek with the clouds. It hid about as well as Ally does, constantly uncovering itself as it dropped past the horizon and we could see it no longer.

We found a non-moving railway car, a nasty old thing that couldn't have been used in years. She laid her head on my chest. I wrapped my arms around her again. And we talked.

"If only this night could last forever," she said.

"If only."

We had left the hospital early in the morning. Brandon said there were news reporters everywhere. I was a famous criminal again.

But in the darkness, while wearing some borrowed clothes that were much too old for my age, I led Ana out one of the back doors of the hospital and into our Sunday car, where Andy greeted us, a knowing expression on his face. It was a look I knew all too well. I'd seen it on Brandon's face. I'd seen it on Jen and Ally's faces. It was same expression I saw on everyone who came to visit me on my last day at the hospital—the expression that said *it's over*. Four wonderful months had come to a close. My second chance had reached its conclusion. Now it was time to return to prison.

The only person who hadn't given me that look was Ana. She was much stronger than everyone else. Ever since that night, the night when Brandon had told us I had one week left, the night when Ana had cried, she had become different. Once the tears were gone and the initial shock accepted, she became a stone.

And she planned the most wonderful last day I could have imagined. First, we spent several hours at the Coffee Shop, doing what we did best, which was a whole lot of nothing. There were five of us instead of six, Reuben's empty seat clearly noted as we raised coffee mugs in a toast.

Then we watched Thomas quit. His boss was not very happy when he tossed his hat and his apron on the desk and declared, "This is my two weeks' notice. And I've got plenty of vacation time to cover those two weeks. So goodbye."

Needless to say, that ended our fun there. Thomas swore he would never go back. I doubt that he will.

My friends let Ana and I spend the rest of the day alone. They said they would wait for us at the warehouse. They wanted one last get-together before this day was over, and I was fine with that.

We sat on her balcony for hours, talking about nothing specifically, laughing about everything. Ana never brought up anything negative, nothing about the sadness we all felt, and nothing about my future. There was no time for that. This was *it*.

"What's the one last thing you want to do before this day is over?" she asked.

"Be with you. That's it."

Ana smiled. "I know. But what do you want to do with me? Just one thing. Surely, we're not going to just sit here all day!"

There was one thing I wanted to do. But I couldn't allow my lust to ruin this day. I would go to prison having never seen her beautiful body. But it would leave me with something to dream of.

"I don't know," I said.

"Do you want to fly with me?"

I laughed. "If that's what you want to do, then I do too."

"I knew you'd say that."

And that's how we found ourselves in the crappiest railway yard in town. But the flying was over now. With the sun disappearing below the horizon, I knew our day was nearly over.

Though I felt sadder than ever, if Ana was as sad as I was, she didn't show it.

"What's the plan now?" she asked. "Lay here for the rest of the night?"

"I wish we could just lay here forever." It was freezing but I didn't care.

Ana flipped over and rested her chin on my chest. "You know, you will always be in my heart. Always."

"I know."

I saw the glint of tears in her eyes, even though her smile was still strong. "I would trade the rest of my life for one night like this," she said. "You know that?"

I did know that. It made me even sadder. "I know," I said again. I was the most wicked man in the world. She was a changed person, a straighter arrow, a less dark human being than she once was.

This Ana, the one who could say something so poetic, was not the girl I'd met three months ago. She would have never said anything like that back then. I'm not sure if it was the beautiful sky or the never-wavering strength Ana had at that moment, but all I could think about was God.

I had left the juvenile detention center alone, but since then, I've been surrounded by friends and family. And I've grown so comfortable with that. I love these people. And the love they've shown a wicked man like me is something that I want to have within me. Forever.

I want what Ariel and Butler Charles have. I want what Brandon has. I want what Ana has. It's hard for me to even say it, but I want God. I want someone who will be with me when these people cannot be. I don't want to be alone. I'm weak, and I know it. I need someone.

It took a millionaire and his family sacrificing for me, a punk princess and her band of misfits accepting me, and even a proud jock named Levi defying me before I realized that I could not go back to what I had been.

"But there's one thing that would make me even—" she began.

"I want what you have," I interrupted her.

She sat up. "And what's that? What do I have that you can possibly want? I just told you that you had my heart."

I sat up too. "I want to change like you. I want God. Whatever that means. I want Him. I don't want to be alone. I want a peace like you have, a peace that even transcends what's going to happen tomorrow when I walk into a prison cell again."

Ana looked shocked. It was the first time in a week that she betrayed her feelings.

"I want to have religion," I continued. "I want to have the opiate of the masses. I want to have what all of those people at our church have. Something to look forward to. Something that can change my heart like it changed yours. If knowing God is what it takes to have that, then I'm not going to fight it anymore. I've seen so many beautiful things in these last few months that I can't deny His existence anymore. I've read the Bible Brandon gave me, like, twenty times, and *I see it*. I see God in the sunrises, the sunsets. I see God in you, Ana. In the way you've changed. Whatever it takes, I want to change like that."

She started crying. "That's what I want for you! Ever since I've let God in, that's what I've wanted to happen. My life is so different now. And yours can be too."

I embraced her as she cried into my shoulder. She laughed and cried at the same time. There was happiness in her tears.

"Can you show me?" I whispered the question in her ear.

She nodded, but she couldn't speak yet. I was willing to wait.

This was the end of the life that I had lived. I used to hate Brandon. I used to hate everyone. I had no friends, only enemies. But all that had changed. Only my heart remained as cold as it had once been. If that could change, then maybe I could continue to live, even if Ana and I were separated by iron bars.

"So you want to know God?" she finally asked.

"Yes, I want to know *your* God."

"Then you must first know Jesus," she answered.

I probably looked dumbfounded. "Aren't they the same?"

She laughed. "They are and they aren't." Her statement was as confusing as her father's sermons. "But it's not just about knowing Jesus or God," she added before I could ask what she meant. "It's about a relationship."

"Okay, then tell me what I need to do to have a relationship with this Jesus guy."

She took my hands off her shoulders and cupped them in hers. "You have to believe, Alex. You have to be able to let go of your shame and guilt and lay it on someone who gave His all for you."

"Someone who died on a cross?" I asked. It still sounded simple and childish, like a fairytale or a myth. But I was beyond that reasoning. I'd never had a childhood, anyway. I'd always been an adult. If I needed to be a child now, then so be it.

"Yes," Ana answered.

Her words alone would not convince me. But the conviction in her voice was enough to make me believe anything she said. For some reason, I remembered reading about people a lot like me. I believe it was in a book called Romans, somewhere toward the end of my little black Bible. I'm not sure how I remembered that. Maybe because the people were so disgusting and made themselves their own gods, something I have done my entire life. But how could I let go of the shame and guilt that I'd held on to for so long? How could I physically give that to someone else? That was *my* burden.

That was the point, I think. "It seems so easy," I said. "Too easy. Like a scapegoat."

"Yes, it sounds easy," Ana countered. "But wait and see. It's not all rainbows and butterflies."

"So all I have to do is believe that this Jesus died for me?"

"And ask for forgiveness. Because you've done so much wrong in your life."

Forgiveness is a word I'd heard few times in my life. Most strikingly when Brandon forgave me for kissing Jen. It's a strange concept, but I remember how it destroyed my pride, my self-loathing, and my shame that night. Brandon's forgiveness and my response changed a lot in our relationship. It made sense that it was such a vital part of starting this new spiritual one.

"Does it have to be prayed out loud?" I know I sounded stupid. I didn't even know how to pray.

"No, it doesn't," Ana said.

I wanted to be forgiven. I wanted God. I wanted Jesus. I wanted to believe in something greater than myself. Because everything that's happened during these past four months is way bigger than me. It always has been. There's been an orchestration of events, a change of hearts, and some general good luck that I can't explain. And I knew that I was a terrible person. I was so sorry for the things that I'd done.

Ana was watching me think. "Are you okay?" she asked.

"I am." I believe I gave her my first genuine smile of the night. The sadness was gone. As stupid as it sounds, as childish as I felt, as simple as it was, *I believed*. And in my head I asked this God for forgiveness for the terrible things that I've done in this short life I've had.

I said the words out loud. "I believe."

Ana started to cry again.

There was no sense of spiritual revelation there. No divine calling in my soul that told me I was a member of the religious masses. No thunder from heaven. This change brought with it no theatrics. I just felt peace. For the first time in forever, the worry, the disappointment, the shame— they were all gone. Gone because of the simple realization that I believed in something more than myself. And the knowledge that I'd been forgiven.

I believed.

I believe.

***

My friends were waiting in the warehouse doorway, shivering from the cold.

"It's about time!" Jess declared as she jumped into my arms. "Oh, Alex, I'm gonna miss you so freaking much!"

Thomas waited for her to release me, then gave me a sideways hug. "We plan on visiting as often as possible," he said.

I knew they would try their best, but with college, careers, and a million others things lying in front of them, I knew it wouldn't be nearly as often as they were planning.

Hannah was the last one to embrace me, and then she handed me a paint brush and a small can of black paint.

"What's this for?"

Jess answered for her. "It's for you to leave your mark," she said. "We thought you'd like to leave behind a message or something. Maybe your name. And even if you really don't want to personally do it, we want you to. We want to be reminded of you every time we come back to this place."

I felt tears welling up in my eyes, then Jess started crying when she noticed them. Thomas consoled her.

"Where do you want me to put it?" I asked Hannah.

She pointed to the main door. "How about right there? That way we'll for sure see it every time we come back."

"Are you guys sure?" I asked. "I'm not that cool."

Jess slapped me on the arm—my bad arm. "Oops, sorry," she apologized as I flinched. "Being cool is overrated," she said. "It's a being a freak like us that counts."

"Whatever you say."

I wrote my name in big, bold letters. That's all they wanted. A reminder.

They didn't seem disappointed.

"Alex Lane!" Jess read aloud.

Thomas took the paint brush out of my hand. "That's not good enough."

"Don't ruin it," Hannah told him.

"I'm not," he replied, and then he added a few words to my autograph.

"Voilà!" He stepped back and pointed.

I read what he'd written. *Alex Lane will be back.*

I sure hoped that was true.

***

We didn't stay at the warehouse long after that. It was getting late, and as much as I wanted to just stay there with my friends forever, I didn't want to give Brandon the idea that I had run away from my due punishment.

So I said goodbye to my friends, one by one. It was a cry-fest. Thomas and Hannah were strong, but Jess bawled her eyes out, which made Ana start to cry again. Thomas and I consoled them, but even we couldn't stop the tears from coming. Finally, there came a point where we just had to go or the crying would have gone on forever. Jess and Ana were both heartbroken.

I waved goodbye. It was so hard, so painful. Ana and I didn't speak the entire drive home. I think it would have hurt too much. Our time together was coming to an end way too fast. Our last day seemed like it had just started, yet it was almost over. Actually, these last two weeks have felt like a heartbeat. I thought I'd lost Ana forever after Reuben's death. Then she was back in my life, only to be gone again, separated by a justice system. And this would be a much longer separation.

Ana broke down again on my doorstep. I held her for at least fifteen minutes as she sobbed uncontrollably. She cried until there were no more tears left to cry.

And then there was silence.

Her composure did come back. But I could tell she was done being strong. Once she had cried on the rail car, and then with Jess, her strength had faded.

As had mine. My legs were weak beneath me. My heart ached. Though it was different than before, when I had nothing else to look forward to. We shared a common bond now. We had both changed from the inside out.

But it made our parting no less difficult.

"I love you," she finally said. "With all of my heart, I love you."

"I love you, too. I always will."

Ana looked up at me and smiled. "I believe you will."

Her emerald eyes sparkled in the moonlight. My tattooed, pierced princess was the most beautiful sight I would ever behold.

"I'll visit you whenever I can," she said. "And I'll be at all of your court dates if I can. I'll never leave you. I'll wait for you."

"I know you will."

We kissed.

Then she left.

As soon as the door to the mansion was shut, I fell to the floor and I cried harder than I'd ever cried before. But it was not complete sadness or despair. I knew that Analeigh would be waiting for me on the other side. I believed it with all my heart.

The last thing I did was look at the ceiling. "Thank you, God."

Chapter 34

December 21, 2013

I dreamed that Kim was still alive. It was nice. There were no needles, no tears, no rehab. She was such a beautiful girl, that is, before the drugs and the abuse ruined her. This was the way I wanted to remember her. My big sister, the only one who really cared for me in my childhood.

I don't know why she dominated my sleep. But when I opened my eyes, I thought about her lot in life. I wished she had been given the opportunities I had. I wished she could have found what her brothers found. I wished she could have had a family, found friends, and found God. I don't know why some are given what others are not. I don't think I'm supposed to know.

Beyond that, there was no despair inside me. I thanked God for one last night in my own bed, one last night in my home.

I quickly put on some clothes. No need to shower. I didn't need to be clean for a jail cell. I grabbed my computer, my Bible, and my cell phone—nothing else. I would need nothing else.

I laughed at the irony of the situation as I left my room for the last time. Four months ago, I woke up in lock-up, and fell asleep in this royal palace. Today, I woke up in the royal palace, but I would be going to sleep in a cage like an animal.

My family was waiting for me at the bottom of the stairs. I could tell Jen had already been crying. Ally seemed unaware of what was happening, and Brandon seemed to be his normal self. Butler Charles and Ariel were standing with them.

Jen hugged me before I could say a word. She squeezed me so tight it kind of hurt my beat-up arm, but I hugged her back. It was an awkward hug, because she hadn't given me time to set my belongings down.

"We love you," she said through fresh tears. This woman had changed so much. This family had changed so much.

"I love you, too."

Butler Charles saluted me and walked into another room. I didn't expect anything more from my dying missionary-butler friend.

Ariel hugged me next. "We will miss you."

I never thought I'd miss this crazy woman, but not having her knock on my door every morning and night will be strange. I will miss that. I will even miss her random talks with God, her poor English, and her manic tendencies.

"I'll miss you too, Ariel. And your pictures are still in my room. Sorry I never got them back to you."

"It's okay," she said, stepping back. "I hope they help you."

"They did," I replied.

Brandon wrapped his arms around me next. "We'll be there for you at every court date. We'll visit you as often as we can. Are you taking the Bible I gave you?"

"Yes, I am." I leaned close to his ear and whispered. "And guess what? *I believe*."

He gave me a skeptical look, but I nodded. "Yes, I really do," I said.

He smiled then. It was a knowing smile. What he and Jen had tried so hard to accomplish had happened. They were victorious. Not only had they changed these past few months, but I had, too. We had taken this spiritual journey together.

The hardest goodbye was Ally's. She could sense that this was a real, final goodbye, that I was not coming home any time soon. But she didn't cry. I was very proud of her. She was doing something I couldn't do.

"I love you so much," I told her as I picked her up and hugged her.

"I love you, too." She wrapped her legs around my waist. "Did you see my dress?" She was wearing a black and white, floral-patterned dress.

"Did you buy that just for me?" I asked.

"Yes. Mommy helped me pick it out."

"Thank you," I said. I could hardly speak. "I'm going to miss you so much, Ally."

She squeezed me again. "I'll miss you, too. But I know you'll come back."

I don't know how she knew that. All I could say was, "Well, in the meantime, tell Wilbur he can save my seat at breakfast. And he can play the piano with you, too."

"I will." The mention of Wilbur put a huge grin on her face.

As I set her down and wiped the tears from my eyes, Brandon put his hand on my shoulder.

"Andy is waiting for you. I love you, brother."

"I love you, too." I looked at each one of them. "I love all of you. Thank you for everything. Thank you for the best four months of my life. Thank you for changing my life. And I'm sorry I can't be here for Christmas."

With that statement, Jen started crying again. "There will be other Christmases. Someday."

I sure hoped so.

***

It was agonizing to leave my home. There weren't enough goodbyes in the world to make it better. But the doors finally closed behind me for the last time. I exhaled. That was it.

Andy was waiting for me in the Sunday car. As soon as the door closed, he turned in his seat. Andy had a very wise face, and he gave me that knowing look that I was becoming accustomed to.

"To the station?" he asked.

I smiled to try to lighten the mood. "We've got one other stop first."

"As you wish."

***

This was not part of Ana's plan. This stop was by my doing. You see, I'd called Levi two nights ago, when Ana was two floors below me grabbing some of that terrible hospital food.

And he had agreed to meet me.

Levi's house was not what I expected. I'd always thought of him coming from some opulent household where mom and dad bought his love and paid to cover his inadequacies. The small, two story house at the end of a cookie-cutter cul-de-sac didn't fit what I'd imagined. It looked like Ana's house, only a darker color.

Levi was sitting on the bottom step of his front porch, waiting for me. He stood up as Andy pulled into the drive way. His face still looked beat up, but he smiled at me.

I felt ashamed and met him halfway down the sidewalk. We shook hands. Levi had changed. Like me, it was because of Ana. He was not the jerk he once was. That's why he'd been with Ana on Thanksgiving. She had wanted me to see that. She had wanted me to see how he'd changed. It was going to be her last-ditch effort to help me. Well, as we all know, it hadn't worked out the way she'd planned.

My rage had put a stop to idealistic plans, but you know what? In the end, the result was the same. He'd found what I had found. And we both had Ana to thank for that. I'm not sure how she did it, but she did.

"Thank you," I said. That was all I could say.

"No," he said. "Thank you. And good luck."

I nodded and smiled at him. I'd already apologized profusely over the phone, and Levi had forgiven me every time.

That was it. Our hate was over. Our brotherhood had just begun.

Another chapter finished.

Levi stood there and waved as we pulled away. It was so strange to see the civility in him. I've heard people say this before, but it must have been a God-thing. (I think I used that phrase right.)

Andy didn't ask me what the next stop was.

I think he drove the long way because we passed through the northern part of Manhattan along streets that would have been the last way I would have taken. I didn't mind the detour. We passed the hospital again, then the industrial area where the warehouse and the automated trains were. I wished I could see both places just one more time, but that would have been torturing myself.

Andy might have taken the long way, but I still felt it was much too short. Then I saw the police station just ahead of us. It should have filled me with dread, but I was fine with it. Somehow, I was fine.

It was the same station I'd been booked at after being arrested nearly three years ago. This time, though, I wasn't trying to kick out the windows in a bloody mess. This time I was walking in of my own volition. I couldn't even imagine voluntarily walking into a police station. I should be on the open road, running away from New York as fast I could.

Instead, Andy parked in front of a long line of squad cars. He didn't say anything.

"I'm going to need about thirty minutes," I told him.

He nodded.

I needed time to finish my story, to write an ending to this four-month roller-coaster ride. I don't think I'll want to write any more when I'm in prison. Not that they'd let me have a computer or anything. I want this to be the end. I want it to be a happy ending. And I don't think that a daily journal of prison life would be a good follow-up to this wonderful experience.

I pulled out my laptop. And here I am now, writing the close.

But before I end, I have to send one last text to Ana. *I love you.*

I know she'll respond right away. For that, I'm thankful. I'm glad her words will be the last. It's fitting

***

But the last thing I plan to do is try my hand at an introduction. But how do you introduce these last four months? I can't imagine I'll do a very good job at it. But I'll do what I can for you.

Attached to my introduction will be a list of things that I've not told you yet. I think it's time for me to show you what I've done. It's time to get these things off of my chest. You should know the terrible atrocities that my life has been filled with. I know writing this will bring peace. I feel it deep inside me. I won't go into detail, but you'll get the picture. You'll see the vileness that is no longer present within me.

"Andy," I said, "I'm going to need you to take my computer home with you when I'm done. I want you to give it to my family."

He nodded. Like I said, he didn't say anything else.

When I hit save on my computer, it will all be done. I will step out of this car. I will walk straight into the fire. They will put handcuffs on me, I will be booked, and then I will be placed in a jail cell. After that, I will only have time. And court dates. And more time. And by God's will, I will either be found guilty of murder, along with a long list of other charges, or I will walk out those doors a free man. It's going to be a long process, but I'm ready for it.

This all started with a car crash. The deaths of two people, which led me into a vagabond life of crime, a long stay in a juvenile detention center, and a four-month experience of normalcy that changed everything. I found family. I found friends. I found love. I found God. I found hope.

Hope is all I need now.

So this is it. This is goodbye.

Chapter 35

February 11, 2014

On the morning of December 21, 2013, my friend, Alex Lane, stepped out of a black sedan in front of New York City's Thirty-Fourth Precinct. He was there to turn himself in. He was there to give up his freedom. But Alex never made it through the front doors.

A small-time junkie named Larry Daniels met Alex on the sidewalk directly in front of a long line of squad cars. There was no conversation. There was no altercation. Alex just stood there as this crook pulled out a gun and shot him three times—point blank—twice in the chest and one time through the neck. The gunman immediately dropped to his knees, set the gun down on the sidewalk beside him, and waited to be arrested.

Alex Lane was pronounced dead at the scene.

There was little doubt who orchestrated the slaying. Larry Daniels was a well-known associate of one of the vilest criminals in the city, a man who was known as Stefan, a man that Alex had nearly beaten to death a few weeks earlier. Stefan was already in prison for a long list of crimes. No formal charges were ever made against him for this crime.

We held the funeral on Christmas Day. I can't describe the sadness that we—his family and friends—felt. But there were few tears. Our sadness was not enough to overtake the peace of knowing something far greater had happened. Alex Lane's life may have ended in a pool of blood in front of a police station, but his soul moved on to a place that is far better than this wicked world that we—the survivors—must continue to live in. Alex found peace, a peace that we will only find in death ourselves.

***

My name is Analeigh Greene. I had to watch the love of my life being lowered into the ground at only eighteen years old. I would be lying if I didn't tell you that a terrible sorrow consumed me for a time. It's the hope that I will see Alex again that gives me the strength to write this. It gives me the strength to move on.

I've been given a task that I didn't even think possible. But by the grace of God, I find myself filling this page with ease. My task—to finish the story of a man whose life was changed. To finish the story of Alex Lane, the criminal turned family man. The criminal turned boyfriend. The criminal turned believer.

You see, Alex left a legacy in both a pile of notebooks and several Word documents on his computer. His family gave everything to me. Why, you may ask? Because in many ways, it's the story of us. His family has read it. I've read it. Our friends have read it. And we believe it's a story that needs to be heard. Though Alex's journals show the many dark shadows, some of the deepest, dirtiest secrets in our lives, we've consented that the end result is worth the present exploitation.

If you've come this far in the story, then you already know what it's about. It's about Jesus. It's always been about Jesus.

But it's also about a criminal whose life changed within months. It's about a dysfunctional family who discovered their inadequacies. It's about a sex addict who found hope outside of the touch of men. It's about a housekeeper who will soon have her family with her again. It's about real people finding their need for change.

It's about all of us.

It's about all of you.

I could end his story here, but before Alex gave his final words to us, he left one simple note attached to the rest of his work. He'd promised it to us. I don't know why, but I'd be wrong not to include it. He wanted it said, and so it will be.

***

My name is Alex Lane. I'm a murderer, a thief, a liar, a cheat, an addict, and an abuser. I'm the worst that this earth has to offer. I deserve to rot in a prison cell for the rest of my natural life. I deserve death. This burning cross, this burning flag, these words of Mein Kampf *inked on my body, they're all testaments to the disgusting nature of my life. I am a criminal.*

But I am changed. I am an uncle. I am a brother. I am a boyfriend. I am a friend. I am a student. I am a piano player. I am sober. I am forgiven. I am loved.

And I am happy. For the first time in my life, I am truly, without a doubt, happy.

The End

About the Author:

Brody Lane Gregg is, first and foremost, a husband and a father. Outside of those blessings, he enjoys the imagination and freedom that writing fiction allows. Over the past ten years, he has been published locally and nationally, and has had the privilege of working with other authors on their projects. Brody and his family currently reside in Lafayette, IN.

Acknowledgements:

First, I would like to thank God for the grace that I don't deserve. No amount of thankfulness is adequate.

Second, I would like to thank my friends and family for their support. I would especially like to extend my gratitude to those who took the time to read my drafts and give me genuine, honest feedback. Your input was invaluable.

I would also like to thank my editor, Barbara Ardinger, for the hours of time spent shaping my draft into something presentable. Without your help, many questions would have been left unanswered. And then there is my publisher, Solstice Publishing. Thank you for believing in my story and working arduously to bring it to the rest of the world. And of course, without readers, all of this means nothing. So, thank you!

Lastly, I would like to thank my wife for putting up with me and my antics, and for listening to all of my ideas over and over again even when she didn't want to. Jessica, you inspire me more than you will ever know.

www.ingramcontent.com/pod-product-compliance
Lightning Source LLC
Chambersburg PA
CBHW061327050726
47504CB00013B/1046